ALSO BY BETSY WOODMAN

Jana Bibi's Excellent Fortunes

Love Potion Number 10

Emeralds Included

Emeralds Included

A Jana Bibi Adventure

Betsy Woodman

HENRY HOLT AND COMPANY   NEW YORK

Henry Holt and Company, LLC
Publishers since 1866
175 Fifth Avenue
New York, New York 10010
www.henryholt.com

Henry Holt® and 🏠® are registered trademarks of
Henry Holt and Company, LLC.

Library of Congress Cataloging-in-Publication Data
Woodman, Betsy.
Emeralds included : a Jana Bibi adventure / Betsy Woodman. — First
Edition.
    pages   cm
ISBN 978-0-8050-9358-2 (hardback)—ISBN 978-1-62779-054-3 (electronic
book) 1. Fortune-tellers—Fiction.   2. Single women—Fiction.
3. Scots—India—Fiction.   4. India—Fiction.   I. Title.
PS3623.O666E44 2014
813'.6—dc23   2013034385

Henry Holt books are available for special promotions and
premiums. For details contact: Director, Special Markets.

First Edition 2014

Designed by Kelly S. Too

Printed in the United States of America
1   3   5   7   9   10   8   6   4   2

This is a work of fiction. All of the characters, organizations,
and events portrayed in this novel either are products of the
author's imagination or are used fictitiously.

To Marjorie Braman

AUTHOR'S NOTE

I have set *Emeralds Included* in 1962 and have used the place-names current at the time—for example, Madras instead of Chennai. The characters speak of Malaya; this country merged with Singapore, Sarawak, and Sabah to become Malaysia in 1963, after the time of our story.

Hamara Nagar is a fictional town; it would be somewhere in today's Uttarakhand, a state that got carved out of Uttar Pradesh in 2000.

The currency exchange rate then was roughly 4.8 Indian rupees to the U.S. dollar. The rupee was divided into 100 naye paise ("new money"), but old coins were also still in use, 16 annas to a rupee. Per capita income in 1962 was less than 300 rupees a year; hence, Mary's salary of 110 rupees a month is well above average.

Some readers may wonder why Tilku enters boarding school at the end of February. With some short breaks, hill station boarding schools were—and still are—in session from February or March through November, with their long vacation in the winter months.

In contrast, at mid-twentieth-century, Isabella Thoburn College started its academic year in July and also provided the opportunity for students to enter in January.

"College" in India can refer to both secondary schools (the fictional St. Bart's College) and to university-level institutions (for example, Isabella Thoburn College, established in 1886 in Lucknow and still going strong).

St. Regis Pre-Military Academy is entirely fictional.

A glossary is provided at the end of the book for terms that may be unfamiliar.

Emeralds Included

Best Foot Forward

Bundled up in a heavy cardigan over a wool pullover over a warm jersey, Jana took Jack's letter and settled down in the window seat of the salon of the Jolly Grant House. She was grateful for the midafternoon sun streaming in. Her son's dutiful missives from Scotland had become quite scarce recently, and she'd wondered why. Had he been sick? Working too hard at that engineering job?

A moment later, she did a double take. Had Jack really used the word "marvelous"? That was pretty gushy for him. She reread: "We plan to be . . ." There it was, in plain, unmistakable English and Jack's strong, forward-slanting handwriting.

"Mr. Ganguly!" she cried. "Jack's going to be married."

Her parrot detected the excitement in her voice; he picked up on any emotion, good or bad. He stopped tearing at the knot in the rope dangling from the roof of his cage, flapped his emerald-green wings, and cried, "Jack zindabad!"

"Yes," said Jana, "long live Jack!"

She turned back to the letter and read on, hungry for details. Just who was the lady who had captured her son's heart? Here, in her small town high in the Himalayas, more than four thousand miles away from Jack, Jana was not able to pepper him with questions and get immediate answers.

The things Jack saw fit to mention or omit in letters never ceased to amaze her. Such as the big promotion he had gotten at his engineering firm the year before—six months had gone by before he'd modestly sent her a tiny printed announcement.

So, how long ago had he met . . . ah, here was her name. Katarina. Katarina Esterhazy. Goodness, Jana wondered, what nationality is she?

Jack, obligingly if surprisingly, had anticipated this question. "She's Hungarian, but she's been here several years. She got out by the skin of her teeth in 1956."

Well, wasn't this all most intriguing! Her more-Scottish-than-thou son was marrying an Eastern European who had escaped from behind the Iron Curtain, and not one of the young women he met at dinner parties around Glasgow.

"As an unattached male," Jack had once revealed, "one is invited to fill in more often than one might expect."

Jana could well imagine the invitations coming in fast and furious. And why not? Jack Laird was definitely a catch. She considered his assets: the MacPherson castle outside Glasgow and the MacPherson fortune, first-class degrees in all his studies, the solid position with the established engineering firm. Not to mention extremely pleasant good looks, if she did say so herself. Jack was a highly successful combination of his American father's sandy hair and athletic build, Jana's good bone structure, and his own steady gray-blue eyes.

Granted, Jack was reserved, even a bit shy, and that could be a drawback when looking for a mate. She wondered whether Katarina was outgoing and had managed to coax Jack out of his shell. Or perhaps Katarina too was shy, and the two of them had been drawn to each other's quiet ways. Had it been a case of opposites attracting or similar people finding that they saw the world the same way?

Moreover, what did Katarina look like? Jack, the wretch, hadn't even put in a photograph. "Hungarian" conjured up two contradictory images in Jana's mind—people fleeing with battered suitcases, and the ultra-sultry Zsa Zsa Gabor, blond with prominent cheekbones and a come-hither look in her eye. If my son has fallen in love with a Zsa Zsa Gabor, Jana mused, he's seeking the opposite of me. She glanced into the mirror at a hazel-eyed woman of sixty, whose olive-colored skin and braided curly hair did not often see the inside of a beauty salon. Plus, she usually dressed for comfort rather than style—layers of sensible Western clothing in winter, salwar kameez in summer. Not exactly Zsa Zsa's evening gowns, with their plunging décolleté.

Jana flipped over the aerogramme and found even more news. "We're hoping that a visit in mid-May would be convenient for you," Jack had written.

"Hoorah," Jana cried. "High time!"

"High time!" Mr. Ganguly repeated.

"Come on, Mr. G," said Jana, "let's go tell Mary."

A moment later, the parrot was on her shoulder and they were heading out of the house to the detached kitchen on the far edge of the side yard.

Mary, at this moment, was not ideally situated for getting big news. She was absorbed in cleaning a chicken she'd bought this morning from the wallah who came around twice a week, shortly after sunup. Fortunately, Mary did not have to behead the chicken; the wallah did that beforehand, as a special favor. However, she still needed to pluck it and remove its entrails, a messy job. The large canvas apron she wore over her old white work sari was spattered with red, like the abstract paintings one saw in the *Illustrated Weekly of India*.

Mary was a sturdy South Indian woman with a round face, dark eyes, and a smattering of pox scars across her cheekbones. Strands of black hair now escaped from the bun at the nape of her neck. Brandishing a blood-smeared knife, she was an intimidating sight.

On seeing the pair of disembodied chicken feet on the floor—or maybe it was Mary with the knife—Mr. Ganguly went into a series of piercing screeches. Jana beat a hasty retreat back into the side yard. Mary wiped her knife on her apron, took the apron off, rinsed her hands, and came out, too.

Meanwhile, the noise brought the other members of the household up from various corners of the compound. Twelve-year-old Tilku appeared first, followed by old Munar, the sweeper, his broom of long reeds in his hand. Last of all, a very groggy Lal Bahadur Pun arrived; Jana felt bad about interrupting the Gurkha's sleep, since he'd been up all night at his watchman's post, keeping them all safe. At least this let her tell everyone the news at the same time.

She looked around at the circle of puzzled faces and said, "Everybody—I have an announcement. Something you will be happy about." She paused to give them a chance to guess.

"Madam is getting married," said Lal Bahadur Pun and Mary together.

Jana burst into laughter; she knew that this was their fondest hope. Their faces fell when she said, "No, not *me*. But . . ."

Mary's glance fell on the aerogramme Jana still had in her hand. "Jack sahib?"

"Yes!"

There was a chorus of *"Jack sahib ki jai!"* and *"Mubarak ho!"* and Tilku did a couple of dance steps. Then came a burst of questions: "Where, Jana mem? When? Who is the lady?"

"I'm not sure when," said Jana. "I think in Scotland, though."

Tilku did not let a lack of information deter him from making suggestions. He said brightly, "We will all fly to U.K. in an airplane and go to the wedding, yes? Maybe one of those double-decker planes, where one can sit upstairs or down." Tilku, who aimed to be a pilot, collected pictures of aircraft.

Lal Bahadur Pun announced, "Yes, the best thing is for us all to go to the U.K. *I* will compose a tune and play pipes for the wedding march."

Munar merely murmured, "Wedding, good. Thanks be to God."

Mary, however, weighed in forcefully with her own idea: "They should come here for their wedding. And then they should stay forever."

"I don't know if we can talk them into having the wedding here," Jana said, "but they *are* coming for a visit, soon."

This brought another round of cheers.

"When?" Mary demanded to know. "When are they coming?"

"In May, if all goes well," said Jana.

"Good." Mary grinned broadly in anticipation. "By then it will be nice and warm."

"But I'll be in boarding school!" Tilku wailed. "This is no good! How can they come then?"

"You can see them on term break," Jana said. "Or maybe they could go visit you at your school. Don't worry, we'll figure it out. You won't miss everything."

Meanwhile, Mary was mulling over another problem. "Jana mem," she said, "where will they stay? Jack sahib stayed at the hotel last time he came."

Jana hesitated barely a second. "They're staying here," she said firmly. "Mary, when you're finished with the chicken, shall we go around the whole house and see what we need to do to get ready?"

She went back into the house to look for the clipboard and a pencil and pad of paper and swapped her cardigan for a coat. When she'd moved into the Jolly Grant House, almost two years earlier, she'd done a lot of repairs, not to mention chasing out the troop of monkeys that had been there for years, and cleaning up the mess they had created. She spent lots of money before she even moved in, but the lower two floors of the look-out tower had never received any attention. The second year she was in residence, a pipe had burst in the large main room that served as her living room, dining room, and fortune-telling salon, and a good number of rupees had gone just to get things back to scratch.

This year, she vowed, the house was going to be perfect. It was going to be up to the standard of her meticulous, observant son, and it was going to give a wonderful welcome to her Hungarian future daughter-in-law. The house and all the people in it would put their best foot forward.

✑ A Prayer to Grandfather Jolly

By the time Mary had found Jana at the front gate of the compound, a cold February wind had come up and the shadows were lengthening. Jana tried to write with her gloves on, finally getting too annoyed and stuffing the gloves into her coat pocket. Mr. Ganguly was plucking at a strand of her hair.

"It's a good thing Jack and Katarina aren't coming until May," Jana said to Mary. "I don't see any way to put central heating in this house. Any affordable way, that is."

She was already realizing that "perfection" was a relative term. Perfection in Hamara Nagar was not what perfection in Delhi would be, or Scotland, let alone some far-off paragon of luxury such as America.

"Still," she said to Mary, "we want to make things as pukka and comfortable as possible."

Jana tried to put herself in the shoes of a complete stranger—Katarina's shoes—and see everything about her home as if for the first time. Stepping out into the street, she cast her gaze on the ornamental wall surrounding the entire compound, the brick pillars flanking the metal front gate, and the shiny brass plaque engraved with "Jolly Grant House, 1890." All seemed in order until she took a close look at the sign that read, "Jana Bibi's Excellent Fortunes." In just two years, sun and rain had taken their toll. The feathers of the parrot pictured in the corner had gone from brilliant emerald to pale yellow, and the ruby-red beak had turned pinkish gray.

"We can't have fading paint, can we now, Mr. Ganguly?" Jana said. "We want the sign to look as good as you do." Also, she was struggling to dispel a niggling worry that her future daughter-in-law might be put off by her small fortune-telling business. She hoped that Jack had already explained it to his fiancée.

Next, she stepped through the gate to survey the general appearance of the house and felt a rush of affection for this fantasy designed by her maternal grandfather, Ramsay "Jolly" Grant. The exuberant spirit of old Jolly seemed present in the lattices and gables and verandahs, and in the six-sided tower attached to the southeast corner.

People in town were proud of this eccentric structure; all one had to tell a team of rickshaw pullers or a porter was "Grant sahib's house" and they knew where to go, even though old Jolly had been dead for fifty years. Jana's friend Rambir, writing in the local newspaper, had mentioned the house as one of the historic spots that tourists should visit (and get their cards read in the bargain).

Of course, the sniffier side of Jana's family had always referred to the place as "Grant's Folly." Jana's paternal grand-father, James MacPherson, had described it as an "Indo-Hebridean vulgarity"—without ever having seen the place in person.

No one, however, regardless of their taste in architecture, could deny that the setting was majestic. The red corrugated roofs of the house and the conical hat of the tower made a romantic silhouette against the forested hills and the enormous expanse of sky.

"Jana mem," Mary said, bringing her back to her immediate surroundings. "Courtyard needs weeding."

"Oh, Mary, of course you're right," Jana said. "It *always* needs weeding. Why are weeds so much quicker than people?" Her eye fell on a broken flowerpot and then strayed to the bench, which was encrusted with bird droppings.

She added "Clean up courtyard" to the list.

"All right, let's go inside," Jana said, and she and Mary went through the ornately carved wooden front door. Jana reached for the old-fashioned light switch.

"Light bulb out in chandelier," she wrote. "Umbrella stand broken. Coat rack too small. Wall needs touch-up paint."

They crossed to the far end of that hall, where a short passageway jutted off diagonally toward the tower. Through a door that also needed paint, they entered a large, echoing room, which had an exit on the far wall to provide access to the side yard and cookhouse. Mary crossed the room and tugged on the door, which finally opened with a long, complaining screech.

"This door always sticks, Jana mem," Mary said. "It's hard to go in and out when you're carrying a tray of food."

Jana went around the perimeter of the room trying to open the ten pairs of French windows; the curly wrought-iron handle of one of them fell off in her hand. She grimaced at the peeling paint of the frames and grimly jotted down "Replace all windows in dining room."

Then she stood in the middle of the huge room, with a sudden pang of nostalgia for things she had never seen but had only heard about.

"My grandfather gave dinner parties in this room," Jana said. "Big *tamashas*."

Jana herself had not had anything resembling a dinner party since she had moved to the Jolly Grant House. Everything about such a project, from making up the guest list to planning the menu, intimidated her.

Her favorite people in the town were of varying faiths, tastes, and dietary restrictions. No meat for some; no eggs for others. Many eschewed alcohol—at least in theory. Editor Rambir and his science teacher wife, Ritu, would certainly accept food cooked on her premises; the more conservative Ramachandran, probably only a piece of fruit. While her Anglo-Indian optometrist, Mr. Niel Powell, would love bacon, her Muslim neighbors Hajji Feroze Ali Khan and his wife, Zohra, would sooner starve than touch it.

Someday, when she solved all the possible problems surrounding what to serve to which combination of people, she would give a party. Maybe even a big one, preceded by cocktails! And bring in the string band from the Victory Hotel, to add to the ambience.

For the foreseeable future, however, she would at least have nice family meals with Jack and Katarina. When they arrived, she couldn't just do what she did when alone, which was to shove aside her music papers or fortune-telling cards on the salon table, make space for a plate, and then eat while reading a book.

"It's time to fix this room up," she said firmly. "Don't you think, Mary?"

Mary agreed. The clipboard list grew: Replaster and paint walls. Fix pockmark in floor. Buy curtains—table—chairs—sideboard.

"Well!" said Jana. "On to the next!"

They climbed the stairs to the second level of the tower, Mary puffing a little and Jana feeling a tug at her knees. Upstairs, the six-sided contours of the floor matched those of the dining room below. This room too had decrepit windows, and the ceiling paint was peeling, although that didn't seem to bother the lizards that stuck up there as if with glue.

The landing also gave onto two small empty rooms. Holes in the wall and sealed-off pipes were evidence that they had been the WC and bath for the larger room. This must have been a very nice guest suite when her grandfather Grant had lived in the house. Well, it would be again, Jana decided.

"We'll put Katarina here," she said.

"And Jack sahib?" Mary said. "Where will he sleep?"

"We could clean out the storage room on the basement level," Jana said tentatively.

"No, madam." Mary said "madam" to Jana only when being emphatic or disapproving. "There is no European WC there. And Tilku will make noise."

Jana ignored this reference to the squat toilet. She pointed out, "Tilku will be away at school."

"*Munar* will make noise," Mary said implacably. "He snores like a bear. No. Servants' quarters are not for Jack sahib."

"Oh!" said Jana, put in her place. "The lookout room, then. Let's go look at it."

Up the final flight of stairs they went, to a sunny hexagonal room with a warm brown wooden ceiling. There was ample space for a bed, Jana decided, on this highest level of the tower. All they needed to do was shift the armchairs and side tables, bring in a luggage rack, and voilà, Jack would have his own domain, out of the mainstream of the household comings and goings. The relative quiet, the views of the gorges and hills on one side and the streets of Central Bazaar on the other—all this would make very nice guest quarters for her private, reserved son.

However, he would have to travel to the main floor for a bathroom—or use Katarina's? He wouldn't actually have to go through her room, Jana decided. Satisfied that the logistics were possible and proper, Jana asked Mary, "What do you think? Would Jack enjoy being up here in the lookout room?"

"Cent percent!" was Mary's verdict. "We will have first-class quarters for both Jack sahib and the lady he is going to marry. Also, I will make first-class food when they come. Like a ten-star hotel. Twenty-star, even." Her eyes gleamed.

She loves a challenge, Jana said to herself. It's a good thing, too; she's had quite a few of them working for me. Mary had been Jana's ayah when Jana's children were small; soon, she'd taken over the cooking; and now, in addition to that, she was a relentlessly efficient and thrifty housekeeper. The word "servant" didn't begin to explain what Mary was: the Rock of Gibraltar.

Mary went off to see whether Tilku was stirring the chicken stew, as ordered, and Jana was left in the lookout room. She stood by the west window and watched the sun sink from the darkening sky into the gray and mauve bands of the winter horizon. Then she switched on the lamp, went to the low cabinet beneath one window, and poured herself a small cordial glass of LPN10. The tonic that had made the local pharmacist famous had turned out to be a delicious aperitif, too. She settled back in one of the easy chairs and thought some more about the implications of undertaking a new round of renovations.

Just think of the expense, said a small, sensible voice in her head. Just think of the bother. Oh, shut up, she told the small voice. You can't let this marvelous old house slide into ruin. Because that's what houses *do*, if you're not constantly improving them. If you're not going forward, you're going backward.

Plus, a spiffier house made it much easier to be hospitable. Hospitality—wasn't that was houses were *for*?

Why, her grandfather Grant had built a whole separate annex for guests. Sold off long ago, that building now housed Ramachandran's Treasure Emporium, beloved by tourists and by Jana herself for its mix of priceless antiques and formidable junk. In Jolly's time, scholars and artists and philosophers, Europeans of all stripes, and Indians rich and poor had stayed there— sometimes for days, sometimes for weeks.

It was an article of faith to old Jolly that Germans and Frenchmen could get along, and (Lord help us) even Englishmen and Irishmen. He broke the ice by serving excellent food and drink, bringing in crates of champagne and caviar and olives and cheese by muleback, even before the motor road to Hamara Nagar was built.

Emulating the emperor Akbar, he'd hosted leisurely conversations between a Muslim imam, a Hindu scholar, and a Jesuit priest, keeping them happy with the best of tea and coffee and whatever delicacies their religions allowed them to eat.

Hospitality was *his* religion. In a letter to a friend, he wrote: "In both the Bible *and* the Qur'an, does not the prophet Abraham kill the fatted calf for his guests? And don't the Upanishads say, 'Guest is God'?"

Dear Grandfather Jolly, Jana now said to the memory of her generous ancestor, I have not yet lived up to your standard in hospitality. But from this point on, I promise you, I'm going to try harder. I will first set the stage.

❦ A Fuse

Late that night, Jana tried to get the list of needed home repairs out of her mind. At least her own bedroom, directly above the salon in the main part of the house, was in good shape. She looked around it gratefully, shed her layers of clothing, and wrapped herself in a woolly robe.

Then she went into her clean but stark bathroom. Not many modern comforts there, but at least the single aging pipe usually delivered an adequate supply of water. She righted the tin tub that had been propped up in the corner, slid it across the bare cement floor, and positioned it under the tap. When the tub was full, she dipped a finger in and grimaced. Icy! It would take a good long while for it to heat up. She got the immersion heater down from the alcove in the wall and plugged it in. Immediately, there was a nasty little spit of electricity from the outlet, and Jana found herself plunged into darkness.

"Oh, blast," she said. "Not again."

She pulled the plug from the outlet and tucked the heating coil into its cubbyhole, then groped her way back to her bedroom, where she found her flashlight in the bedside table drawer.

The faltering little beam lasted for about five seconds, just long enough for her to locate her bedroom slippers.

Now in pitch-darkness, she heard some activity on the ground floor of the house. Mary's voice floated up the staircase.

"Power has gone, Jana mem."

"Yes, I know," Jana said. "And so has my torch."

"I have a candle, Jana mem."

A few moments later, Mary appeared, holding a candlestick with a burning taper. Her black hair was unloosed, reaching almost to her waist; the kohl that usually rimmed her eyes was smudged.

"I was washing my face," Mary said. "And pfft—no light."

Jana followed Mary down to the ground floor and out to the cookhouse, where Lal Bahadur Pun was already up on a ladder, inspecting the fuse box.

"*Khatm hogya,*" the Gurkha announced. "Gone. Finished. See, this looks all black."

"Have we got another?" Jana said.

"This is the last one, madam," Lal Bahadur Pun said. "I can put a one-anna coin in place until morning."

"Won't that be dangerous?" Jana asked.

"Not if we are careful," said the Gurkha. "Don't turn the lights on. And don't use the hot water coil or the electric hot plate."

"I do very little cooking at this hour of the night," Mary said dryly.

"No coin in the fuse box, I think," said Jana. "We'll get along without power tonight. Thank you, Subedar-Major."

Back in her room, she put on her pajamas and a thick sweater, snuggled down beneath the blankets and quilts, and blew out the candle. No reading in bed this evening, nor listening to All India Radio. She settled down to sleep.

In the morning, she took up the clipboard again and added to the list of improvements: hot-water tank. It was the dratted heating coils that always blew the fuses. Besides, she regularly gave herself an electric shock when she dipped her finger in the bathwater before taking the immersion heater out.

"We can't have Jack and Katarina electrocuting themselves with bucket baths," Jana said to Mary. "And there should be a hot-water spigot downstairs, too. As for the cookhouse—just think how much easier running hot water would make the washing up."

"If we get a tank, we also need new pipes," said Mary.

"I suppose you're right," Jana said, and added "hot-water pipes" to her list.

The Arc of the Day

℘ Jigs for Posterity—and Cash

Though still excited over her son's news, Jana began feeling overwhelmed by the prospect of all the preparations. She sat at the
salon table staring at her list of repairs, which now stretched to
two and a half pages.

Mary poked her head around the door from the front hall.
"Jana mem, are you ready to look at the book?"

"Yes, come on in, Mary," she said. "Sit down."

Jana stacked her own papers to the side, and Mary opened
the account book on the table.

"Chikens," Jana read aloud. "Three small; one large—very
old." She glanced inquiringly at Mary.

"Yes," Mary said. "The old one was for the stew we had Tuesday night. I had to boil it forever."

Next Jana looked at the vegetable bill, totaled up day by day.

"Karot, onion, brinjal, nuts," Jana read.

"Nut!" cried Mr. Ganguly from his perch.

"We're going to have to start spelling that word around here,"
Jana said, but she gave the bird a groundnut to shell and told
him, "Work on that for a while, please. A long while."

Then she continued reading Mary's list: "Tomato, kabaj."

Mary's spelling, Jana had learned, was not random; her
departures from conventional English all had a logical reason.

Why use the ambiguous letter *c* when there was never any question about how *k* could be pronounced? Moreover, thought Jana, Mary was right. The teaching of English spelling amounted to warping children's brains to accept absurdities.

Mary was now also reminding Jana about other commitments. "On Monday, we need to pay the wallahs: vegetable, chicken and egg, milk, bread, charcoal. And the *dhobi*."

"Don't worry, Mary," Jana said. "I'll go to the bank for cash."

"Okay, Jana mem." Mary retreated, clutching the account book.

They hadn't mentioned household salaries, but those would have to be paid soon, too. Last Christmas, Mary had gotten a raise, from 100 to 110 rupees a month; Jana would have gladly doubled that, if she'd been able. *Chokidar* Lal Bahadur Pun and sweeper Munar were now also on the payroll. They'd both started out on a barter basis, Lalu swapping watchman services and Munar sweeping the floors in exchange for room and board. Over time, the Gurkha's duties had increased to the point where payment was only just. Munar, on the other hand, did little work, but his gentle nature made people feel happy and so Jana decided that a token stipend was in order.

As for Tilku? Oh my goodness! As a messenger boy swapping miscellaneous services for his keep, he had cost little to have in the house. All that was about to change explosively, now that Jana was financing Tilku's boarding school education. She was happy to do it, of course—it was the first step toward the boy's dream of being an airline pilot—but it was a daunting prospect.

Getting him into a school had been a struggle to begin with. Jana had considered entering Tilku in the humble local school that served Hamara Nagar and a few surrounding villages, but it was desperately overcrowded and only went up through standard six. The government had promised a secondary school sooner or later; Jana did not find that reassuring. There were no vacancies at the exclusive boarding schools adjacent to town.

A bit of string pulling at St. Regis Pre-Military Academy by her wealthy Bombay friends the Kings finally resolved the matter. Tilku got an offer of admission for the spring term and a small reduction in fees. That partial scholarship had lulled Jana into complacency; also, she'd underestimated the other expenses: school uniforms, books, the fare for the four-hour bus ride, sports supplement, registration fee, and Lord knows what else.

In short, all those *Punch* cartoons about Scottish parsimony aside—and she had seen quite a few of them—Jana was having a lot of trouble being thrifty. How could she pinch pennies—or annas—if she wanted to do the right thing by people? She decided that she couldn't. She pictured the way Tilku's eyes had shone when the acceptance letter from the school had arrived. Scrimp on the boy's kit, send him off ill-equipped to forge a bright future? Never.

And now there was the house.

Face the facts, Janet Louisa Caroline Elizabeth MacPherson Laird, she told herself firmly. You've got to come up with more money. Unbidden, a thought tiptoed into her brain: There's always the emeralds . . .

Yes, sale of the emeralds would float her whole waterlogged ship for quite a while. Yet, yet—now that Jack was getting married, how dearly she would love to wear the emeralds at his wedding.

Also, she thought of the ornate, old-fashioned jewelry as bringing her good luck. When the idea of Jana's becoming a fortune-teller had first come up, Ramachandran had fished a necklace and matching earrings out of a box of discarded jewelry from the back room of the Treasure Emporium and had given them to Jana for her costume. At the time, no one had recognized the gems' value.

She wasn't ready to sell them yet. I will just have to earn more money, she vowed. Increasing the number of her fortune-telling customers, that would help. And how about giving more music lessons? She sighed. Few students came through her door, and most wanted discounts.

There was one more project in which she put her hopes: the music collection she was working on. Perhaps some publisher will offer a thousand pounds! she said to herself. She tried to stifle a little voice inside her that dourly told her, You're clutching at straws.

But the tunes are lovely, she said back to the voice. Original Scottish tunes, worthy of taking their place in the fiddle repertoire beside those of William Marshall or James Scott Skinner. Long ago, Grandfather MacPherson's patient old butler, Ian, had composed them in his spare time and taught them to Jana, in the pantry of the drafty castle that Jack now owned.

She picked up her violin and played one of Ian's catchy little jigs. Mr. Ganguly danced on his perch, always an auspicious sign. If he liked a tune, chances were good that humans would, too.

"One of my favorites," said Jana to the parrot. "Ian used to call it 'A Jig to Cheer Up Miss Janet.'"

Now to get it down for posterity—and cash. Jana picked up her pen, inserted a new nib, and reached for a fresh piece of music staff paper.

⌗ The Age of Aquarius Hits the Why Not? Tea Shop

Three hours later, when Jana entered the Why Not? Tea Shop, V. K. Ramachandran, the proprietor of Ramachandran's Treasure Emporium, and Rambir Vohra, the editor of *Our Town, Our Times* and the owner of the Aaj Kal Printing Press, had already settled at their usual table, the one with the steadiest legs and the best view of the street.

"Welcome, Mrs. Laird!" cried Ramachandran. "Here, sit, sit; we have already given one order, but what's to prevent us from giving a second? I say, Mr. Joshi's new dishes are quite delicious." He pointed to the blackboard, where a new menu was chalked up:

Aquarian Puris with Conjunction Chutney

Heavenly Halwa

Double Roti with Celestial Vegetable Masala

Astronomical Omelets

(Two—Three—Any Number of Eggs You Want!)

The menu was bordered by symbols of planets and stars and topped by a happy injunction to "Celebrate the Arrival of Love and Harmony."

Ah yes, thought Jana, the Aquarian Conjunction. Just a few days ago, on the fourth and fifth of February 1962, the sun and moon and Mercury and Venus and several other heavenly bodies had lined up, delighting some astrologers (although worrying others).

"Namasté, Mr. Joshi," said Jana as the jovial owner of the tea shop arrived to take her order. "I can't decide what to have."

"I am also serving all of the usual favorites," Mr. Joshi said. "Samosas, *pakoras*, whatever you want. Fresh by the minute." He gestured toward his nephew, who was deep-frying savory pastries in a huge conical pan in the back of the shop.

"I'll try the Aquarian puris with your new condiments," Jana said.

Mr. Joshi beamed. "Try, try, you will like, guaranteed." He retreated for a moment to his tea-making corner and returned with a glass of hot tea with milk and sugar already boiled in. "Just the way you like it," he announced. "Puris coming just now."

"So, Mrs. Laird, what is new?" Ramachandran asked. "Is your son coming to visit again?"

"He is, in fact," said Jana. "But there's bigger news than that."

"Bigger news?" The roly-poly Ramachandran and the lean, serious Rambir leaned forward with curiosity.

"He's bringing someone with him." She paused for effect. "His fiancée!"

"Fiancée!" Ramachandran's face lit up, and Rambir's eyes opened wide.

"Yes. Jack—is getting married."

"Oh, bravo, Mrs. Laird," said Ramachandran. "That is truly excellent news."

"Yes," said Rambir. "Congratulations! And please convey my sincere congratulations to *him,* as well."

The other customers were now turned toward them and listening, and Mr. Joshi hurried over from the back of the shop. "Madam, the stars are truly smiling on you! See, the age of love and harmony *is* upon us. Oh, this is very good, very good."

"What's the lady's name?" Ramachandran asked.

"Katarina," said Jana. "Katarina Esterhazy."

"That doesn't sound British." Ramachandran, originally from South India, took an interest in names and what they revealed about origins.

"It isn't," said Jana. "She's Hungarian. Although she's a British citizen now. She escaped over the border into Austria in '56."

"My, my," said Ramachandran. "A *refugee.* How dramatic."

"Apparently it was," said Jana. "Although I haven't heard all the details yet. When I hear the phrase 'Hungarian refugee,' I picture a shipwreck victim, waifishly wrapped in a man's huge overcoat."

"She'll have had time by now to get herself some clothes," Rambir sensibly pointed out. "Does she have a profession?" Rambir's own wife, Ritu, was a physics teacher who had given a paper at a national conference; he was always interested in professional couples, people who forged ahead two by two, shaping the modern world.

"She translates Hungarian into English. And vice versa,"

Jana said. "And she knows Russian, too, so sometimes she translates that."

"Goodness!" Rambir said. "How brainy!"

"I imagine she must be," Jana said.

"They will have lots and lots of brainy children," Ramachandran said.

"Perhaps," said Jana, more convinced about the "brainy" part than the "lots and lots."

"And when is the happy event?" Ramachandran said.

"The date hasn't been set yet," said Jana.

"They should ask my wife's astrologer," said Ramachandran. "Not just leave everything up to chance and chaos."

Rambir arched an eyebrow. Unlike his old university chum Ramachandran, who was steeped in tradition and family, Rambir was a modern man, all science and socialism. However, Jana had noticed, even Rambir bowed to customer demand and published in his paper a column called "What the Stars Foretell This Week," plus an annual list of auspicious wedding dates. One had to find ways to boost circulation, it seemed. "Once the newspaper is in the reader's hand," Rambir had remarked hopefully, "then that same reader will look at the news about the nuclear arms race and consider the issues of neocolonialism and nonalignment."

The man at the next table leaned over and asked, "Where is this wedding taking place?"

"In Scotland," said Jana.

"Oh. U.K." said the man in disappointment, as if he would have planned to attend otherwise.

Ramachandran said, "But why not here? We can supply everything you need. And you have your own live-in bagpipe player. Furthermore, Mr. Joshi can provide a feast! Is that not right, Mr. Joshi?"

"Oh yes, oh yes," Mr. Joshi said happily. "Any wedding specialties you like. Small wedding, three–four hundred people, no problem. Just give me a modicum of notice."

"Wait, wait," said Jana, "all this is *not* in my hands. For all I know, they intend to go down to the registry office someday after lunch and elope."

Rambir, who had done just that with his wife, Ritu, looked sympathetic, but Ramachandran, whose marriage to the lovely Padma had been arranged and taken place with a feast for seven hundred people, shook his head.

"Anyway," said Jana, "the task ahead of me at the moment is to get my house ready for them. I never did fix up the dining room or the guest room when I moved in. I've got to do that now. *And* put in a hot-water tank. And improve the plumbing. And the wiring. Get some new fixtures. I don't even know where to begin."

"Oh, I put in hot water last year, so I know all about that," Ramachandran said. "Go to Modern Inconveniences."

"Conveniences," Rambir corrected. "Modern *Conveniences*."

"Yes, yes, of course," said Ramachandran. "Go there. They have lavabos, showerheads, whatever you want. For heating water, order an Anand boiler. It burns newspapers, straw, wood chips—anything you have on hand."

"I want to make sure everything's really pukka," said Jana. "Jack's an engineer, you know. It wouldn't do to have him walk in and find things jerry-rigged and higgledy-piggledy."

"Not to worry, Mrs. Laird," said Ramachandran. "Everyone is rooting for you and your house. Let me know if you need to find painters and carpenters and the like."

"Oh, thank you, Mr. Ramachandran, you always help out when I'm doing battle against the house."

"Don't think of it as *against* the house, think of it as *for*."

The three friends by now had eaten an ample quantity of Mr. Joshi's Aquarian specialties and were lingering over a final glass of tea.

"Speaking of conveniences," Rambir said, "Mrs. Laird is not the only one with news." Now it was his turn to pause dramatically.

"Oh, do tell, Rambir," Jana said.

"The telephone," said Rambir, "has been successfully installed at Aaj Kal press."

"Ah!" Jana exclaimed. "Then congratulations are in order to you, too."

"Thank you." Rambir leaned forward. "My friends, now that they're extending the phone lines, don't you think you should get connected, too? The Victory Hotel has a phone. So does Dr. Chawla's surgery, and Mr. Powell's Sharp Eyes Vision Care. Mr. Powell's even got one at home. The police station has had phone service practically forever."

"The law never sleeps," said Jana dryly.

Ramachandran said, "Oh, if I get a phone, my wife and children and everyone else in the house will be fighting to talk into it, and I'll get no peace. Who would I call, anyway?"

"You could call me," said Rambir. "We could talk."

"We already do," said Ramachandran. "Right here. With the important benefit of Mr. Joshi's samosas. And Mrs. Laird's presence, of course," he added gallantly.

"The problem is," Jana said slowly, "it's such an expense."

She thought of her expenses, already ballooning alarmingly. And here was another expense, albeit small: Mr. Joshi came by and put the bill on the table. In an unspoken agreement, the three rotated signing the chit, and Jana now reached for it.

"My turn," she said.

"Ladies paying, oh my," said Ramachandran. "This is indeed the brave new world." He always said that when Jana paid.

"My pleasure," said Jana.

Ramachandran reorganized his shawl around his plump shoulders, Rambir picked up his briefcase, and the three of them went down the broad shallow steps from the Why Not? into the street.

"Cheerio, Mrs. Laird. Cheerio, Rambir," said Ramachandran.

"Good-bye, friends," Rambir said.

"Namasté-ji," Jana said first to one, then to the other. Then she started home for the Jolly Grant House.

⸲ᴓ A Reading Lesson

While Jana was at lunch, Tilku had been amusing Mr. Ganguly, teaching him to play dead. This was not the first such lesson; the act was well on its way to perfection, and highly realistic. When Jana entered the salon, Mr. Ganguly was lying rigidly on his back on the table next to her stack of music papers, his claws in the air. Though she had seen this before, Jana couldn't prevent herself from letting out a little squeal.

Mr. Ganguly righted himself and said, "Hiya hiya hiya."

"Say 'namasté-ji' to Jana mem," Tilku prompted the bird.

"Hiya!" Mr. Ganguly repeated.

"His manners really are slipping," Jana said. "He used to be so polite. 'Namasté-ji' to the people outside the temple, 'salaam' to those outside the mosque, 'Sat Sri Akal' to the Sikh police officer outside the jail. Now it's just 'hiya' to everyone."

"Walk?" cried Mr. Ganguly.

"I could use one," said Jana. "I ate too many Aquarian puris. And I *must* go to the bank before it closes. Tilku, do you want to come with us?"

Tilku did, and fifteen minutes later, they were making their way westward through the Central Bazaar. All along the way, Jana used the signs to coach Tilku in his English reading. *Mother India* had returned to the Bharat Mata Cinema, and *West Side Story* was playing at the Europa; Tilku deciphered both titles.

"Did you read the English letters or the Devanagari ones?" Jana demanded. Most of the signs had both, and also Urdu script, making the whole street a miniature multilingual textbook.

"English, Jana mem!" Tilku insisted. "I read them in English!"

The Giant Skating Rink presented more of a challenge, since

there was only English on its sign. Tilku made it through "Under New Management" and "Special Events!"

"*Shabash,* Tilku," Jana said. "And across the street?"

"Kashmiri Palace," Tilku said. Jana suspected that the Kashmiri rugs hanging in the storefront and the picture of a palace on the sign might have helped.

Once they'd moved on to the English Bazaar, the street was wider and straighter, the buildings a mix of European architectural styles, from Tudor to Swiss chalet, and the stores more expensive-looking. This was particularly true the closer they got to the bank; money seemed to coalesce in this part of town.

Three jewelry stores clustered together, as if for mutual protection, and their signs gave Tilku plenty of reading practice.

The bright yellow sign over the door to Nanda Lal Goldsmith warned, "All that glitters is not gold. Trust only Nanda Lal." Janki Dass Silversmith's sign had a more rhythmic promise: "Your school ring will always ring true. The brightness of silver is here for *you.*" Lastly, snuggled in between them was a store called Priceless Gems, which proclaimed to have the "best possible jewelry north of Chandni Chowk."

"Have you been to Chandni Chowk, Jana mem?" Tilku asked.

"I have," said Jana. "Many years ago." Many years ago, she *had* visited the jewelry district of Old Delhi, with its endless temptations, but she hadn't been able to afford to buy anything.

" 'Gems sold—and bought,' " read Tilku. " 'Reasonable loans against col—lat—er—al.' "

Reasonable loans. Very interesting, thought Jana, and tucked the fact back into her mind.

Not far after that, the bank, with its pillared front verandah, came into view. The sign said, "No animals or birds permitted in banks. Municipal ordinance."

"Mr. Ganguly can't go in," Tilku said, after squinting at the sign.

"You're right," said Jana. "Well done, Tilku. Good reading."

She transferred Mr. Ganguly to Tilku's wrist and entered the bank.

·⚭ *A Withdrawal of Funds*

Jana always felt uncomfortable in banks. They acted as if they were doing you a huge favor by taking your money, and then they made it difficult for you to get it back again. She stopped at the first counter and picked up the necessary forms, then proceeded to a table and filled them out, pressing down heavily with her pen so that the carbons would be legible.

While waiting her turn in line, she had ample time to study the bank teller's jowly face. It always put Jana in mind of a camel, although she told herself that this notion was uncharitable. When she handed the man the forms and he frowned in disapproval, the camel image got reinforced in her head.

"You're getting low on funds, Mrs. Laird," he said. "Anything wrong at the Jolly Grant House?"

"Nothing at all," she said.

He looked down into a drawer of banknotes, as if reluctant to surrender any of them to her. Among the wad of notes he finally gave her, a few of the single rupees were faded and soft as cloth.

"If you please," she said, "I'll need newer ones than this. The tradesmen do not like getting banknotes that are worn out of recognition."

After a silent little tug-of-war between them, he gave in and swapped the old notes for crisp new ones, which she tucked triumphantly into her billfold.

"Will you be bringing your balance up to a respectable level before long?" Mr. Camel-Face asked.

Really, the cheek of the man, she thought.

"I will be making a deposit next month," said Jana with dignity. By then, the small quarterly check she received from her inheritance in Scotland would be in.

Outside on the verandah, she let Mr. Ganguly climb once again to her shoulder. The day's errands were done. Sagging bank balance, home repairs, the manners of parrots—all of these would eventually be coped with, one step at a time.

"Okay, Tilku, off we go," she said.

"Off we go," repeated Mr. Ganguly. *"Chal."*

Mary's Day Off

✍ Woolgathering

Mary had the day off, but she was moving through her activities as purposefully as when she was working. Likki Ram's cupboard-size shop in the Upper Bazaar was her first destination. The grizzled *kabariwalla* was her favorite of all the rag-and-bone men in town; he assiduously made the rounds of private homes in order to obtain the most ample supply of used clothing. He now sat cross-legged among the billowing piles of his wares, resting one elbow on a stack of sweaters.

"Namasté, Mary-ji," Likki Ram said. "What is happening at the Jolly Grant House?"

"Big news," said Mary. "Jana memsahib's son in U.K. is engaged. He is bringing the lady for a visit. I am going to knit scarves for them both. As a wedding gift."

Likki Ram handed her a large gray man's pullover. "Here, look at this sweater. It is hardly worn at all. The wool is thick and soft, and there's plenty of it."

"But not enough for *two* scarves," Mary said.

"Well, then, take this red cardigan and use that wool, too. Red and gray together, very nice."

"I am thinking red, white, and blue," said Mary. "Colors of the Union Jack. The sahib's name is Jack, and marriage is a union, no?"

"You have very precise requirements," grumbled the *kabari-walla,* but he searched around and came up with two more sweaters, one white and one blue. "Here, perfect. One rupee for three items."

"Eight annas," said Mary.

"Mary, sister, you drive a hard bargain," the *kabariwalla* said, reproach written all over his face. "I have a family to feed. Do you want to put me out of business?"

"Put you out of business?" Mary said, just indignantly enough. "I'm keeping you *in* business. I'm your best customer. Who else is as good?"

"Twelve annas, then."

"Ten."

The *kabariwalla* gave a huge sigh. "All right, all right," he said. "This time I will think of your welfare more than my own."

Mary quickly handed over the ten annas and bundled up the articles in a cloth she had brought along for the purpose.

"Namasté, Likki Ram," she said.

"Namasté, Mary-ji," he said. "Knit quickly."

"I always knit quickly," Mary said.

Next, Mary stopped at This and That Dry Goods and bought herself a dozen hairpins and a drawstring for her sari petticoat. Picking up these small personal articles gave her the pleasure of purchasing something without making a large dent in her purse. Thrift was a high virtue, in Mary's opinion, but that didn't mean you had to deprive yourself *all* the time. In any case, she still had a good chunk of money saved this month to make a deposit.

The next stop, accordingly, would be at the bank, all the way across town in the English Bazaar. Mary retraced her steps through the Central Bazaar, passing the Jolly Grant House.

Good house, she said to herself. Of all the places she had lived with Jana mem, this was the best: nice servants' quarters with a private room for each person, and two washrooms with good, strong water pressure. Plus, from the basement level of the house, you could walk out a door straight onto the back terrace and dry your hair in the sun or air your bedding.

The town, too, suited her, in spite of the cold at this time of year. People in this town didn't know about her origins, and probably wouldn't care if they did know. Here, she was respected.

In her native Madras, she'd been beneath contempt—the youngest daughter of a leatherworker, married off at thirteen to a man twenty years older. There, people called her "girl" and "you there" and "useless one." In contrast, here in the town of Hamara Nagar, she was "Mary-ji." At the bank, in fact, she was even "Mrs. Thomas."

Moreover, in this part of the country, she was not afraid. Many years ago, back home in Madras, she'd often been afraid, particularly of her husband, a rough man who'd smelled of home brew and cow skins and blood. When he was in a good mood, he'd have his way with her; when he was in a bad one, he'd beat her. Actually, she'd always felt, there wasn't much difference between the two treatments.

Enjoying the chilly but bright day, she continued down the main street of the town, glancing inside a bracelet shop without going in. The rainbow of glass bangles on the racks looked pretty, but why buy something that would break in two days? Mary wanted her possessions to endure. The studs in her ears and nose were twenty-two-karat gold; a lesser grade, she believed, would make her skin rot.

"Gold never loses its value," her mother and grandmother in Madras used to say, although they'd learned, back in the times of starvation, that this was not true. In 1931, when Mary risked all and fled to an unknown future in northern India, she found that her gold wedding anklets and bracelets *had* lost their value. In those days, nothing would bring in money, neither leather, nor rice, nor human labor. Mary had traded one anklet for a train ticket and another for a bus ticket. She'd bartered her earrings for a few *dosas* and a couple of *idlis* to keep from fainting with hunger.

But that was in 1931, and this was 1962. Shuddering, she reminded herself firmly that the bad times were over. Her work brought rewards, and the rewards were her own. Now that gold was again worth its weight in, well, gold, she had a basic quota of ornaments—*and* a bank account.

She entered the bank, went to the counter and got the deposit form, and filled it out in triplicate. Her handwriting had been wobbly and childish when she had learned the English alphabet from Jana mem all those years ago, studying at the table alongside little Jack. It was now firm and clear.

"Good morning, Mrs. Thomas," the clerk said, and wrote the date and deposit amount in her passbook. "You'll soon have enough for your own house," he joked, his jowly face lifting in a smile. "You could buy the Jolly Grant House."

Mary was startled. How did the man know she was saving for a house? She was indeed dreaming of a little whitewashed brick bungalow with a plot of vegetables next to it. But the big, old Jolly Grant House, with its rooms laid out this way and that and up and down? The house looked very pretty from the street, but it gobbled rupees.

"I am saving for a rainy day only," she said to the jowly clerk.

"Very prudent," he replied.

Nine Yards in Full Measure

After leaving the bank, Mary headed for the turnoff to Maharajah's Hill. Half a mile down the road, however, the saris hanging in the storefront of All-India Saree Jubilee caught her eye. The shopkeeper, who was leaning against the side of the wide entryway, saw her hesitating. Oh, oh—he had made eye contact

with her and was trying to pull her in like a fish in a net. "Just
come, look," he called. "Looking is free. You don't have to
buy."

He'd thrown down the gauntlet, but she was unafraid of this
test to her willpower. When had she ever failed such a test?
When a shopkeeper looked as well fed as this one, she said breezily to herself, it was easy to keep one's guard way up high. With
a resolutely noncommittal look on her face, she went into the
shop.

My, what a lot of saris! Stacks of them in glass cases, on
shelves on the walls. "There are many more in the back room,"
the shopkeeper said, "if you don't see exactly what strikes your
fancy."

However, Mary *had* seen something that struck her fancy.
Following her gaze, the shopkeeper carefully took a sari from a
shelf and spread it on the small platform in front of her.

"It's a nice deep yellow, isn't it?" he said.

Mary gave a grunt, trying not to smile too much with admi-
ration. The rich patterns at the end of the sari would show off
so nicely when draped over one's shoulder or head.

"That design gives a feeling of richness," said the man.

Mary frowned. A feeling of richness didn't often come
cheap.

"Nine yards, full measure, I tell you," the man coaxed. "Best
Benares silk. Just feel."

Mary picked up a fold of the sari very briefly, feeling the
soft, light fabric slide as smoothly as a liquid against her hand.

Nine yards—not the everyday six. It was a special sari, for
special occasions.

"I'll think about it," she said.

"Don't think too long," the man said. "It might not be here
when you come back."

As she walked off, she hated the way the man smirked, as
if he could see right into her heart and detect the twist of
desire.

∾ Mary Visits a House on Maharajah's Hill

Mary's next destination was Ramachandran's house on Maharajah's Hill, where her friend Meenakshi was employed. Meenakshi polished the family's brass pots and bowls and trays, of which there were many, and the brass plaque at the gate that said, "*Shanti Niwas*": The Abode of Peace.

Spying her from a window, Meenakshi came out to meet her. The girl was a younger, slimmer version of Mary, even to the band of smallpox scars spread across her face. She addressed Mary as Mary-*akka*, elder sister, mixing this Tamil expression into a mishmash of Tamil, Malayalam, Hindi, and English; Mary understood it all. Meenakshi too had left South India, but not in a stealthy flight like Mary's. She'd had a happy send-off by her family, who depended on the money order she mailed back to them each month.

"I will show you the whole house," Meenakshi said. "All the Ramachandrans have gone to see their son playing cricket."

She led Mary around the servants' quarters and introduced her to the numerous people who washed, cooked, and cleaned for the family. After that came the Ramachandran family's many rooms, arranged around a central courtyard. On the east side, Meenakshi pointed out the pride of the house, Mrs. Ramachandran's new *puja* room.

"Memsahib spends a lot of money on flowers and fruits and incense for her prayers," Meenakshi said.

No doubt, thought Mary. She gazed at the statues of Radha and Krishna in the alcove, the shelves for fruits and flowers, the shiny brass bowls. Blessed are the poor, Pastor Mitra of All-Saints Church often said, but it was Mary's observation that the rich tended to be even more blessed. In the white house that I shall build one day, she resolved, I too shall have a nice prayer room, with an alcove for the Bible alone and a shelf for figurines of the Nativity scene. Mary and Joseph will look down on baby Jesus, and the kings and shepherds will march in a line to see them.

Once the tour was done, Meenakshi and Mary drank coffee, and then they sat in the sun, Meenakshi knitting and Mary pulling the wool from the sweaters she had bought and rolling it into neat balls. Thus they worked and chatted until the shadows lengthened.

"I must go," said Mary.

On the long road back her feet hurt, and briefly she stopped walking and considered taking a rickshaw. Then she steeled herself to go on. At the end of a rickshaw ride, what did you have to show for it? Nothing; you were at the same place you would have been if you'd walked, with your purse a little thinner.

Reaching the Jolly Grant House, she went down to the basement, stored her balls of wool and small purchases in the recessed shelves of the wall, and stretched out on her charpoy. Her mind flitted briefly back to the nine-yard silk sari she'd seen at the Jubilee. Should she have made that shopkeeper a low offer? How much might he come down on the price? Never mind, she told herself, don't think of that now. There are plenty of saris and sari merchants in the world.

On the whole, she was pleased with her day. Her feet ached, but, in her experience, feet generally healed with a little rest.

A Tourist Destination

·◦ Diplomatic Pouch

The morning mail brought a package from Kenneth Stuart-Smith, Jana's American diplomat friend who did travel writing in his spare time. Jana found her scissors, cut open the package, and pulled out the second edition of his *Globe-Trotter's Companion*. My, that was fast work on Kenneth's part, she thought. The first edition, which had brought a huge influx of tourists to Hamara Nagar, had barely been out a year, and now here was the new book, greatly expanded, with more pictures, a better index, and cartoons about travel. What tickled her most, however, was the cover, which featured a parrot in sunglasses with a suitcase and a camera. She flipped quickly through the pages to see what Kenneth had said this time about the town she'd come to call her own.

There, topped by a picture of the clock tower in the Central Bazaar, was his cheerful description: "The long trip up the winding road is well worth it. Step into this friendly little corner hidden from the world, where optimists outnumber naysayers, the tailors are philosophers, and the local pharmacist is the creator of the multipurpose Love Potion Number 10. Spend a night—or a month—at the newly renovated Victory Hotel. Buy a pair of bookends at Ramachandran's Treasure

Emporium—you may find that they belonged to Mahatma Gandhi."

He's overdone it a bit about Mahatma Gandhi, Jana thought, but never mind the occasional hyperbole.

"Finally," she read, "don't forget to stop in at Jana Bibi's Excellent Fortunes, where a sympathetic ear, encouraging word, and uncanny parrot wisdom await you."

She turned to the personal letter that was folded up in the book. "I hope to be back to Hamara Nagar soon," Kenneth had written. "Hard to believe, but the *third* edition of *GTC* is in the works. Best regards to Mary, Lal Bahadur Pun, and old Munar."

His signature was a scrawl of initials with a slanted line underneath.

Jana grabbed a pen and an in-country letter form from the sideboard and quickly wrote:

Dear Stu,

Thank you ever so much for the second edition of *GTC*! You'll be happy to know that the Why Not? has some new specialties you can include in the third edition. Something for everyone, no matter what their sun sign is.

The big news is that my son, Jack, is engaged to be married.

He's bringing his fiancée here on the 17th of May, and they're staying for a long, lovely month! I'll soon be up to my ears in home improvements.

Cheerio, Jana.

She folded the letter, licked the flap and grimaced at the taste, and addressed the outside. Then she glanced at her watch. With luck, she could get one more tune down on paper before she was due at the Why Not? for lunch.

✑ *Only Brainstorming*

"Gentlemen!" said Jana, when she and Ramachandran and Rambir were established at their favorite table and had given their order to Mr. Joshi. "*Guess* what I have."

"I'm truly dreadful at guessing," Ramachandran said. "Let's see—you now have an understanding of the meaning of life."

"You credit me with a bit too much wisdom, I'm afraid," Jana said.

"You have a new dog," said Rambir.

"Oh, Lord no, Mr. Ganguly would have a nervous breakdown. He has the greatest disdain for dogs," Jana said. "Mary's not fond of them, either, although Lal Bahadur Pun would probably like one to help him keep watch."

"I give up," said Ramachandran.

"Me too," said Rambir.

"Here it is!" Jana took the new edition of *Globe-Trotter's Companion* out of her satchel and handed it to Ramachandran.

"Oh, jolly good!" Ramachandran said. "Jolly good! But I didn't know that it was in the stores already."

"It's not," Jana said. "Kenneth sent me an advance copy."

Rambir looked a tad jealous. "I wish he'd sent *me* one so I could put a review in the newspaper," he said.

"Oh, you're welcome to borrow this one for a while," said Jana.

Ramachandran said, "I do like the new cover! Don't you, Rambir?"

"Yes, yes, very colorful," said Rambir. "I gather it's supposed to be Mr. Ganguly?"

"I assume so, too," Jana said.

"That book certainly has helped the town," said Ramachandran. "I estimate that the number of tourists who came into the Treasure Emporium last year was double that of the previous year."

Rambir was flipping through the book. He checked the index, looked up a few things, and nodded. "It seems quite well done," he said.

"Gentlemen," said Jana, "I think we really *have* put this town on the map. No one will want to drown us now."

A shadow of Rambir's characteristic worry, however, had passed over his bony face. "We still shouldn't rest on our laurels," he said, and took a swallow of tea.

"Why not?" Ramachandran said. "Aren't laurels exactly for the purpose of resting on?"

"No," said Rambir. "If we're not going forward, we'll soon find ourselves going backward. And backward is just where we don't want to go. We didn't fend off the threat of a government dam by resting on our laurels, now, did we? Don't you agree with me, Jana?"

To tell the truth, Jana secretly agreed with Ramachandran—resting on one's laurels sounded like an excellent idea. She was proud of having done her part to boost tourism, and she'd grown to like telling fortunes in her sunny living room; it gave her a chance to meet people of all ages and hear their life stories. She supposed that it was like doing what the *Illustrated Weekly of India* called "psychotherapy": making people feel better by talking with them. (No mystery about *that*, she often said.) She also looked back on last year's project—writing a column for the newspaper in which she interpreted readers' dreams—with satisfaction.

Now, however, Rambir was saying, "We need a new twist. This year's column could be a Miss Lonely Hearts sort of thing. You know, advice to the lovelorn."

Jana almost choked on her samosa. "You want *me* to give advice about love?" She shook her head adamantly. "I'm not qualified."

The two men seemed surprised at how quickly she rejected this suggestion. "You were married a long time," said Ramachandran. "Doesn't that count as a qualification?"

"You're barking up the wrong tree," Jana said.

Then she felt bad about being contentious; conversation between the three of them so rarely struck a negative note. "I'm sorry," she said. "I didn't mean to be rude."

"All right, all right," said Ramachandran. "Let's leave that one aside for another time." He took a large bite of his *aloo paratha* and chewed thoughtfully, then said, "How about something flashier for this year's tourist attraction? Perhaps we could have a *son et lumière* in the Central Bazaar, with narration. I was reading about how they do that at the Palace of Versailles."

Rambir chuckled. "Picture the Jolly Grant House all lit up . . . a spotlight sweeping over the Treasure Emporium . . ."

"Yes, yes, that's the ticket," said Ramachandran. "Throw in some music, dancers making their way down the street, that sort of thing."

"That sounds very disruptive to the life of the quarter," Jana said.

"No more than the normal wedding," Ramachandran said.

"Oh! Weddings! That gives me another idea." Rambir turned to Jana. "How about renting out the Jolly Grant House for special functions? Graduation parties, birthday celebrations, weddings? Especially since you're about to get the house all fixed up. It would bring in income for you and be one more asset for the town."

"It sounds perfectly dreadful," Jana said in dismay. "I don't want to be a bad sport, but really, I don't think I could handle the noise and mess and breakage. I'm accustomed to a quiet life, you know."

Unlike the normal pleasant conversation with her friends, this discussion was starting to give her indigestion.

"Don't worry, don't worry," Ramachandran said. "We're only brainstorming, as the Americans say. When *does* the work on your house start, anyway?"

"Tomorrow," said Jana.

∽ *Jana Lays Down the Law*

By the last week in February, the Jolly Grant House had been
turned into a chaotic construction site. Workers banged through
the hallway carrying pickaxes and hammers and window frames
and miscellaneous pieces of lumber. They dropped buckets of
nails on the staircase. They interrupted Mary's cooking to ask for
drinks of water and samples of what she was making. Jana had
thought she would be able to get at least *some* work done during
the renovations, but this was turning out to be wishful thinking.

"*Shanti,*" screamed Mr. Ganguly. "*Shanti!*"

Yes, thought Jana, that's exactly what I need. Peace. Peace
and quiet so that I can get the last few tunes down. In the dining room, the workmen were yelling at one another, their insults
floating through the hall into the salon.

"*Buddhu!*" one cried, delighting Mr. Ganguly, who repeated
the word several times. Jana groaned. She did not want to add
"stupid" to his vocabulary.

The next moment, *thud! crash!* Jana's arm jiggled, and a drop
of ink fell from her pen nib onto her music manuscript. Was it
just her imagination or had the *house* actually shaken? She rose
from her chair and went into the dining room, where she found
that one of the new windows had tumbled to the floor, leaving
broken glass from several panes scattered about. Eight men were
arguing about whose fault this was.

"What has happened here?" Jana cried.

"Difficult work, memsahib!" complained one.

"Old house," said another. "It doesn't want new windows."

"It's going to *get* new windows," Jana insisted. "And why does
it take eight people to put them in? I thought four of you were
going to work on *this* floor and four upstairs in the guest room."

"You see, madam," said one of the workmen, a foreman of
sorts, "these fellows are lazy fellows who need to be watched so
they will get the work done."

"Lazy fellows, eh?" Jana's voice rose. "Do you want me to get my *chokidar,* Subedar-Major Lal Bahadur Pun, to encourage you to do the work?"

The mention of the Gurkha with his stick and his razor-sharp curved knife made them shake their heads. Jana said forcefully, "This work has to be finished by the first of April, *samjhé*? Understand?"

Vigorous head wiggling confirmed that all understood.

That will mean they'll get it done by the first of May, Jana calculated silently, and then I'll have a couple of weeks to furnish it.

"I *should* dock your wages for the cost of the glass," Jana said.

Their look of utter alarm was a cold dash of water to her anger, as she knew how close to the edge of survival they lived.

"From now on, everyone is working carefully, right?" she warned. "Carefully! You understand? *Samjhé*? Using your brains! Or else I fire the lot of you and get new men on the job."

Recognizing that this was an unlikely threat, they all said, "Yes, yes, memsahib," and she turned, closed the dining room door against the noise, and went back to the salon.

"Buddhu!" cried Mr. Ganguly, greeting her happily with his new word.

"Mind your manners," she said, and tried to go back to work.

‧⊕ Open to Interpretation

As the banging continued in the dining room, all of a sudden Jana became aware that the doorbell was tinkling, first tentatively, then more insistently. A customer, she thought, oh dear. If noise was bad for music transcriptions, it was even worse for telling fortunes. What people wanted when they came in off the street into Jana Bibi's Excellent Fortunes was a quiet little refuge where they could ask their most sensitive questions. How

could she give them hope for the future or understanding of
the present when their very brains were being rattled?

She looked at her watch and saw with relief that it was getting on to five P.M., when the workmen would quit and all would
be peaceful again.

Mr. Ganguly imitated the ringing of the doorbell.

"Yes, I know," Jana said. "I'm going to answer it immediately."

She opened the door to find an earnest-looking young man
with tortoiseshell glasses and a shock of black hair that fell over
his forehead. He wore an expensive-looking tweed jacket, with
a muffler wrapped around his neck.

An anxious line between his eyebrows marred his pleasant
face, and he had a tense expression that Jana had seen on many
other customers. She was always gratified when someone came
in with that worried wrinkle and walked out with a smooth
forehead.

"You are Jana Bibi of Jana Bibi's Excellent Fortunes?" the
young man asked.

"Yes, I am," she said.

"My name," he began, and his voice was blotted out by several loud thumps from the dining room.

Jana gestured for him to come in, yelling, "So sorry, the
noise will stop in a minute." She led him into the salon and
pulled out a chair from the table. "Do sit down. Would you
like tea?"

He shook his head. "No, no, I have just had."

"Water, then?"

He nodded, and she went to the sideboard and filled a tumbler from the jug.

The hammering from the dining room abated, making the
sudden silence seem even more delicious than an ordinary
silence.

"Finally!" said Jana. "I'm so sorry you had to sit through that.
The workmen have been making this place a madhouse. Now
that we can hear ourselves think, do tell me your name again."

"I am Deepak," the young man said.

"Namasté, Deepak-ji," Mr. Ganguly called from his perch. At least the bird's going to be on his best behavior, Jana thought. She was glad; the lad looked as if he needed an extra dose or two of TLC.

"Tell me what brings you here," she said.

"Worries," young Deepak said. "Worries about the future."

Worry is such a curse, thought Jana. She listened sympathetically, while Mr. Ganguly leaned forward from his perch, his head tilted at a thoughtful angle.

"I need courage," said the young man.

Jana sighed. "Oh dear, so do I. So does *everyone*. I wish we could have Mr. Abinath bottle it and sell it in his apothecary. May I ask what you need courage for?"

"I am an MA candidate in geology," the young man said.

Jana, herself largely self-educated, couldn't help being impressed by letters after a person's name. "Why, that's excellent," she said. "Congratulations! You must have had to pass all sorts of terribly difficult exams to get to this point."

"Yes, I did," said the young man, with some pride.

"Have you another big exam coming up?" Jana asked. "Is that your worry?"

"No, no, exams are all finished. I have passed. First-class," he added matter-of-factly.

"First-class on your MA exams! That *is* impressive," Jana said. "Have you a thesis to write?"

"Thesis is finished," said Deepak. "Only formalities are left."

"Perhaps . . . you're worried about employment?" Jana asked.

Deepak fell silent for a moment, and Jana was sure she'd finally identified the problem. There were so many educated, unemployed young men like Deepak; all that study, and then— crash. Massive disappointment as they found dull jobs they considered way beneath their station—or no job at all.

However, she was wrong again. "I have had an interview with Standard Oil Company," said Deepak. "You know Standard Oil?"

"I should say I do," said Jana. "Everyone does."

"There were one hundred candidates for the job," said Deepak.

"One hundred!" said Jana. "Oh dear me."

"No, no, that's not the problem," Deepak rushed to say. "They have offered me the position."

At this point, Jana burst out, "Bravo for you!" For the life of her, she could not fathom what the young man's dilemma might be. He sounded like the epitome of success. Perhaps it was unrequited love that was causing his distress? A romantic triangle?

It was not. "The problem is," the young man said, "that my father wants me to go into *his* business."

"Ah. I see," said Jana.

"I barely *hinted* to him that I had other plans, and he got such an insulted look on his face. Family tradition," said Deepak gloomily. "If it's good enough for him, it's good enough for me. Or so he thinks. He is a narrow man."

"Is he really?" said Jana. "You're sure about that? He allowed you to go study for the MA."

"Only because I told him geology was related to gemology. He is a gem dealer, you see. You probably know him. M. L. Shah—he is the owner of Priceless Gems."

"Oh, yes, of course, I've seen the sign," said Jana.

She cast about for something to say. She'd heard many versions of the tug-of-war between generations. A girl saying, "My parents want me to get married, and I want to go to university." A dad complaining, "My wife and I have given our *lives* to our daughter, and she turns down our choices for a husband." A dismissive son: "My parents are behind the times." An aggrieved mother: "My children are ungrateful."

Deepak broke into her thoughts, saying, "So, I need courage. The courage to tell my father that I am going to accept that job. And leave home. And go to Malaya to work. Or maybe Burma. My question to you is: If I do this, will things go well?"

Jana had a sense that if young Deepak summoned up some

gumption, things would indeed go well for him, and that surely any card she drew would confirm that. She picked up the new set of divination cards she had recently bought at Muktinanda's Stationers and School Supplies. The cards bore beautiful pictures of Hindu gods and goddesses, verses from the Bhagavad Gita, scenes from the *Ramayana*, and inspirational thoughts.

Jana moved Mr. Ganguly from his perch to the table and spread a few cards facedown. "All right, Mr. Ganguly, please choose one of these for Deepak."

Mr. Ganguly looked from left to right as if deciding, then picked a card and handed it to the young man.

"Hmm, " said Jana. "Lord Rama saying good-bye to his father, Dasaratha . . ."

Just the ticket, she thought: a man setting out from his ancestral home. She glanced up and was horrified to see Deepak's face twist in dismay.

"But his father *told* him to leave," Deepak pointed out. "Lord Rama is *obeying* his father. The lesson of the card is filial obedience."

"It might be," said Jana. "But I can't help thinking that the actual leaving is important. You can emphasize the obedience— or you can emphasize the leaving."

"That sounds a bit subversive to me," Deepak said.

"Could you get your own way without insulting your father?" she asked. "Make him feel honored and respected without giving in to him? Still be his loyal son without being his underling? At the very least, I think you should play for time. Ask Standard Oil *when* they want you to come on the payroll."

This attempt at compromise struck a chord with Deepak, who nodded slowly.

"I know you want to be on good terms with your father," Jana said. "Because, in spite of your differences, the two of you love each other deeply, is it not so?"

With a faint intake of breath, Deepak admitted, "Love is not lacking."

"And your father would be so proud to tell his friends about 'my son working in Malaya' or 'my son working in Burma.'"

Hope flickered briefly in Deepak's eyes. "I believe he would." After a moment, he asked, "Have you any children of your own, madam?"

"I have a son," Jana said.

"And does he obey you?"

"Good heavens, no!" Jana burst out laughing. "The idea wouldn't even occur to him. Nor to *me*, for that matter. I don't think I've ever given him any orders anyway. Not since he was seven years old."

"And his father?"

"His father is no longer among the living, but no, I don't remember my husband giving orders to Jack."

"I see. But you Europeans are different from us," Deepak said.

"Not that different," said Jana.

The young man looked at his watch. "I must go. I told my father I would help in the store this afternoon."

"Don't despair, Deepak," Jana said, as she showed him to the door. "Have faith in your own bright future. And don't underestimate your father, either. He might well be very proud of you if you leave—in spite of his desire to keep you with him. As you yourself put it, love is not lacking."

After this encounter, she sat in the window seat, staring out at the fair-weather clouds drifting by in the bright blue sky. She was reminded of a soothsayer she'd met who read clouds. What could one predict from clouds, she'd asked him, besides rain?

"If you are looking for a story," the sky-reading man had said, "the clouds help the story spring to your mind. See how clouds are sometimes angry and sometimes playful. Sometimes they frown down on you and sometimes they skip across the sky. The customer's story is inside him—or inside her. The clouds help bring it out."

Into Hot Water

✒ Two Boilers

When Mr. Aram from Modern Conveniences showed up to figure out whether an Anand hot-water boiler could be installed at the Jolly Grant House, Mary and Jana met him at the gate. He was a tubby, clean-shaven man with a receding hairline, round cheeks, and a dimple in his chin.

"Good morning, Mrs. Laird," he said merrily. "I'm so pleased you sent for me."

"Why, thank you, Mr. Aram," she said. "I'm so pleased you came."

"You and I," he said, "both want to bring more happiness to mankind, isn't it?"

"Well, yes, I suppose so," said Jana. The sales pitch she was expecting had started on a high-minded note, indeed.

"Your business is telling people excellent fortunes. My business is getting people into hot water." He paused. "In a *good* way of course. Ha ha."

Jana made herself smile politely.

"You know what my name means, do you not?" Mr. Aram asked.

"Well, yes," said Jana, remembering that an *aram kursi* was an easy chair. "It means comfort, doesn't it?"

"Exactly. And you also know what the word *anand* means, no?"

"I thought it was a name," Jana said. "The name of the family that owns the company that makes the boilers." A new twist on the old nursery rhyme popped into her brain: that heats the water that bathes the people that live in the house that Jack built.

"It *is* a name," Mr. Aram said. "But the meaning is . . . happiness. Contentment. Joy!"

Mary said suspiciously, "You are selling joy? I thought you were selling fixtures."

"They are fixtures to make you joyful," Mr. Aram said. "You will see."

"Comfort and joy," said Mary. "Just like Christmas."

Mr. Aram beamed. "Quite right."

Jana and Mary led the merry vendor first to the cookhouse, where he examined the narrow, shadowy kitchen, with its built-in hearth on one wall and recessed shelves on another. Mr. Aram noted the position of the cast-iron sink and took some measurements; then he inspected the aging pipes and rubbed his finger along a patch of corrosion.

Next, they went around the outside of the house and down a stone staircase to a terrace, and through the double doors into the basement. Over the years, this floor had lodged domestic staff members numbering from two or three to a couple of dozen, in a warren of small rooms with high windows. A narrow hall led to a Turkish toilet and a couple of bathing cubicles, where Mr. Aram took notes about faucets.

On the ground floor, he examined a tiny washroom, and on the next level, he checked out Jana's gray austere bathing cubicle and WC with the high toilet tank. In the proposed guest bath, he tapped here and there with a little hammer.

"We can easily go through the wall," he said, his face lighting up.

Pipes going through walls, Jana thought with alarm—was the house strong enough for this kind of treatment? Did one subject elderly patients to unnecessary surgery? Her heart sank at the prospect of more banging and clattering, dust and chaos.

Mr. Aram clearly sensed her dismay. "Mrs. Laird, do *not* worry. We will drill the smallest holes possible; the pipes will fit nicely. There will be no problem whatsoever." At the end of the inspection, he gave his breezy verdict: "Old, but still serviceable."

For a moment Jana thought he was talking about *her* and threw him an offended and inquiring glance.

"Your house," Mr. Aram explained. "It is suitable for adaptation. I recommend two hot-water boilers. A small geyser for the kitchen and a large one for the house."

Jana drew a deep breath. "Can you tell me how much all this will cost?"

Whipping out a notebook, Mr. Aram did some quick calculations, the total of which made Jana's head swim. "Does this include labor?" she asked.

"Yes, yes, labor is included," he assured her. "For only a small extra fee. I will send my own workmen—they are highly skilled, just ask anyone. How can you turn your back on comfort and joy, Mrs. Laird?"

"I'll give you my decision soon, Mr. Aram," she said gloomily.

When Mr. Aram had gone, she asked Mary, "What do you think?"

"It would be better than blowing the electric fuses all the time," Mary said. "But there would be one more wallah to pay. Wood costs money, Jana mem. Pay for wood or pay for electricity—that's the choice. Hot water costs money."

"It does rather boil down to that, doesn't it?" Jana said.

Oh, decisions, decisions.

✑ *Young Master Tilku*

Back in the salon, Tilku was holding up a printed paper bearing the St. Regis Pre-Military Academy crest of castle, cannons, and winged lions. "Jana mem?"

"Yes, Tilku?"

"The school list, you remember?"

Oh, my word. Mr. Comfort and Joy and his bathtubs had driven clear out of her mind her promise to go shopping with Tilku for his school supplies.

"Give me just a few minutes, would you, Tilku?" she said.

Twenty minutes later, they were going up the broad entry steps to Muktinanda's Stationers and School Supplies. Over the storefront, painted right on the building in large capital letters, were the words "The Right Tools for the Right Job." Inside, the lanky, fastidious merchant was straightening the already tidy stacks of notebooks, pencils, pencil cases, pencil sharpeners, rubber erasers, logarithm tables, and everlasting calendars.

"Mrs. Laird," said Muktinanda. "How pleasant to see you. Hello, Tilku. When are you leaving for boarding school?"

"Tomorrow," said Tilku.

"Tomorrow!" exclaimed Muktinanda. "You're here not a moment too soon." His eyes lit up at the length of the list that Tilku now took from his pocket. Without delay, Muktinanda went from shelf to shelf, murmuring. "Black ink. Blotting paper. Compass. Protractor. Ruler. Hmm, where are the slide rules? Oh yes, there they are."

Tilku's eyes grew wide as Muktinanda added to the pile of items on the counter. Jana remembered the day when the cheerful messenger boy had moved into the Jolly Grant House with his single possession: a broken comb.

Textbooks were next. "I can supply one hundred percent of requirements," Muktinanda said happily. He thumped down a mathematics book. Then history. Geography. English grammar and *Lamb's Tales from Shakespeare*. An up-to-date atlas that showed all the new African nations.

Finally, Muktinanda reached with a long pair of grippers to the ceiling rack and took down a canvas school satchel. "Most commodious," he said. "You need this. We'll pack everything into it right now."

Tilku, shouldering the bulging satchel, looked like an eager young mountain climber.

"On account, Mrs. Laird?" Muktinanda asked.

"Yes, please," said Jana.

They got home to the Jolly Grant House to find Hajji Feroze Ali Khan of Royal Tailors in the courtyard, accompanied by one of his employees carrying a huge bundle.

"The school uniforms," Feroze said.

"Yes, of course, Feroze sahib, please come in," said Jana.

In the salon, Feroze ceremoniously untied the bundle of clothes. "White shirts—four. Khaki trousers—two. Sports uniforms—two. School blazer—one. Wool overcoat—one."

"Go try them on," Jana said, and Tilku scooped up the clothes and pelted down the stairs.

While Tilku was gone, Feroze and Jana made polite chitchat. Mary arrived and briefly hefted the satchel Tilku had left on the table. "Oof," she said, raising her eyebrows. "That child now owns too many items!"

Finally, rapid footsteps sounded on the stairs, and Tilku burst back into the room.

"Oh my," said Jana.

"You are one pukka sahib," Mary said.

Tilku turned from left to right to let them admire the dark green blazer with St. Regis's castle, cannons, and lions on the pocket. His green-and-brown-striped tie contrasted nicely with his cream-colored shirt; his khaki trousers had a sharp crease. Suddenly, Tilku was transformed into a young gentleman. The only humorous note was the short haircut he'd gotten the day before, which made his ears appear to stick out.

Feroze checked the sleeve and pant lengths and deemed everything in order. Then, quietly, he handed Jana a meticulous bill, and, finding everything correct, she counted out the payment.

After everyone else had left, Jana was alone in the salon with Mr. Ganguly.

What was that Shakespearean speech Jana had had to memorize in school? "Costly thy habit as thy purse can buy"—that was it. Only problem was, it wasn't Tilku's purse that was in question here; it was her own.

"Mr. G," Jana said to the parrot, "I'm glad *you* don't need new clothes. You are quite splendid as you are."

Mr. Ganguly preened, his red beak and black neck ring providing an elegant contrast to his brilliant green feathers. Jana reflected that her pet, at least, was always in his dress uniform, at no extra cost.

The next day, Jana got up early to accompany Tilku to his school. During the long bus ride, they both fell asleep, waking up to take a tonga from the bus terminal to the campus. St. Regis Pre-Military Academy favorably impressed Jana, with its Gothic buildings, neat paths and courtyards, and glass-fronted display cases containing sports shields and cups. The school had a most tony appearance, and the parents of the other boys certainly looked tony, too, sweeping up in their Mercedes-Benzes and Cadillacs. Next to the mothers in their silk saris and the fathers in their business suits or uniforms dripping with medals, Jana felt conspicuously humble. She hoped Tilku wouldn't be intimidated by his classmates, and that his horizons would be expanded.

At Tilku's dormitory, they stashed his trunk under the cot to which he'd been assigned. To be sure, the room gave Jana a momentary chill, with its cement floor and long rows of metal cots. But, she told herself, it was no worse than Jack's school in Scotland, which she'd seen once or twice during her rare visits.

She was also reassured when, during the reception for newcomers, the headmaster, Mr. Chopra, clapped Tilku on the shoulder and said to Jana, "It's meritorious of you, Mrs. Laird, to sponsor this young fellow. Have no fear whatsoever—we'll make a real man of him."

"He's prepared to work *very* hard," Jana said, and Tilku corroborated this with a spirited wobble of his head.

Only at the last moment, when Jana said good-bye at the school gate, did a look of terror flash across Tilku's face.

"Good luck, Pilot sahib," she said, lingering a moment to put her arm around him. Throwing off her hug with a half-affectionate, half-embarrassed look, he squared his shoulders and headed back along the path to his dormitory. As his small, spunky figure faded into the distance, it seemed to her more and more solitary and more and more vulnerable.

The following Tuesday brought the first of Tilku's obligatory letters home. Jana could picture him squinting in concentration as he penned a few words, enough to satisfy the St. Regis rule that all boys put a letter to their parents or guardians in a box in the dormitory each Sunday afternoon. He certainly wasn't going to risk the penalty of no dinner and a demerit, especially the dinner part.

"Dear Jana mem," Tilku had written, "if I leave this school, will you get your money back? Very truly yours, Tilku."

Oh dear, sighed Jana, this is hardly evidence of unbridled enthusiasm.

The next week's letter wasn't much more encouraging. "Dear Jana mem," it said, "this school is difficult. Very truly yours, Tilku."

Poor lad, though Jana. He's coping with everything from longitude and latitude to lining up for meals and sitting still in assembly. Her normal optimism was shaken, but she consoled herself that this week, at least, Tilku hadn't mentioned quitting.

We Are All Trying Hard

⚡ Cleanest Toilets on the Planet

Jana wavered for a few days over whether to buy the Anand hot-water boilers. The household had gotten along fine heating up a couple of gallons at a time, as needed, hadn't they? But one morning, after she'd given herself a particularly stinging electric shock with the immersion coil, she received a note from Mr. Aram at Modern Conveniences, saying that he would, just this once, reduce the price by 20 percent.

"They'll never be cheaper," she decided, and with that, she dashed off her answer and sent it back to Mr. Aram with the same messenger boy.

The two white enameled metal cylinders were in the courtyard within hours, as if Mr. Aram were afraid that Jana would change her mind if he delayed delivery. Then came porters bearing copper pipes and tools so crude-looking that Jana just had to turn away. It reminded her of a visit to the dentist, when she'd made the mistake of glancing at the instrument tray. Not in *my* mouth, she'd thought—but that was exactly where they were going.

The cacophony in the house increased; Jana pictured a music score marked with *fffff*. A couple of days later, when the pipes were in place, a small army of porters trudged through the gate with the bathroom fixtures on their backs. The Jolly

Grant House rang with people shouting things like "Watch out, stupid! You'll crack the porcelain."

Mr. Ganguly heard the word *buddhu* so many times that it became now firmly established in his vocabulary.

Then came the first quiet morning, when only the painters in the dining room were left, the soft *swish-swish* of their brushes music to Jana's ears. She didn't even mind that the house smelled of paint. Soon the workmen would be finished and gone.

She settled down at the salon table and examined her manuscript of Ian the butler's tunes. She loved the look of sheet music—just about any sheet music—and she'd taken infinite pains over these pages. The grace notes, the tails, the clefs, the rests—all were tidily drawn and satisfyingly well proportioned.

"Jana mem," came Mary's voice from the hall. "Sorry to bother."

"No bother," said Jana. "Oh, you've found someone to help out when Jack and Katarina are here."

"This is Harmendra," said Mary, beckoning a scared-looking young man of about fifteen years of age to come forward. He was dressed in a khaki shirt and trousers and a pullover with yellow roses embroidered on the front.

"He can manage the boiler and help in the kitchen," Mary said. "Two hours in the morning and two hours in the afternoon."

"Have you had work experience before?" Jana asked the young man.

"Yes, madam," he said, without looking up.

"What kind of work?"

"This and that," he said.

"I see," said Jana.

"Jana mem, this is a willing fellow," Mary said. "Not to worry, I will supervise."

"Very well," said Jana. "We'll try each other out for a few weeks. Oh! For starters, let's give Mr. Anand's boilers a shot. Have him load them up with wood chips."

A half hour later, Jana went up to the guest bath and turned the lavabo tap that was marked with a red dot. Out of the spigot gushed a glorious jet of hot water—if anything, a little too hot, Jana thought, testing it with her finger. Before she could add cold from the other faucet, however, she heard Mary on the stairs. To Jana's surprise, Mary's eyebrows were crunched up with annoyance. She swept past Jana and turned on the tap with the blue dot.

Out gushed another stream of water, steaming as exuberantly as the first.

"You will see—same thing with the bathtub," Mary said, and turned on the two taps there. Then she flushed the toilet.

Dismayed, Jana watched tendrils of steam spiraling from the toilet bowl.

Mary said, "Jana mem, we have the cleanest toilets in India. Boiled and sterilized. But no cold water anywhere."

Jana went down to the salon and penned an irate note to Mr. Aram. Two hours later, the noisy workmen returned, and again the decibel level rose to *fffff* in the Jolly Grant House.

❧ Encounters in the Park

"Walk?" screeched Mr. Ganguly, above the clanging of pipes and the shouts of the workmen.

"Best idea you've had today," Jana said. She grabbed an unopened letter from Tilku off the sideboard, stuffed it into her satchel, and let Mr. Ganguly climb to her shoulder. Once outside, she heaved a sigh of relief; compared to the house, the normal clattering of rickshaws and hawking of street vendors suddenly seemed restful. She made her way across town and into the sanctuary of the Municipal Garden.

School was out for the day, and she smiled at a group of little girls in navy skirts and white blouses who were skipping rope. Half a dozen others (burgundy skirts, this time) were going dizzily round and round on the spinning platform, latecomers running up and jumping on with triumphant shrieks.

At some distance away, Jana's optometrist, Niel Powell, was taking his habitual walk with his two dachshunds, Albert and Victoria. Mr. Ganguly gave a flutter on Jana's shoulder.

"Dogs," he said. *"Buddhu."*

"Mind your manners," she said.

She was reminded of a saying: Dogs look up to people, cats look down on them, and pigs consider them equal. Parrots, Jana was sure, considered themselves superior to *all* other creatures, and she wasn't sure they were wrong.

"Hello, Jana," Mr. Powell said.

"Good afternoon, Niel," she said. "All finished seeing patients today?"

"Yes, I've closed up the office."

Indeed, he was not in his high-necked white professional coat but in a woolly cable-knit pullover that set off his thick black hair and dark eyes and gave him a sporty and dashing look.

Jana and her eye doctor had started out on a formal basis, addressing each other as "Mrs. Laird" and "Mr. Powell," but later they'd gotten to know each other socially. Jana had made friends with Niel's cousin Miriam Orley and had been a guest at Miriam's birthday party at his house. Moreover, she had returned frequently to visit Miriam's aunt, the aged Mrs. Sylvia Foster, whom Niel had lodged for many years. Niel and Sylvia were not actually related by blood, but by various skeins of marriage and years of friendship.

Niel traced his heritage back to a Rajput woman and a Scottish businessman who'd come to India in the early eighteenth century and never left. His musical parents had named him after Niel Gow, the Scottish composer. Spying an old piano in Niel's living room, Jana had once asked if he played it.

"I used to in school days," he'd said. "But, alas, with my optometry practice, I rarely have time."

Jana liked Niel Gow Powell very much—he was a patient and exacting optometrist and a kind man. Moreover, as both her son, Jack, and Kenneth Stuart-Smith had told her, Niel was unusually brilliant, although not flashily so. His hobbies included making optical instruments of a highly professional standard. In fact, one of his telescopes was at that very minute sitting in the lookout room at the Jolly Grant House, on indefinite loan to Jana.

Niel was now face-to-face with Jana, the two dogs wiggling their long sausage bodies beside him. "Sit, Albert. Sit, Victoria," he said, and the two dogs instantly sank onto their short haunches.

"How are things at home?" Jana asked. Seeing Niel had given her a twinge of guilt that she hadn't visited Aunt Sylvia lately.

"We're muddling through," Niel said. "Although I *am* concerned about Sylvia."

"What's wrong with her?" Jana asked, her guilt intensifying.

"Nothing specific," said Niel. "Just—she seems a bit blue. And slowing down, I fear."

Sylvia, blue? That was hard to picture. Jana knew her ninety-two-year-old friend to be relentlessly cheerful. As for slowing down?

"I can't believe it," Jana said. "Last time I saw her she was discussing India-China relations." She remembered quite clearly Sylvia saying that brotherhood between India and China—*Hindi-Chini bhai-bhai*—was *Hindi-Chini* bye-bye.

Mr. Powell sighed. "She doesn't even seem to care about politics anymore. And she's stopped joking—if it really was a joke—about finding a fourth husband. I hate to put a burden on you—I know you're dreadfully busy—but do you think you could come over and cheer her up sometime? And bring Mr. Ganguly; she loves him."

"Of course I will," said Jana.

His face brightening, Niel said, "I hear you've got family coming to visit!"

"I have!" Jana said. "How did you hear that?"

"Jacob John told me. Mary told him." Niel laughed. "No secrets in this town. But anyway, that's wonderful. It must be so nice to have a grown son. And you must very excited to meet his fiancée."

"I am indeed," Jana said. She knew that Niel had no children. He *looked* like the archetypical life-long bachelor, but Miriam Orley had told her that he'd been married once, to a woman named Celeste. The union had been anything but celestial: Niel's wife had run off with a Panamanian businessman, and Niel had moved from Calcutta to Hamara Nagar to escape the humiliation and heartbreak of the experience.

"What fun for you!" Niel said, but a wistful expression came over his face, making Jana wonder whether he was nursing some painful regret about the way his life had turned out. If he'd had a blissful marriage and a fine collection of children, he might be walking his grandchildren in the park right now, rather than two dachshunds. However, she'd always thought of him as a happy man, self-sufficient and content to stay that way.

Now, although not wanting to pry, she asked, "Are you all right?"

"Of course," he said. "A bit tired, that's all."

Mr. Ganguly, losing patience, pulled on a strand of Jana's hair.

Niel said, "It looks as if your parrot is eager to move on." Albert and Victoria, until now placid at his feet, also were getting restless.

"It's lovely to talk to you, Niel," Jana said. "When the renovations are done, perhaps you'd like to come by and have a quiet meal. And bring Aunt Sylvia, of course."

"A delightful idea," Niel said. He looked down at the dachshunds. "Okay, kiddies, let's go."

As Niel and the dogs disappeared, Jana reflected on how she'd never before seen him subdued. Delightful as Aunt Sylvia was, Jana concluded that having charge of her was beginning to press heavily on him, even with the help of Jacob John.

Walking over to the birdbath, she put Mr. Ganguly on the rim, then settled down on a bench and read Tilku's letter.

"Dear Jana mem, I am trying hard. Very hard. Yours truly, Tilku."

She put the letter back in her bag. Poor darling, she thought, I'm sure you *are* trying very hard indeed. I hope you get your bearings soon.

Loud cawing came from the birdbath, and she saw that a crow had settled on the opposite rim from Mr. Ganguly. It cawed again, and the parrot imitated the sound in a higher register. Was the crow going to attack? It wouldn't be much of a match, Jana thought. The raucous, gray and black creature looked enormous next to Mr. Ganguly's gemlike dash of green. Its great wedge of a beak could tear him to pieces.

Yet the two did not fight. Mr. Ganguly was evidently curious about his visitor, and the crow, for his part, seemed fascinated, too; they observed each other, cocked their heads, and called back and forth.

"*Kya kya*—what, what—*kya kya*?" interrogated Mr. Ganguly, and "Caw, caw," the crow replied.

"Beautiful, marvelous," Mr. Ganguly called, and flapped his wings.

Meanwhile, a young man with a muffler around his neck approached Jana.

"Namasté," he said.

Now, where had she seen him? Oh yes, it was Deepak, the fellow who'd wanted help gathering courage for a talk with his father. "Hello, Deepak," she said, gesturing for him to sit down next to her on the bench. "It's nice to see you again. You are well?"

"I am," said Deepak. "And you?"

"Very well, thank you."

Deepak's face was still as pinched and anxious as when Jana had first met him. She asked cautiously, "Well, have you told your father about your job?"

"Not yet," said Deepak. "Just today he was talking happily about how his business was growing and how he would put me in charge of the Dehra Dun branch of Priceless Gems. If you knew how terrible I am as a salesman, you would laugh."

Jana shook her head. "I'm sure I wouldn't laugh, Deepak, knowing how you feel about it."

He scuffed one shoe in the dirt and said, "Time is *ticking* away, Madam Jana. I must give my answer to Standard Oil soon or they will withdraw the offer."

All Deepak needs, she said to herself, is the tiniest little nudge.

"Just tell your dad about the offer," she said. "It can't do any harm to let him know that the rest of the world thinks highly of you."

"I suppose you are right," Deepak said.

"If you take the first small step," said Jana, "the rest will fall into place."

"One small step," said Deepak, getting up from the bench. He turned and looked at her for a long moment, indecision still pressing heavily on his shoulders. "One small step, you say."

"I do."

He nodded. "Good afternoon, Madam Jana."

She gave him what she hoped was an encouraging look. "Good afternoon, Deepak. Take heart."

• • •

When Deepak was gone, she got up and approached the bird-bath, making the crow flap furiously and lift off into flight.

Mr. Ganguly let out his version of the crow's caw, and she could swear, from the way he cocked his head, that he was love-struck. I am getting daft, she thought.

"You made a new friend, eh?" Jana said.

"Good bird," cried Mr. Ganguly, watching the crow disappear from view.

Marveling at how love could strike unpredictably, she let him climb up her arm onto her shoulder, and headed for home.

Mary Looks Ahead

⁓❦ *A Warm Water Rinse*

Her arms folded across her chest, Mary watched Mr. Comfort and Joy's workmen struggling to find the source of their plumbing mistake.

"It is valves!" one said.

"It is water pressure," said another. "Too much water pressure."

"It is the juncture of the pipes," said a third.

"It's all three," said Mary, pointing to where an old water pipe entered the geyser in the main house. "You should have attached this pipe lower down. Steam is pushing up in the wrong place."

After much discussion, the workmen tried it Mary's way, shamefacedly discovering that she was right.

The next morning, Mary had her first warm shower in the Jolly Grant House. She had rejected a bathtub, figuring that she would have to wash off completely before getting into it, and then what would be the point of just sitting there? So, standing on the cement floor, she wet her hair and rubbed shampoo into her scalp. How easy it is compared to sluicing yourself with a dipper, she thought as the water gurgled down the drain in the corner.

As a child, she had learned to wash fully clothed, in a river with other women and girls; the bath had been a social event.

But you get cleaner in a shower, she thought now, and it's nice not to have mud between your toes.

Back in her room and wrapped in a clean sari, she folded her quilt neatly on her charpoy. Then she faced the wall that held two pictures: a color print of Lord Jesus holding a lamb and a framed black-and-white photograph of the late Dr. Bhimrao R. Ambedkar, who had drafted the Constitution of India. Mary revered both as champions of the poor and suffering, and though she no longer considered *herself* poor and suffering, she still felt they deserved gratitude.

Accordingly, she gave thanks for daily bread, health, and the roof over her head. Then she prayed for health for Jana mem and Jack sahib and for the unknown far-off lady who was going to be Jack sahib's wife.

Her devotions done, she glanced at herself in the mirror. The sunlight slanting through the high window suddenly allowed a good, clear view of her face—and her hairline. She frowned at a few white hairs. Did that hot water wash *too* well, she wondered? A visit to Abinath's Apothecary was in order.

·⁂ Goddess Hair

That afternoon, Mary ran down to the apothecary, where she found Mr. Abinath putting up a poster. Three generations of a family were depicted: a grandfather in round spectacles and a white *dhoti* and shawl, a mother stirring something in a cooking pot, and boy and a girl doing their homework at a table. All looked alert and extremely happy.

"Namasté-ji," Mary said to Abinath. "That's a fine poster."

"I think so, too." Abinath stood back and admired it.

"What is it selling?" Mary asked.

Abinath pointed to where "R2" was written large, in the top right corner. "R2," he said. "Recognition and Recall—my new aid to memory. It halts the ravages of time; it helps mothers remember recipes and children learn their lessons. Would you like some?"

"No, thank you," said Mary. "I remember everything that I want to, and a few more things besides."

"Perhaps you are the exception that proves the rule."

Mary didn't know what rule he was talking about, but she refrained from asking, because when Abinath got chatting, he could be difficult to stop. However, she did indeed want to stop the ravages of time. Her glance traveled to the shelf where there were a good dozen hair dyes. She said to Abinath, "I need one bottle of Goddess Tresses."

Abinath took down a box that pictured a woman's back with jet-black hair streaming to a belted waist.

"Two rupees, eight annas," he said.

"Still very expensive," said Mary. Even though Abinath's was a fixed-price store, could one hand over money just like that, without a word of protest?

"Mary-ji, I told you before, this lotion is nationally advertised. I can't change the price! It's right there in the magazines. Just look, you will see."

"I don't look at magazines much," Mary said. "Very well. How about throwing in a pinch or two of cotton wool to rub off the excess?"

Abinath took some loose cotton fluff out of a box and handed it to her along with the Goddess Tresses box. Now feeling she'd gotten her money's worth, Mary paid for her purchase and bid Mr. Abinath a good afternoon.

⁓ *Who Knew Him First?*

When Mary got back from Abinath's, Lal Bahadur Pun was playing his pipes on the terrace. Mary felt her shoulders rise in irritation. She liked bagpipe playing well enough, but not at close range, like this. To make things worse, Lal Bahadur Pun was experimenting first with one phrase, then with another, without actually finishing a tune. It made Mary want to scream, "Make up your mind!" She let out an "oof" of relief when he finally put his instrument down.

"Which one did you like the best?" the Gurkha asked.

"Which what?" Mary asked.

"Which ending. For the march I am composing. For Jack sahib when he arrives."

Now Mary was doubly irritated. Lal Bahadur Pun was a brave man and had been, by all accounts, a good soldier. Yes, Mary was glad that he kept watch at the gate, so they could all sleep soundly at night. Yes, when Mary and Jana mem had first arrived in Hamara Nagar, he'd blasted the resident monkey troop out of the Jolly Grant House with martial tunes played at top volume.

But now, really, his attitude was too much. He thought he *owned* Jack sahib—just because, when Jack sahib had visited two years ago, Lal Bahadur Pun had given him a few pointers on how to play those self-same pipes.

Who knew Jack sahib *first,* anyway? Who knew him when he was a solemn little boy with pale gold curls? Who bathed him and tied his shoes and showed him how to do cat's cradle? Who sponged his forehead when he had a fever? Who snatched him away from that rabid cat before he could be bitten?

I, Mary Thomas, she thought. That's who.

You, Subedar-Major Lal Bahadur Pun, she said silently, you are very full of yourself, but you have only known Mr. Jack Laird since 1960. *I* have been his ayah since 1931, and *that* is a long time. Thirty-one years, to be precise.

"Use the second ending of the tune," she said, knowing that whatever she said, Lal Bahadur Pun wouldn't pay much attention anyway.

In Anticipation

⁓ A Visit from Padma

"It's very nice of you to drop by," Jana said. "I'm so very honored. Come, come, have a seat."

Mrs. Padma Ramachandran rarely came into town, as she was not needed in the Treasure Emporium. Her husband handled all the business decisions; her daughters Asha and Bimla waited on customers after school and on weekends; Aunt Putli attended the back desk; and a half dozen minions carried the merchandise around, wrapped parcels, and delivered large items to purchasers' homes. Meanwhile, Padma kept herself fully occupied with her household of seven children and numerous relatives, hangers-on, and domestic servants.

Padma settled herself in an armchair, adjusted her yellow-and-fuchsia sari around her generous curves, and looked around the room. A delicate fragrance of sandalwood and jasmine wafted to Jana's nose. Padma, not yet forty, had jet-black hair and flawless skin and exuded an ageless elegance. Her eyes now traveled from Mr. Ganguly's birdcage and the statue of Saint Francis feeding the birds to the painted Rajasthani peacocks and the table carved in the shape of an elephant.

"Quite a lot of animal motifs you have here," she noted.

"As you know, many of these things were bought at your very own Emporium," Jana said. "Will you take tea, *Shrimati-ji*?"

"I have just now taken," Padma said.

"One small cup?"

Padma swayed her head in polite but final refusal.

"I just came to congratulate you," Padma said. "About your son. Very good news. How old is he?"

"Thirty-six," said Jana.

"Oh my goodness, he's *so* old," said Padma. "He could be planning his *own* children's weddings by now. But, I suppose, better late than never. Being a bachelor . . ." Padma shook her head as if being a bachelor were a fate worse than death. "Everyone should get married. Parents cannot rest until their children are married, don't you agree? Myself, I am thinking about this one hundred percent of the time."

"Surely you don't have to worry for a while yet," Jana said. "Asha and Bimla are young yet. And so bright, I must add—tied for first place in their physics exam and off to Isabella Thoburn College in July. You must be proud."

"Yes, yes, of course, I am proud," Padma said dismissively. "But—why would my girls need to know physics? Do *you* know physics? Did you go to university?"

"Sadly, no," said Jana. "But I would have *loved* to get a bachelor's degree."

"Bachelor vachelor, that's the problem. Who wants lady bachelors?" Padma's face darkened. "By the time Asha and Bimla are bachelors, there won't be any gentleman bachelors left for them to marry!"

"Don't panic, Mrs. Ramachandran," Jana said. She pointed to an issue of *Filmfare* magazine on the side table. "You know the movie stars the Travancore Sisters?"

"Of course, they are my favorites," Padma said.

"I was just reading that the oldest two married quite late—closer to thirty than twenty. And the third is soon twenty-four, and not married yet."

Padma shuddered. "What on earth is their mother *thinking*? But anyway, the rules for the rich and famous are different from the rules for the rest of us. Mrs. Laird, when is the happy occasion for your son and his bride?"

"They haven't set a date yet," Jana said.

"I can have my astrologer draw up their charts and tell them the auspicious day and time," Padma said. "He would charge you a very reasonable price."

"Why, thank you for the offer, *Shrimati-ji*. I'll be certain to tell them about that when they arrive." Jack consulting an astrologer—fat chance, she thought.

They chatted some more—about young Vikram's cricket triumphs, about little Sonny's asthma, and about how Ramachandran's nephew and his wife, Teddy and Twinkle, had come to visit for two days and were still here two years later.

When all her concerns had been aired, Padma said, "All right, then, I must go."

Jana walked her guest out to the front gate.

"Namaskar," they bid each other. Padma climbed into the rickshaw that had been waiting the whole time, and rolled off.

The auspicious day, just the right moment . . . People do want to get the details right about something as momentous as marriage, Jana thought. She walked back into the house and went into the dining room to see how things were getting along.

"Oh, hell," she said.

One of the workers had overturned a bucket of brown paint, leaving a splash on the white wall and a growing amoeba-shaped puddle on the floor.

"No problem, no problem," the foreman said. "This will be cleaned up in one minute flat."

For a moment, she considered telling the men to leave the splatters on the wall and the stain on the floor and pretend it was a deliberate artistic decision. The workers, however, were already grabbing dirty rags and starting to scrub. They were making things worse by the minute, and Jana decided that it was often better not to watch work in progress.

"Carry on," she said with a sigh, and left the room.

◌ *Celebrity Weddings*

A couple of days later, Jana was reading newspapers at the salon table when the front door opened and two young female voices called, "Auntie Jana! Can we come?"

"Come along," she called, and in bounced Asha and Bimla Ramachandran. The eighteen-year-old twins had their mother's dark eyes and heart-shaped face, but in contrast to Padma's traditional style, they wore sporty turtleneck sweaters and jeans. Their braided hair was looped up and tied with jaunty ribbons. Actresses pictured in *Filmfare* were wearing their hair like that.

"Hello, girls," Jana said. "You're just in time for tea. Mary's been trying out some new cake recipes."

Mary's entrance with a huge chocolate cake brought cheers from the girls, which set off ecstatic wing flapping and girlish-sounding cheers from Mr. Ganguly, too.

"Triple layer with cream filling," Mary announced.

"Hoorah for Mary," cried Asha.

Jana cut large slices, which disappeared in no time, so she cut a second round.

"Dads told us your son is getting *married*," Asha said.

"Ooh, how did he meet his sweetheart?" Bimla wanted to know.

"I don't know," Jana said. "I'm still waiting for the full story. You know how it is with letters—you ask a question and then the person writes back but doesn't answer it."

"It's always so romantic with Europeans," said Asha. "They meet—and zing! Cupid shoots his arrow into their hearts." She pantomimed drawing back a bow and releasing it.

"I love weddings so much," said Bimla dreamily.

Asha turned to Jana. "Your son should have his wedding *here*. Don't you think so, Mary?"

"Of course," Mary said.

"And we could be bridesmaids," Bimla said. "With wide-brimmed hats. Just like Princess Grace of Monaco's bridesmaids."

Asha and Bimla, it turned out, knew the details of every celebrity wedding of the century.

"Princess Grace's dress cost forty-five hundred pounds," said Asha.

"Her dowry was two million dollars," Bimla said.

"They had six hundred guests at the cathedral," Asha said.

"And three thousand guests at the garden party," Bimla added. "Everyone in Monaco was invited."

"Your son and his bride could invite everyone in Hamara Nagar," Asha said to Jana. "Why not? It's not that big a town. What—five thousand or so?"

Meanwhile, Bimla was continuing on the matter of trousseau. "The maharani of Jaipur got hers in Italy."

"Plus, nightgowns from France," Asha added. "And two hundred saris from India—don't forget those."

"Someone gave her a house in Mussoorie. And a Bentley," Bimla said. "And a Packard. Wouldn't you love to have a Packard? Ride around in a car as big as a sitting room? Jana, will you give Katarina and Jack a car?"

"A rickshaw," Jana said, sending the twins into yet more laughter.

"What did *you* get for wedding presents, Auntie Jana?" Bimla asked suddenly.

Jana was startled by the very question; and silence fell abruptly, as if a teacher had just walked into a class of misbehaving students.

"Not very much," she said.

"Why not? Did you *elope*?" Asha asked.

Jana took a breath before admitting, "I did, actually."

"Oh, that's so *daring*," Asha said. "So romantic. Tell us *all* the details."

"Some other time," said Jana, thinking of her departure for India on an unglamorous steamer.

In spite of her wet blanket of an answer, however, the girls were only briefly subdued.

Bimla said, "Mums is terribly afraid that when we go to Isabella Thoburn College, we'll meet boys from La Martiniere and run off with them. She's sure that someday after class, we'll leap merrily over the garden wall and that will be the end of it."

"Well, don't do that," Jana said. "Leap over the garden wall, that is. You know what they say: marry in haste, repent at leisure."

Mary came in to get the used tea things, and Asha turned to her. "Mary, you got married once, right? Did you run away and elope?"

"Oh, no," Mary said. "These people came to my parents and said, How about marrying your daughter with my son. My parents had to pay a lot of money, which they had to borrow, but they said yes. They told me, We've found you a good boy. Now you go and be a good wife."

"What happened to the husband?" Asha asked.

Mary hesitated awhile, then said, "He died."

Bimla said, "Oh, how sad for you."

Mary made a noncommittal motion of her chin. "Yes, very sad."

◦ꝝ *Good Pood*

When Asha and Bimla had left, Jana carried the plates across to the cookhouse and placed them next to the sink. Harmendra, the young man Mary had hired recently, looked up, startled.

"Wash carefully now," Mary was saying. "Don't break anything!"

With a huge display of caution, Harmendra slowly swished a cloth around each plate.

Jana and Mary went out into the side yard and Jana said, in a low voice, "How is he working out?"

"He's good enough for temporary help," Mary said, with a shrug. "Which cake did you like better, Jana mem, the lemon one we had the other day or the chocolate one?"

"Chocolate," said Jana.

"Okay," said Mary, "we'll have a big chocolate cake the first day Jack sahib is here. But tomorrow, I'll make sponge cake, just for practice."

"Mary, you'll wear yourself out before they even get here," Jana said.

"No, I won't," said Mary. "Cooking is easy for me."

"It's a good thing," said Jana, "because it's not easy for me. Remember that pudding you used to make when Jack was small?"

"Rice pudding," said Mary. "With currants."

"Oh, yes," said Jana.

Her eyes blurred for a moment at the memory of three little towheads sitting at the table on the verandah of the mission house, Jack holding up his spoon, his two little sisters watching him adoringly.

"This is . . ." Jack would say authoritatively, "good pood!" Then all three children would collapse into gales of laughter. Mary would shake her head and tell them that they were silly babas, which only had the effect of making them laugh even harder.

Mary broke into Jana's thoughts: "Jack sahib liked mango fool the best when he was little. You remember that tree at the mission, Jana mem? In the month of May? There were mangoes all over the place."

Jana smiled. She did remember now, but she wouldn't have thought of it if Mary hadn't mentioned it. It was good to have someone else's memory supplement one's own.

"Mangoes will be in season when Jack and Katarina are here," she said.

"I'll make mango fool," said Mary. "Everyone likes that. Oh. One thing—does Katarina memsahib eat Indian food?"

Jana said, "I don't know, Mary. I suppose she must. Yes, actually, Jack mentioned in a letter that they'd gone to an Indian restaurant."

"I'll make my Madras specialties," Mary said, with a gleam in her eye.

"Perhaps not too spicy at first," Jana said. "Give her a few days to get settled, and then see." She remembered Jack on his last visit, manfully forking down Mary's Madras specialties and wiping perspiration from his brow. He liked things on the bland side—meat, potato, two vegetables, and gravy—but would never have hurt Mary's feelings. Katarina might be more gastronomically adventurous, of course, but one never knew. They'd find out soon enough.

"I'll make exactly what each likes," Mary resolved.

"Mary, you're a good sport," Jana said.

There was an ominous clink from the cookhouse; had something broken? "I'll go watch that boy Harmendra," Mary said. "He still needs training. Don't worry. If he breaks anything, I'll give him a good tight slap."

"No need to be fierce," said Jana. Sometimes the force of Mary's personality felt like a strong wind that swept away obstacles in its path.

Mary Does Some Errands

✧ A Handsome Man

"Vanakkam, Mary." A voice startled Mary as she made her way through the Central Bazaar, on her way to get supplies for her own cooking. Mrs. Sylvia Foster's bearer, Jacob John, had just come out of a shop that dealt in secondhand books.

"How are you keeping, Jacob-*anna*?" she asked. She addressed him as "older brother Jacob," since he was easy to talk to, the way an older brother should be. In her experience, real older brothers weren't necessarily that way.

She was always glad to see this make-believe older brother, since, like Meenakshi at the Ramachandran house, he spoke the same mixture of Tamil, Malayalam, Hindi, and English that she did. Plus, she found him handsome, in his snowy-white high-collared coat and trousers and tidy flat turban. How old could he be? Maybe sixty, sixty-two, she figured. Certainly he had lived longer than her own forty-six years. His serene face, however, had very few lines.

"How is Mrs. Foster?" Mary asked politely.

"She is as well as can be expected, at her age," said Jacob John. "Almost ninety-three. Can you imagine living that long?"

"Yes, I can," said Mary. "I imagine myself at that age, sitting in the sun outside my small whitewashed brick house, admiring my vegetable garden."

"And at that age, who will bend over to pick your vegetables for you?" asked Jacob John.

"I'll adopt a girl to be my granddaughter," Mary said. "Someone who has run away from home." Adopting a runaway was one of Mary's pet dreams. In a sense, Jana had done that, long ago, when she'd given Mary, then fifteen, a refuge and a job. One day, Mary would pass on the favor to some other desperate girl.

Jacob John smiled at these plans. Then he asked, "How are things at the Jolly Grant House? And Mrs. Laird?"

"Oh! She is most excited about her son coming to visit. And bringing the lady he is going to marry."

"Really, now! Much work for you, I am thinking," Jacob John said.

"Yes, some extra work, that is true," Mary said, making light of it. "What's that book in your hand?"

He held out a paperback with a cover picturing the elaborate façade of the Madras Central railway station. Mary shuddered, remembering how she had escaped through that very arcade on her way to her new life.

"It's a history of Madras," Jacob John said. "I like short stories better, but this was all that man had in Tamil today. I'll sell it back to him when I'm done. Or shall I save it for you?"

"That's very nice of you, but, no, sell as soon as possible; I don't have much time to read. Actually," she found herself confessing, "I don't read or write Tamil. Except for my name."

"But you read and write a good amount of Hindi and English," Jacob John said matter-of-factly.

"Yes," she said. "I learned those after I started working for Jana memsahib and her husband."

"After your husband died," said Jacob John.

Mary hesitated. "Yes, well, maybe around that time," she said.

Jacob John looked momentarily puzzled by this vague response; but Mary did not want to be interrogated about her marriage. She said briskly, "I must continue with my shopping."

"I will see you in church," Jacob John said.

"Very good," said Mary.

As she continued to the South Indian grocery store, she felt her shoulders shiver, as if she were shaking off that conversational reminder of her old life. If her husband wasn't literally dead—which she didn't in fact know—he was certainly dead to her.

⁓ᢗ *Employed in Education*

"Mary has come!" Mr. Ramesh said, as Mary stood in front of the little grocery store. "Do we have the kind of black gram she likes?"

"Yes, yes," Mrs. Ramesh answered, her ample rear end bumping into him as she turned around. There was hardly enough room for both halves of this long-married pair in the minuscule stall topped by the brave sign reading, "Best Madras & Kerala Foods." Far from home, Mr. and Mrs. Ramesh especially liked it when their South Indian customers came by. Whether it was the Ramachandrans, Jacob John, Mary, or any of three or four others, the Rameshes knew exactly what each would ask for.

"This flour makes the best papadum," Mrs. Ramesh said, holding up a small packet. "As you know. Now. One or two coconuts?"

"One," said Mary.

"And Vizagapatnam vegetable oil?"

"One small bottle," said Mary.

"Very hot chilies?" Mrs. Ramesh asked.

"Are they really hot? Last time they weren't hot enough," said Mary. "They get cold sitting here in the north."

All three laughed as if none had ever made that joke before.

"So. How are your people in Chingleput District?" Mrs.

Ramesh asked. "Keeping well?" Though the Rameshes had wormed out of Mary roughly where she was from, Mary never admitted that she had no contact with and no interest in her kin. Instead, she now said, "Quite well, quite well."

"That Mabel Thomas from Chingleput, she had diabetes," Mrs. Ramesh remarked to her husband. "And Joseph Thomas—he died two weeks past." She picked up a Tamil newspaper and found the death notices. "Yes, here it is. Joseph Thomas, school headmaster. Some relative of yours?"

"Maybe," said Mary. "There are many people named Thomas in that place." She put the chances at a headmaster being related to her at less than one in a thousand.

"Must be," said Mrs. Ramesh. "You are so clever, with your good English. Surely you are coming from a family of school-masters."

Mary thought about it for a moment and remembered that a cousin had cleaned school toilets. "Now that you mention it," she said, "some of my people are employed in education. But again, there are many Thomases. Some are related to me and others, not."

May all of them stay away from me, she added, mentally.

"Well," she said brightly, "I'm going to cook myself some good food tonight." She hefted her cloth bag, now bulging with purchases.

"Bye-bye," the couple said as Mary turned toward the street.

Furnishings

◦ Eighty Yards of Velvet

"Eighty yards," Feroze said, putting away his measuring stick.

"Eighty?" Jana repeated.

"Forty for the guest room and forty for the dining room. These rooms are full of windows, madam."

They stood in the dining room, Mr. Ganguly on Jana's shoulder. She wished she could sit down and absorb the news of the latest thing she'd have to shell out money for, but there wasn't anything to sit down *on* in this large, bare echo chamber. The immaculate ceiling and smooth, unpocked walls were dazzling white. The room was a clean, empty slate, ready to be written on.

"Curtains will absorb the sound," Feroze was saying. "Otherwise, it will be loud in here. Your digestion may suffer."

"I suppose that's true," Jana said. Mr. Ganguly let out a whistle, which reverberated around the room. Excited, he then tried a sequence of even more earsplitting notes, which made Jana wince. She set him down on one of the windowsills.

"I recommend velvet," Feroze said. "Velvet has a big appetite for sound."

It also has a big appetite for money, Jana thought.

"Brocade is heavy enough," Feroze mused. "It would keep out the light. But velvet will do that, too. And—one thing, madam. Instead of having just plain things . . ."

"Yes?" said Jana, remembering that Feroze disapproved of "plain things."

"You can put some extra cloth horizontally across the top. With two-three scallops. And consider braid trim, too. And heavy cords with tassels."

"I really don't know about the valences," she said. "Or the braid trim." This is a simple dining room in an old house, she thought, where we're going to *eat*, not conduct royal ceremonies.

Feroze broke into her thoughts. "Lining, too, is necessary. You need eighty yards of *that*, also. Keram Chand at Fabulous Fabrics can tell you what kind to get."

"Keram Chand will be very glad to see me coming," Jana said. "Has he even got big enough lots of cloth for a project like this?"

"Oh, yes," said Feroze. "No problem. Big projects are our specialty, remember? Take gym suits for the Far Oaks School. They needed three hundred of them. He supplied cloth; I supplied labor. They were done in no time."

"Feroze sahib," said Jana. "This project is making me feel— well, it's making my head dizzy. Every day there is something new to build, buy, have made . . ."

"Dizziness is an unfortunate part of life," Feroze said. "But when you see the curtains hanging, nice and soft against the hard walls, the dizziness will fade away."

Toe Appeal

Two days later, Hajji Yusuf Baig of the Kashmiri Palace arrived at the Jolly Grant House, followed by several pairs of men, each duo bearing a long rolled-up rug. A series of thumps resounded on the paving stones of the courtyard as the porters put their burdens down.

"Madam," Yusuf Baig said to Jana. "I understand you are getting dizzy."

"Dizzy?"

"Feroze Ali Khan told me." Yusuf Baig was Feroze's oldest friend; Jana could just picture them strolling back from the mosque after Friday prayers and bringing each other up-to-date on their mutual customers—such as Jana herself.

"Oh, I see," she said. "All I meant was that there is a lot to do before my son and his fiancée arrive."

"If you are dizzy," Yusuf Baig said, "you need a carpet under your feet. What if you fell? Better to fall on a nice thick carpet than on a cruel stone floor."

He saw her hesitating, and added, "Carpets will make it more quiet, too. Let me just roll out two-three here in the courtyard, so you can see the colors. No charge for looking."

"Well . . ." Jana began.

The pairs of men were already unrolling the carpets, and they did not stop at two or three. Soon the courtyard was completely transformed with sumptuous designs. The colors dazzled Jana's eyes: red and cream here, soft brown with lemon and black accents there. Unable to resist, she took off her shoes, stepped onto the nearest carpet, and felt the luxurious wool and silk underfoot. With a practiced eye, Yusuf Baig registered which rugs she lingered on longest.

"Try the red one in the dining room," he said. "No harm in trying. And the brown one in the room above."

A half hour later, the two carpets had been spread out in the dining room and the guest room and left "on approval," as Yusuf Baig put it. Half amused and half appalled, Jana thought, That man seduced my *toes*.

Bumps in the Road

Two and a half months had gone by since the letter bearing Jack's momentous news. Winter had withdrawn; mild sunny days had brought out young parents walking with newborn babies and tourists from the plains looking for escape from the heat, bargains, and fun. At the Jolly Grant House, the painting was done, the new furnishings in place.

Now to get the music manuscript out the door, resolved Jana. Yet, on that day in late April, the violin tune transcriptions were going poorly. She'd wasted several sheets of music paper and still hadn't a complete tune to show for the morning's effort.

"Post, Jana mem," said Mary, putting the pile of letters on the salon table.

"Thank you, Mary."

Jana gently laid down her violin and reached for her letter opener.

"Goodness!" she said. Could the newsletters from *four* societies for the prevention of cruelty to animals really arrive on the same day? The Bombay SPCA, Nagpur SPCA, Gujarat SPCA, and Delhi SPCA had all sent her an appeal for funds. A particularly gruesome story from Bombay on the bad treatment of fortune-telling birds made her wince at man's inhumanity to bird.

Such stories inspired her to send in bigger contributions than she could afford, but one had to do *something*. She wrote a small check to the Bombay SPCA. When the dust had settled from Jack and Katarina's visit, she promised herself, she would send donations to the other organizations, too.

"Good bird," Mr. Ganguly said from his perch. Had he read her mind? No, he was merely buttering her up. "Walk?" he asked hopefully.

"Maybe later," she said.

She picked up an envelope from St. Regis Pre-Military Academy. Cannons were still blazing and mythical lions still flapping their wings on the school crest. She opened the envelope to find a form letter on which handwritten particulars had been entered in the blanks. Below the letterhead, in curly letters, was the motto of the school, *"Semper Sursum"*: Always Try Hard.

"Dear Mr. (dec) and Mrs. William Laird," Jana read.

Enclosed you will find the marks for *Pratap Singh Mangat Rai, a.k.a. Tilku,* for the marking period *1st Mar* through *15th April, 1962.*

Please note that these marks are provisional. Kindly give this report your careful attention and sign in the indicated space on the back of the card.

Accordingly, Jana turned to the stiff, buff-colored report card. On a scale of 1 to 100, Tilku had earned:

English	23
Hindi	15
Geography	32
History	18
Maths	29
Moral Development	38
P.T.	70

Dismayed, she clutched at straws. At Tilku's school, was a *lower* score better than a higher one, like coming in first in a race rather than one hundredth? Alas, no. The card explained that 40 or above was passing and 39 and below was failing; 50, she saw, was considered "fairly meritorious."

She looked up to see Mary watching her.

"What's wrong, Jana mem? You look very pulled down."

Jana took a deep breath and let out a "phew."

"I *feel* pulled down! It seems that Tilku is struggling at that school." She handed Mary the report card. Mary studied it and thought for a moment.

"There aren't any zeros, Jana mem," she said.

"Well, no, there aren't," Jana admitted. Trust Mary to point out that the glass was only 85 percent empty, which was better than bone-dry.

"He got a good mark in Physical Training," Mary observed.

"I'd be appalled if he hadn't," Jana said. "Running around is one thing at which he excels. But why do you suppose he failed Moral Development? What does that even mean?"

"These are not final marks," Mary reminded Jana. "They can go soaring up any minute now. Like a bird."

"You think so?" Jana said.

"Yes, yes."

Seeing the confident wiggle of Mary's head, Jana started to feel less discouraged. "Mary, your spirit always cheers me up. You're a veritable lifesaver."

"A Life Saver is a small American sweet," Mary pointed out. "I'm not small. Or American. Or a sweet."

"You're still a lifesaver," Jana said.

An Unexpected Bill

Trying to dispel the anxiety created by Tilku's grades and sal-
vage a heretofore unproductive morning, Jana once again
picked up her fiddle. She tried out a phrase, decided it wasn't
exactly the way old Ian had played it, and tried another way.
How had that rhythm gone? Short note, long note? Or long note,
short note?

Transcribing these tunes felt like doing archaeology, at least
as she imagined the archaeological process. One grubbed around
and found a broken bit of pottery, and then tried to imagine
what the original artifact had looked like. For museum exhibits,
people reconstructed Greek vases by filling in gaps between
potsherds with plain clay, and then they painted the plain
parts to complete the picture. Jana had filled in so many of the
missing bits in these tunes that some were almost her own cre-
ations.

"*Ta*-duh *ta*-duh *ta*-duh," chirped Mr. Ganguly from his perch.

"What's that again?" said Jana, startled.

"*Ta*-duh *ta*-duh *ta*-duh," the bird repeated.

Oh, of course, Jana thought. Mr. Ganguly had figured out
the rhythm of the tune. Three long-shorts—that sounded exactly
right, much better than three short-longs.

"Thank you, Mr. G," she said. "You're a good bird and a fine
musician."

"Nut?" said Mr. Ganguly.

"Of course, I should have known—you don't work for free."
She gave him a walnut to shell and went back to her task, getting completely engrossed and not even noticing the passage
of time. When the work went like this, it didn't even feel like
work. Suddenly, however, a cough from the archway to the hall
broke into her concentration, and then a soft "Madam?" and a
louder "Excuse me, Jana mem."

Lal Bahadur Pun was standing there with a peculiar blend

of irritation and disdain on his face. "Police Commissioner Sharma is here, Jana mem."

Jana's heart sank. She asked, "What on earth does he want?"

"Some government business," said the Gurkha.

Jana would never forget the night she had spent in the Hamara Nagar jail after Mr. Ganguly had flown at Police Commissioner Bandhu Sharma and taken a chomp at his ear. Now she quickly got up and put the parrot in his cage, from where he protested wildly, puffing up his chest and flapping his wings. In desperation, Jana slipped the sleeping cover over the cage, then turned to Lal Bahadur Pun.

"You'd better ask the commissioner to come in," she said.

A moment later, Bandhu, all starched khaki, was standing in her salon, and behind him an obsequious lackey carrying a briefcase and umbrella.

"Good morning, Commissioner," said Jana. "May I invite you to take a seat?"

"That will not be necessary," Bandhu said. "We will be walking around."

"Yes, Commissioner?" Jana said. "Where will we be walking?"

"Mrs. Laird," said Bandhu. "Word has come to me that you are improving the Jolly Grant House. Regulations impel me to conduct a thorough inspection of the property."

He was twitching with his usual impatience, and Jana, her heart sinking, said, "Very well, then. I will lead you through."

The inspection, as Bandhu had promised, was thoroughgoing. In each room, Bandhu circled the floor, gazed at the ceiling, and took in the furnishings. All the while, he gave orders to his assistant. "Open and close that window. Flush that toilet. Try that water spigot. Inspect that cupboard."

You'd think he was trying to track down a fugitive from justice, Jana thought. Or, Lord help us, to *buy* the house. She kept her mouth clamped shut as she led him up and down the stairs to the tower, out to the cookhouse, down to the terrace and the numerous basement rooms.

They ended up back in the salon, Bandhu with an "I *thought* so" expression on his face.

"Mrs. Laird, I am required to tell you that you owe a substantial improvement tax. In addition to your normal annual house tax, we must now levy luxury tax, convenience tax, and site and situation tax."

Jana felt her heart descending to the pit of her stomach. Bandhu was not yet finished.

He said happily, "We are also reviewing all our records for accuracy. If last year's assessment contained an error, you will be sent a corrected bill."

"But what if I have overpaid?" Jana asked.

"In the unlikely event that you overpaid, the assumption is that you intended the surplus to be donated to the Homeland Purity Society. Don't you read the fine print on official documents?"

"I shall from now on," Jana assured him, doing her best to keep calm and polite.

"Oh, one last thing," said Bandhu. "What is the purpose of all these improvements? If you are going to have some new permanent occupants to the Jolly Grant House, I will need to add them to the latest town population statistics. These things can't be taken lightly."

"No, Commissioner Sharma," said Jana. "There will be no additional permanent occupants. My son will be visiting from Scotland with his fiancée."

Bandhu paused, and Jana tried to read the look that came over his face.

"Fiancée? Your son is getting married? No one told me that." To his assistant, he said, "Did *you* know that?" The sheepish affirmative response brought such an enraged flush to Bandhu's cheeks that Jana thought the commissioner might actually pop like a balloon before her very eyes.

She caught a trace of another expression, too—that of a schoolboy who is the last to know about a birthday party he hasn't been invited to. She wondered, Could Bandhu possibly feel *hurt*?

"Your son is to be married here," Bandhu stated, an aggrieved line deepening between his eyebrows.

Jana said, "Oh, no, Commissioner; the wedding will take place in Scotland."

Commissioner Sharma said flatly, "You're sure of that."

"Why, yes," Jana said. She refrained from adding, "No wedding site tax will be necessary, sir."

ᴄᢅ *Emeralds Included*

The next day, when the official envelope arrived by post, she saw that Bandhu had added even a few more embellishments than expected to the new assessment on her house. "Tower," "View" . . . She scanned the list of reasons why she should pay more. There was an assessment for "Occupation of Historic Property" and, right underneath that, a fee for "Modification of Historic Property." She also read, "Unnecessary Modern Conveniences." Well, if that wasn't the limit!

Worse yet, the "total payable, owed, and due upon receipt" stuck out like a flag in bright red, underlined numerals. It was a sum, in Bandhu's words, not to be taken lightly.

The emeralds, she thought with a sigh. The time had come to cash them in.

Jack had told her to keep the jewels in a vault at the bank, but Jana hadn't taken his advice. She figured she'd never wear them if she had to fetch and return them every time. Nor did she padlock the cupboard very often, since this made putting laundry away inconvenient. Now she fished way back in the almirah behind a stack of socks and got out a long, slim jewelry box. Inside, on black velvet, twinkled the emerald necklace and earrings. Holding the necklace up to the light, she saw that

every stone was a little different from the one next to it. Quirks
of nature, they were not the uniform and predictable products
of some assembly line.

She remembered Tilku reading the words "Reasonable loans
against collateral" at M. L. Shah's jewelry store in the bazaar.
Disregarding Grandfather MacPherson's voice in her head boom-
ing, "Neither a borrower nor a lender be," she put the necklace
back in the box, snapped the lid shut, and changed into her
walking shoes.

"I'll be back in a couple of hours," she yelled to Mary on her
way out the front door.

In the street, she threaded her way through the foot traffic,
standing back periodically to let rickshaws clatter by, and occasionally dodging an errant cow. Reaching the English Bazaar in
good time, she stopped briefly in front of the entry to Priceless
Gems. The two guards on either side of the door cast a quick
evaluative glance at her and, apparently deciding she wasn't a
jewel thief, nodded to her in greeting as she went in.

The front door now having closed behind her, she found
herself in a quiet little antechamber, with benches attached to
all four walls, low lighting, and twin back doors. "Kindly Be
Seated," said the sign on the wall, so she followed this instruc-
tion, wondering which door would open first, and who would
emerge from it.

When the left-hand door finally opened, it was a uniformed
chaprassi who came through with a tray of tea.

"Oh, no thank you." Jana shook her head.

"Something else, memsahib?" the *chaprassi* asked. "Coca-
Cola?"

"No, no," said Jana. "No need."

As you will, the *chaprassi's* attitude said as he took the tray
away. "Shah sahib will be coming right away."

A few minutes later, a well-built man of about fifty years of age
came through the right-hand door.

Jana had heard via the grapevine that Mr. Shah was from a prominent New Delhi jewelry family that also had a store in London's Hatton Garden. Now she believed the gossip. Every aspect of his dress spelled worldly success: the expensive-looking jacket, the immaculate trousers, the Swiss watch, the ruby ring, and the highly polished Italian shoes. With his calm, assured demeanor and his observant gaze, he was at the same time charismatic and intimidating, and Jana could see how his son, Deepak, might be afraid of him.

"Mrs. Laird, I take it. What a pleasure," Mr. Shah said. "I've been eager to meet you. Actually, I owe you a vote of thanks."

"You do?" Jana said, rattled that he knew who she was. "Whatever for?"

Mr. Shah said, "I was in the audience at the Futurology Convention two years ago, when you made a speech greeting the visitors to town. That put many of them in a good mood for jewelry shopping. And later that year, the jewelry enthusiasts of the American Women's Club of New Delhi came by en masse—after they had emptied out the Treasure Emporium, of course."

"I'm . . . I'm glad they did," said Jana. "Come by here, I mean. I'm sure they found some lovely things."

"Lovely things is our specialty," M. L. Shah said. "I've got a number of them you might be interested in. Let's go into the showroom."

He led her back through the mysterious right-hand door, into a room full of wonders. Looking around at the glass wall cases, Jana felt utterly dazzled. Her head swam with ornate gold necklaces, ruby pendant earrings, and sapphire brooches in the shape of birds and flowers. Artful lighting brought out the fire and sparkle of each gem and made the gold settings glow like honey. The hushed atmosphere suggested that further riches waited in unseen vaults.

"What may I show you today?" asked Mr. Shah. "Perhaps

you were thinking of having something made to order. Many of our customers themselves design very beautiful things. We always make them up precisely to specifications."

Faced with Mr. Shah's assumption that she was a prosperous customer, Jana felt a flush rising to her face. "I'm actually not buying today," she said.

"Not to worry," said Mr. Shah consolingly. "Have a nice look, make yourself at home. There's no hurry."

Be brave, Jana told herself, and get it over with. She took a deep breath and said, "I'm here . . . I'm here to show you something."

His eyebrows went up briefly. "Yes, of course. Please show me anything, Mrs. Laird."

She reached into her satchel for the jewelry box and opened it. The lights in the ceiling shone down on the sparkling green stones, making them appear to dance mischievously in their settings.

"Ah," said Mr. Shah. "The Treasure Emporium emeralds."

"Yes, they are," said Jana.

"It just so happens that emeralds are my favorite gemstone," Mr. Shah said.

"Mine, too," said Jana.

Mr. Shah turned the necklace over and remarked, "You know, I'm happy to get a look at them. One never knows the real truth behind local gossip."

Jana looked at him inquiringly.

"I'd heard that some Mughal pieces had turned up, quite unexpectedly." Mr. Shah glanced casually at her face, then went back to his examination. "The setting is nice and open, so we can fully inspect the back of the stones. You see—foil has not been used to give a false depth of color. Happily, we have not been foiled."

Jana smiled politely at his joke. Meanwhile, Mr. Shah had taken a jeweler's loupe from his pocket and was peering through it with increased concentration.

"The settings are worn," he said, "but the stones have life and personality. Of course, they're full of inclusions."

"Inclusions?" asked Jana.

"Flaws. You see the little bubbles and lines?"

As Mr. Shah talked, Jana became convinced that the little bubbles did indeed bring the stones to life, making them like champagne instead of ordinary table wine.

"Emeralds," Mr. Shah mused, "are very much like human beings. Perfection is virtually impossible. They are full of little zigs and zags and cracks and extraneous matter. That's true of emeralds more than of other gems, because they are born from violent geologic struggle. Chromium and vanadium come to the rescue to give them that characteristic green color, but other materials find their way in."

Jana listened raptly, in the grip of Mr. Shah's erudition. "Both the Romans and the ancient Hindus believed that emeralds had healing powers. They thought they were good for eyesight as well as for fidelity in love, good health and general well-being. Plus, traditionally they're thought to assist in childbirth. Well. I'm rambling. Do you wish me to clean these pieces? Or to appraise them for insurance purposes? Or would you like them copied in another stone? Rubies, perhaps?"

The time had come. Jana steeled herself and took a deep breath. Then she said, "I came to ask if I could leave them with you in safekeeping, for a small amount of cash, for a limited time. I'd come back for them very quickly, and . . ."

"Ah, I see," said Mr. Shah. "You are here for a loan."

"Yes, that's right." She was grateful that he'd said it first.

Sympathy streamed from Mr. Shah's dark eyes. "Even very well-situated people have an occasional cash-flow problem." He paused, then said, "We can handle such a request. I'll just now send in my cashier, and he can make up the papers."

And then he was gone, carrying off the emeralds in his well-manicured hands. For what seemed like hours, but was actually fifteen minutes, Jana could hear a typewriter clacking in the next room. Finally, a clerk emerged with a number of papers, already signed by Mr. Shah. Jana forced herself to read them.

Fourteen percent interest—was that high or low? Jana pushed her unwilling brain to calculate: fourteen divided by twelve, multiplied by 15,000, move the decimal point over two places— that would be the monthly fee, but, of course, that was only the interest; it would have to be added to the principal repayment.

Damnation. Never mind: she was going to repay the loan within a month, and then all those calculations would be irrelevant. She scanned the repayment schedule and noted the penalty for late payment. The dry language made everything distant and abstract. One thing, however, was clear. If one fell too far behind in the payments . . .

If one fell too far behind, the emeralds would be gone, for good.

"I won't let that happen," Jana said to herself as she left the store. On the way home, from time to time she patted her satchel, checking that her now fattened wallet was still there.

What Is Love, Anyway?

◦ϐ *Zero Value?*

"Nose to grindstone!" Jana told herself every day for the next week.

Finally, the last of old Ian's tunes was down on paper, and she'd painstakingly made a copy of all fifty of them. Gazing down at the two neat stacks of sheet music, she was euphoric. A burden had been lifted, a long-overdue duty accomplished. Transcribing the tunes had been a battle against time and forgetting, and she had won.

Moreover, it was a charming collection. How could it fail to find favor with fiddling enthusiasts in Scotland?

One last task remained. She picked up her pen and wrote a brief letter of explanation: "The following tunes were composed by Ian Marshall (no relation to composer William Marshall), who was in the employ of Mr. James MacPherson, Glasgow, from 1898 to 1939. I have recorded them to the best of my memory and ability. Very truly yours, Janet Laird, Hamara Nagar, Uttar Pradesh, India." She added the date: 1 April 1962.

She felt a thrill to be part of music history, a link in the chain of tradition. The famous William Marshall had composed *his* classic tunes while serving as a butler; surely Messrs. Duff and Ferguson, Music Publishers, would find this coincidence significant.

She pictured the parcel arriving at Buchanan Street, Glasgow. Mr. Duff would answer the door and accept it from the postman. He'd slit it open and eye the first few sheets, and his eyebrows would shoot up in excitement. "I say, Ferguson," he would exclaim to his colleague. "There's something rather good here." They'd look at some more tunes and send her back an offer of a thousand pounds by return post.

She now hunted about in the sideboard and found a large envelope, in which Jack had sent her the carbon copies of some family correspondence. Judging the envelope still serviceable, she pasted on a new label and addressed it. From Glasgow the envelope had come; to Glasgow it could go!

"Mr. Ganguly," she said, "shall we go to the post office?"

"Post office!" cried Mr. Ganguly, flapping his wings.

Walking through the bazaar, Jana felt carefree and liberated. Mr. Ganguly rode on her shoulder, infected with her own good mood. "Salaam!" he cried, as they passed Royal Tailors. "Namasté," he said to one and all as they entered the PTT.

Today, Jana found even standing in line enjoyable. Instead of being impatient, she savored each moment of anticipation before the manuscript would finally be out of her hands.

"Airmail or sea mail?" said the clerk, putting the packet on the scale.

"What's the difference in cost?" Jana asked.

The difference was considerable, enough to make her deliberate for a moment or two. Then she told herself that the sooner she got the manuscript out, the sooner she'd get the thousand pounds back.

"Air," she said firmly.

"We must do a customs declaration," said the clerk. "What's in here?"

"Music," she said.

"Oh?" said the clerk. "I hear nothing."

"Sheet music," she explained. "Paper. Paper with black dots on it."

The clerk frowned; he was accustomed to people sending manuscripts, but not those consisting of dots. "Please to be assigning a monetary value."

"Oh! Put . . ." She quickly translated pounds into rupees. A thousand pounds would be more than thirteen thousand rupees. Should she say that? She wavered, worried that proclaiming such a large amount might get the packet stolen.

Tired of waiting, the man entered a large zero, bearing down heavily on the carbon. He ripped the top sheet off and gave her the second copy.

She paid, got her change, and left the PTT. Zero value, eh? That took a person down a peg. Then she reassured herself that claiming a value of zero was just as well; it formed a cloak of anonymity around precious cargo. All the better surprise for Messrs. Duff and Ferguson.

✑ More than a Friend?

Kenneth Stuart-Smith was back in town, on a *Globe-Trotter's* mission. Among the local attractions of the region, he planned to list in the guidebook a small, unnamed temple six or seven miles out of town. Jana had been meaning to make the trek but somehow had never snatched the time to do so, like the inhabitant of Paris who has never gone up inside the Eiffel Tower. Now Kenneth was making it easy for her, offering to carry lunch and water, binoculars, compass, first-aid kit, and other practical essentials. By nine o'clock, looking forward to a day of unaccustomed athleticism, she was dressed in rough cotton trousers, a cotton shirt, and her walking shoes. She added a windbreaker, which eliminated the need for a handbag; its pockets were big enough to hold a comb, her glasses, a handkerchief, and a few rupees. Donning her sunglasses and a porkpie hat, she was ready to go when Kenneth arrived.

"Do you really think I can keep up with you?" Jana asked, as they left through the gate of the Jolly Grant House.

"The halt, the lame, and the elderly do this little trek all the time," said Kenneth Stuart-Smith.

"Thanks for the compliment," she said.

"No, no, I wasn't including you in those categories. Just saying that, as an able-bodied person, you should have no trouble at all. In fact, people claim that visiting the temple cures whatever happens to be ailing them."

They walked through the Upper Bazaar to the limit of the town and then continued east, coming after an hour to a trail that led sharply uphill. On the way, they passed a few groups of travelers—whole families, including grandparents leaning on their walking sticks and mothers carrying tiny babies. In turn, Jana and Kenneth were overtaken by a quartet of American boys from the Far Oaks School, who were apparently on some speed-hiking challenge.

"That was me, a few years ago," said Kenneth.

"Only a few," Jana said, doing some math in her head. In his early fifties, Kenneth was lean and fit, striding along easily without getting winded. He did stop from time to time, ostensibly to peer through his binoculars and identify a bird, but really, Jana suspected, to allow her to keep up.

An amusing man, she thought, who did much of the work of conversation. As they went along, he kept her laughing with stories about Jacqueline Kennedy's recent goodwill visit to India.

"The press got their quota of elephant pictures," Kenneth said. "Jackie garlanding an elephant, Jackie riding on an elephant, Jackie patting an elephant. That's what the folks back in the U.S. will remember about Jackie's trip: elephants and the Taj Mahal."

The last stretch of the hike was sharply steeper, ending in a stone staircase that led to a small, one-story structure plastered in white and pink and largely open to the winds. A small archway off to the side held a bell that arriving pilgrims reached up and struck, so a continual clanging sound carried on the breeze. Most of the visitors laid small offerings of fruit or flowers on the shrine. Kenneth left a handful of rupees in the pot strategically placed to receive them, then led Jana down some steps and along a ridge heading away from the temple.

"What an amazing view," Jana said as they perched on some boulders at a lookout point. The drop-off was sharply vertical, giving her the feeling of being about to make a parachute jump from a plane. She let her eyes roam over a sky that was white at the horizon and deepened to blue way up high.

"Water?" said Kenneth, offering her the canteen.

Jana drank by holding it up and letting the water fall into her mouth without touching the rim, then passed the canteen back to Kenneth, who did the same. You can always tell someone who has grown up in India, thought Jana, by the way they can drink that way without spilling a drop.

"Now, the lunch," said Kenneth.

"Let me guess: cheese sandwiches," said Jana.

"No, samosas and *aloo paratha*," said Kenneth.

"From the Victory?" Jana asked, astonished at this departure from tradition.

"New picnic menu," said Kenneth. "But they still give you a banana and a tangerine. And chocolate bars."

The talk turned to Jack and Katarina's upcoming visit, and then to weddings.

"I sometimes have dreams—maybe you should call them nightmares—about Sandra getting married," Kenneth said.

"I can understand that," Jana said, remembering how strong-willed his daughter was. When Jana and Kenneth had first met, Kenneth was putting Sandra in boarding school in hopes of controlling her; earlier, in Paris, Sandra had crashed a party at the Belgian embassy by claiming to be a relative of Princess Grace of Monaco. Boarding school, however, had not worked very well, and Sandra was once again living with her father.

"What happens in these dreams?" Jana asked.

Kenneth laughed. "In one, she insists on getting married at the Taj Mahal. In another, at Notre-Dame de Paris. The common theme seems to be that she'll have some monstrously expensive shindig and have to jet people in from all over the world."

"Tell her to elope," Jana said.

Kenneth said, "Maybe I will, when the time comes."

"It's funny, isn't it, this business of weddings," Jana said. "I didn't really have one. I ran down with William to the registry office and signed my name in a book, with my suitcase already packed. That afternoon, we jumped on the steamer for India. My grandfather disowned me."

"But you stuck it out until death did you part," Kenneth said. "Congratulations on that, in any case."

He sat quietly for a moment, apparently thinking about his own marriage to a Boston socialite.

"We had a huge affair," he said. "We rented Trinity Church and damn near filled all the pews. Ten bridesmaids. Ten ushers. Flower girls. Ring bearers." He shook his head. "With all that for prologue, you would have thought the marriage would stick. Both sets of parents were all for it, too."

Jana finished her chocolate bar, then wadded the foil up tightly and gave it to Kenneth.

"Would you marry again?" she asked.

"Is that a proposal?" he joked.

She felt the flush rising to her cheeks. "I merely meant at *some* point," she said.

"I don't know," he said. "For a while I thought I *had* to fill that gap. Divorce isn't a huge amount of fun, and it can make you feel very imperfect and incomplete. Second-rate, somehow. Embarrassed. Guilty."

Jana knew that Kenneth's wife had been the one to run off; how could the experience have made *him* feel guilty?

He finished a samosa and brushed off the crumbs that had fallen into his lap. "The funny thing is, the single state doesn't seem so bad to me now. It's not a catastrophe to go to an official function without a woman on my arm."

But what about coming home from the reception and getting into an empty bed? If that was indeed what he did, thought Jana.

The conversation felt like making one's way over a bed of eggshells. Here was Kenneth, in some senses close and confiding, and yet—unreachable. There had never been any romance between them, only a very easy comradely feeling, based on common experience in India. Should it—could it—be any more than that? she wondered. An overture toward something more intimate might backfire, embarrassing them both and resulting in the loss of a friendship.

Still, if I suddenly kissed him, she thought, what would happen? She stared at his bare arm, light brown hairs visible against the tanned skin. It would be the simplest thing in the world to reach out and run her finger down his arm. One impulse, followed by one tiny little action. In her indecision, she was reminded of a chameleon she had once seen crossing a strip of tarmac, swaying back and forth before putting a foot down.

The moment passed; Kenneth was now standing up, hoisting his backpack onto his shoulders.

"Ready?" he said.

They hiked back largely in silence and then, reaching the Jolly Grant House, paused at the gate.

"I'm going to bring Sandra back to Hamara Nagar as soon as the American School in Delhi gets out for the year," he said.

"That's good," she said, giving him a hug. "Keep me posted."

That night, she ate a solitary bowl of Mary's tomato soup at the table in the salon, feeling tired and subdued. Usually she paid little attention to the years galloping along, but now she thought, with a shock, I'm sixty, and if I want to find a partner in life, the time is running out.

Mr. Ganguly picked up on her mood. "Sad bird?" he asked.

"A bit," she admitted. It was easier to admit to a bird than to a human that all was not exactly right.

Not ready to go to bed, she put Mr. Ganguly on her shoulder and went up to the lookout room.

"Kya? Kya?" Mr. Ganguly cried, puzzled at the new arrangement of furniture—the cot moved in against one wall, the armchairs and side tables closer to each other in the center of the room.

"The room *is* going to be different for a while, you're right," she said to the bird.

Going to the sideboard, she got out a small cordial glass and poured herself the last few drops of LPN10 from its small brown bottle. "Going, going, gone," the drops seemed to say. Love Potion Number 10—what an irony the very name now seemed to her. Abinath's potion may have once soothed a toothache for her, but it had never brought her any romance. What did she expect? It was essentially an apricot tincture. What *is* love, she asked herself, and would I recognize it if I saw it? Pensively, she crossed to the window and looked out at the lights of the boarding school dormitories across the dark gorge.

Had she loved William Laird, whom she'd married thirty-seven years ago, after spending only a few hours with him? Was that sudden elopement proof of love? Granted, William had had good looks and good humor, and she'd found his innocence refreshing. But even at the time, some small part of her had stood back and observed, recognizing not love but the urgent wish to get out from under Grandfather MacPherson's domination. Also, even after several years in Scotland, she was still so painfully homesick for the India of her childhood that William's impetuous proposal had seemed a perfect escape route.

If she hadn't loved him, however, why had she stayed? After their two daughters had died from smallpox—because of *his* adamant opposition to vaccination—and after William had survived scarred and blinded, she'd forced back despair and rage and accepted a mission: the duty of taking care of her husband, now a bewildered, stricken man. Jana had watched over him and shaved him and led him on walks and done all his correspondence and generally served as his manager and his nurse. When he died, after collapsing midsermon from a heart attack, she'd felt an unexpected piercing grief, but that sorrow had gradually been replaced by a huge sense of relief.

Duty and pity, she now mused, did not constitute love—at any rate, not the type of love she wanted to experience again.

Romance, fun, and adventure: none of those had been possible during the twenty-two years Jana had lived with William at the mission station. The eight years as a music teacher and dance musician in Bombay, the five years as a violin tutor at the nawab's palace, the two years to date in Hamara Nagar—now, those years had been much more amusing, if not always easy. Fancy dress balls, playing music for Prime Minister Nehru, the Jolly Grant House, the fortune-telling: those things had been adventures.

A few times since William's death, she had searched for romance, putting a toe in that fascinating but treacherous water, but nothing had lasted. The men who'd seemed promising—or who had pursued her—had all disappeared. Ruefully, she thought of the English businessman in Bombay who'd been married all along and of the French-Parsi hotel magnate whose widowhood lasted only until he found a bright young replacement. As for the sweet Anglo-Indian gentleman in Bombay who'd dropped dead with Jana's name on his lips, the memory of him brought a spasm of tenderness mixed with guilt.

Now, what to do about Kenneth? Perhaps, she reflected, one shouldn't tamper with a friendship so perfectly balanced—so unmarked by conflict, so stable—and so very pleasant. Try to change the balance, she warned herself, and you might not only fail to get a lover, you might lose a friend.

The Daughter-in-Law

❧ A Marigold Welcome

"There was shortage of marigolds today in the bazaar, Jana mem," said Mary. "They were costly. But what could I do?" She held up two long loops of marigolds interspersed with fringes of silver tinsel. "I paid eight annas."

In this part of the world, Jana reflected, a welcome without marigolds would be a sorry welcome indeed. She fished in her bag and handed Mary two four-anna coins. Nonetheless, she was a touch worried that Jack and Katarina might be put off by the fuss. Jack never liked being the center of attention; he was more comfortable standing back and observing. And Katarina? Was she going to enjoy being garlanded with pungent orange flowers and being followed, as they surely would be, by a group of giggling and pointing children—all the way from the taxi stand to the Jolly Grant House? Jana would soon find out.

Meanwhile, she asked, "Mary, is that a new sari?"

"No, Jana mem," Mary said. "You know this one. Same-same as before."

"You look very nice," Jana said. "Ten years younger!"

She caught the scent of jasmine and realized that Mary had tucked the tiny white flowers into her glossy black hair bun. Her eyes, ringed with fresh kohl, looked dark and lustrous. With a fresh yellow-and-magenta sari, gold earrings, and gold bangles jingling on both arms, she was unrecognizable from the woman in worn white cotton who'd been up to her elbows in flour a couple of hours ago.

At the gate, Lal Bahadur Pun was waiting for them, also dressed in his best attire: green-and-black kilt, velvet waistcoat over ruffled white blouse, and yellow-and-black argyle socks. A cloth of a second plaid, fuchsia and yellow, protected his bagpipes.

"Subedar-Major," Jana said. "You are quite splendid."

Next to Mary and Lal Bahadur Pun, and dressed as she was in a beige-and-cream salwar kameez, Jana felt like a sparrow among birds of paradise.

As for real birds, Mr. Ganguly had been left in his cage. Bagpipe music put his nerves on edge, and it would not do to have him screeching at top volume when they were all trying to make a good impression on Katarina.

"Ready?" Jana said to Mary.

"Ready!" Mary replied.

It was a pleasant two-mile walk to the taxi stand, where they took up watch next to a sign that said, "No Autos Permitted Without Special Permit." All peered down at the hairpin bends of the road that led from the train station in Dehra Dun. As soon as they glimpsed a battered taxi hurtling up the mountain, Lal Bahadur broke triumphantly into the march he had composed for the arrival.

The taxi lurched to a halt by the barrier, and out of the driver's door jumped a gray-bearded man in a turquoise turban. Jana tried to remember: Hadn't Mr. Kilometres's turban been pink last year? The man was quite the fashion-setter, as well as a fearless driver. Jana pictured him elbowing aside the competition and heaving Jack and Katarina's bags into his boot before they even dreamt of hiring anyone else's cab.

"Mrs. Laird," shouted Mr. Kilometres, his glee sounding above the din of the bagpipes. "I've got them! I've got them! Here they are, safe and sound!"

As Lal Bahadur Pun blasted away at his tune with renewed vigor, Mr. Kilometres proudly flung open the back door on one side of the taxi, allowing a slim woman with long honey-brown hair to edge herself across the seat. She was even more elegant than in the one picture that Jack, under duress, had finally sent. Even after the long journey by several modes of transportation, Katarina's skin and eyes were clear, and her simple skirt and cardigan unwrinkled. For a second, a wince crossed Katarina's face as her foot touched the ground, but it vanished as Jack uncurled himself from the other side of the vehicle.

"You're here!" Jana cried, hugging Katarina before any introductions could be made and then holding her son for a long moment.

"Jack, darling," she said. "How fit you look!"

Lal Bahadur Pun's music was still blaring, while Mary, all smiles, moved forward with her armful of garlands.

"Ayah-ji!" Jack said. "You're looking so well! You better be careful or talent scouts will ask you to be in films."

Mary said, "Jack baba, we have been waiting so long for you!"

Roped in marigolds, Jack and Katarina stood side by side as the street children who had been watching with interest pressed in closer. Contrary to Jana's worries, Katarina did not seem at all fazed. At one point, she gave Jack a quick smile, and a second later, Jack's face broke into a similar smile. It was as if a magic current had passed through the air between them.

Lal Bahadur Pun had finally reached the last and most elaborate variation of his tune. When the sound fell away, both Katarina and Jack clapped vigorously.

"Bravo!" Jack turned to Katarina. "Subedar-Major Lal Bahadur Pun was in the Tenth Princess Mary's Own Gurkha Rifles. He plays at least two hundred Scottish pipe tunes and has composed a few dozen of his own. Was that a new one, Subedar sahib?"

"'Mr. Jack Laird Returns to Hamara Nagar with the Future

Mrs. Laird,'" said Lal Bahadur Pun. "I finished it one-two days ago."

"It's an excellent tune," Jack said. "Perhaps you'll teach it to me."

"Of course, Sahib!" said the piper.

"No one's ever written a tune for me," Katarina said. "I'm honored. Thank you so very much."

"My pleasure, madam," said Lal Bahadur Pun.

"Well," Jana said to Jack and Katarina. "Do you two feel up to walking or shall we find a rickshaw?"

"Katya?" Jack turned to Katarina. "Can you make it? It's a couple of miles."

"Of course I can make it," Katarina said. "But the suitcases?"

She looked around and saw their luggage being carried away at a fast clip on the heads of two porters. Jana laughed at the astonishment on her face.

"Not to worry, madam, they know where to go," Lal Bahadur Pun said.

They walked back rather more slowly than Jana usually did, Katarina with her hand tucked into Jack's elbow, stopping occasionally to look more carefully at a sign or a shop.

"We're in full tourist season," Jana told Katarina, as they made their way along the main road of the town.

"I see that," said Katarina, her eyes wide as she took in the families strolling along, women in pastel holiday saris, little girls in frilly dresses and matching hair ribbons, small boys in sailor suits. Nearby, a little girl spilled her pistachio ice cream on the front of her dress but caught it in the cone before it could hit the street.

"I understand that this is a historic hill station?" Katarina said.

"It is, rather," said Jana. "But it's nowhere near as big or as well known as Simla or Mussoorie. The government was even ready to sacrifice it to a hydroelectric dam. If that had worked, we would all be underwater by now. But we're developing our own modest fame."

"I read that in *Globe-Trotter's Companion,*" said Katarina. "It is the Town of Philosophers, right?"

"Yes," said Jana. "To turn a phrase. Actually, people in this town are always turning a phrase. Trying to make the ordinary seem extraordinary."

"How very wise," said Katarina.

Jana found Katarina's voice musical and restful to listen to, with a lilt giving away that English was not her native language. Her *v*'s and *w*'s overlapped, so that she asked Jana about her "wiolin playing," and she had a soft way of pronouncing *t*'s and *d*'s. Katarina's beauty aside, Jana could tell—she could *hear*—why Jack had fallen in love with her.

"And here we are in the Central Bazaar!" Jana announced. "There are three business districts in all. The English Bazaar is to the west and the Upper Bazaar is uphill over there, to the east."

"And here are the shops they list in *Globe-Trotter's,*" Katarina said. "Abinath's Apothecary." She read the sign and chuckled. "'Shipping Love Potion Number 10 all over the world, but always keeping some for you, too.' That's considerate of them."

Finally, across the street from Royal Tailors ("Highest-Quality Stitching from Mughal Times Until Now") was the gate to the Jolly Grant House.

Katarina said, "The view from here—with the forest in the background—makes me think of the house where I lived when I was small."

"In Budapest?" Jana asked.

"Oh, no, far outside. After the war, the house was taken over to be an administrative building."

On either side of the gate, Munar and Harmendra stood at attention, Harmendra saluting smartly and Munar giving a gentle namasté.

The two porters had long since arrived and were standing in the courtyard, waiting to be paid. Jack fished in his pockets and handed each of them a few bills, and Jana noted the warmth of the salaams he got. Meanwhile, Lal Bahadur Pun told Harmendra to carry Katarina's suitcase to the guest room and grabbed Jack's suitcase himself.

As their bags disappeared, Jack said, "I'd forgotten how one doesn't really manage one's *self* in India. Other people grab your bags, or push you into a taxi, open a door here, guide you down a street there. The trick is to relax and enjoy it. Oh! Look at the front door! Someone's polished it."

"It's lovely," Katarina said, admiring the oak panels carved with flower and leaf motifs.

Jana led them through the uncharacteristically tidy front hall and under the broad archway into the salon, where mountain light poured through the newly washed windows.

"Enchanting," said Katarina. "So exotic and friendly at the same time. And here's the famous parrot."

Jana lifted Mr. Ganguly out of his cage and onto her arm, from where he looked curiously at Jack and then at Katarina and back at Jack.

"Namasté! *Salaam aleikum! Bonjour!*" said the bird.

"Namasté to you, too, you beautiful creature," said Katarina.

"Beautiful, marvelous!" cried Mr. Ganguly.

"He's giving you his highest compliment," said Jana. "He sizes people up quite quickly."

"Like Jack," Katarina said.

Jana glanced at her son, surprised at this characterization. Careful, deliberate Jack sized people up quickly? Perhaps he was evolving in a way she hadn't anticipated.

"But I've kept you standing here," Jana said. "Come on, I'll show you your digs."

"Jack sahib," Mary broke in. "There's chocolate cake for tea."

"We'll be in the dining room in ten minutes," Jack promised.

Santa Claus Falls in Love with a Soothsayer

It was more like a half hour than ten minutes later when Jack finally came down to the dining room, followed a moment later by Katarina, her hair brushed into a twist. Jack looked around at the well-fitting windows and the new furnishings and let out a long whistle.

"Mother, you've really outdone yourself. But have you spent the *earth* on all this?"

Jana said firmly, "We do not talk about filthy lucre in this house."

"*Samjhé?*" cried Mr. Ganguly.

"I do *samjhé*," said Jack. "Oh! Here comes Mary. Good show!"

Through the side door, which now swung quietly on well-oiled hinges, came Mary, triumphantly carrying the tea tray. The large chocolate cake was topped with pink swirls of icing bearing the message "WELCOME!"

"Sit, sit," said Jana, and they settled down as Mary put the tea things on the table.

"Jack baba, you cut," said Mary, handing him the knife.

"Katya?" Jack said.

"A small piece for me," Katarina said. "Thank you."

"A large one for me," said Jack, and loaded his plate. "Mary, will you have some?"

"Later," said Mary. "I'm going now to tell that new boy to fire up the hot-water boilers." Smiling, she put the teapot down so Jana could pour and left the room.

Jana picked up her own fork, overflowing with happiness. How relaxed and rested Jack looked, in spite of the long journey! Katarina, too, appeared very at home. Jana studied her mobile, intelligent face.

"Now, you must tell me how you met," Jana said.

Jack and Katarina exchanged their magnetic glance again,

as if silently and jointly deciding how much to reveal to the outside world.

"It was at a charity bazaar," said Jack finally. "A Christmas fair. You know, tables of homemade jam, fruitcake, smocked baby dresses . . ."

"How did *you* happen to be at a charity bazaar?" Jana wanted to know.

"Jack was Father Christmas," said Katarina, a dimple forming as she smiled.

"Jack was what?" asked Jana, incredulously.

"I was paying back a favor," said Jack. "You know how these things are. I couldn't get out of it—I was on the board of directors of the charity."

Jack doing good works? Good heavens, thought Jana.

Jack went on: "It was a very long day. I had a dreadful costume—stiff red felt and imitation ermine. I had to arrive in a horse-drawn carriage and march into the hall carrying a huge bag of toys."

"He made a beautiful entrance," Katarina said to Jana. "The children were in tears of excitement."

Jack continued: "The entrance was all very well and good, but then I had to spend the day in an airless grotto with children crawling all over me and sneezing in my face. Plus, I had to wear a long white beard that itched like the devil. And the mustache kept falling off."

Jana asked, "Katarina, why were *you* at the fair? Surely not to get a toy from Father Christmas?"

"Katarina had a booth, too," said Jack. "Right next to mine. At one point, I looked over and she happened to be looking up, and she winked."

"I did not *wink*," said Katarina. "I had an eyelash in my eye. I was trying to get it out."

"And what was *your* booth?" Jana asked.

"I was a fortune-teller," said Katarina. "The ladies putting on the fair came up with the idea. They thought that since I was

Hungarian, I could easily play the role of a Gypsy soothsayer. I couldn't refuse. The dear ladies had raised money for me when I'd arrived from Hungary. One had even put me up in her house for ages."

Jack chuckled. "There she was with huge hoop earrings and a print scarf on her head, sitting in front of a crystal ball with a deck of cards! She was very convincing, actually. She told marvelous fortunes. I listened in. Finally, I took a break and had my own fortune told."

"Several times," said Katarina.

"What did she tell you?" Jana asked Jack.

"Oh, optimistic things. Success in career, robust health . . ."

"And luck in love," Jana said, which, she was amused to see, made Jack blush. "And then what happened?"

"When they closed the fair down," Katarina said, "Jack came over again and invited me to dinner. He suggested that we both go change into more normal clothes and then he'd come and fetch me. So I went home and put on a long-sleeved wool dress. When the doorbell rang, it occurred to me—I don't know what he really *looks* like. I opened the door, and here was a clean-shaven man in a dark suit."

"With an upper lip still crimson from where the whiskers had been pasted on," Jack said.

Katarina continued: "We went to Sloans. The waiters know him there; they gave him the best table."

Another interesting little detail, thought Jana. How ignorant one is about one's own children.

Katarina finished her story: "During dinner, he told me about his mother telling fortunes up in the mountains of India. I said, Oh, I do so want to go there. And, as you see, I got my wish."

"Katya, aren't you going to eat that?" Jack said and, when Katarina shook her head, took her plate and finished her cake. Slowly, he scooped up a final blob of frosting and licked his fork.

"When did you each know that you'd found the right person?" Jana asked.

"That afternoon," said Katarina. "After observing children climbing on Jack for several hours straight, I said to myself, There's a patient man."

"And you?" Jana turned to her son.

"When she winked," Jack said.

"I did not *wink*," Katarina said.

"In any case, it was that afternoon," said Jack.

Love at first sight, thought Jana. Who would have predicted it? She glanced at Katarina, who winked.

"Katarina, you must tell *my* fortune," Jana said. "I haven't had that done in ages. Let me see. When I first arrived, an old fellow outside the train station in Dehra Dun foretold long life from my shadow. Then a man who used to practice at the Victoria Hotel—before it was the Victory—predicted that the Jolly Grant House would bring me joy, because of the first letter of my name."

"I'll certainly tell your fortune," Katarina said. "But perhaps not this very minute?"

"Of course, what am I thinking!" Jana said. "Here, you've only just arrived and I'm making you perform. We'll do it when you've had a nice rest."

◦ℬ *Wish Cards*

They didn't get to fortune-telling that day, nor the next. Katarina and Jack took a couple of days to adjust to the high altitude. Neither slept very well the first night, which made Jana feel bad. She wondered whether the new platform bed she'd had made for the guest room was comfortable after all. Maybe the mattress wasn't thick enough. Also, that cot in the lookout room—was it long enough for Jack? Then she remembered the patches of sleeplessness during her first few nights in Hamara Nagar, and how she, too, had taken a while to feel clearheaded and energetic during the day.

Jack and Katarina started their mornings buoyantly enough, going out after breakfast to explore the bazaar, but by lunchtime they looked overwhelmed. Jana and Mary had planned simple lunches, which Jack ate enthusiastically, but Katarina pecked at her food and proclaimed herself falling asleep.

"It's the bright sun and mountain air," she said.

"Go take a siesta," Jack said. "We're on vacation."

"Excellent idea," said Katarina. "Jana, do you mind?"

Jana said, "Of *course* not," although she found that, after all the preparations for the visit, it was something of a letdown to have one's guests fast asleep for hours at a time. By the third day, however, Jack said he had not only adapted but felt tip-top, and he reported that Katarina was rallying, too. After tea, Katarina asked if Jana wanted her cards read now.

"Yes, please!" Jana said.

Katarina looked up at Mary, who was clearing the tea things. "Mary, would you like your cards read, too?"

"Not today, madam," Mary said. Jana glanced at her sharply, wondering why Mary was giving Katarina the "madam" treatment.

"Maybe another day, then," said Katarina, unfazed.

Once in the salon, Jana fished in the drawer of the sideboard and found a pack of ordinary playing cards, and then she and Katarina settled at the table. Jana counted the cards and Katarina removed the twos through the sixes from the deck, Mr. Ganguly watching everything intently from Jana's shoulder. "Cards?" he asked hopefully.

"Not for you today," said Jana, putting him in his cage with a supply of groundnuts.

"Very well, then," said Katarina to Jana. "You are here to consult Madam Katarina on a matter of great importance to you. Sit quietly and allow the cards to speak."

She is an artist, Jana thought. She is creating a mysterious atmosphere right from the start. Even if you consider card reading absolute rubbish, she charms you and calls to some hidden unused corner of your heart to be receptive.

Katarina spread the reduced deck facedown on the table, made Jana pull thirteen cards, and arranged them in a fan.

"Aha," she said, "here is the queen of clubs. It's you. A woman alone, dark-haired, warm-hearted. A widow. Madam Katarina asks: In your heart of hearts, what is it you long for? What is it you want most?"

Jana was taken aback. "I have everything I want," she said.

Katarina raised an eyebrow. "Maybe."

A thoughtful expression playing across her face, she counted and pointed and manipulated the cards. Finally, she selected several diamonds. "I see a money worry," she said. "A loan that can't be repaid. Does someone unreliable owe you money?"

Jana shook her head, thinking of the emeralds. Were the cards saying she was going to lose them?

"Oh! Here's an arrival of a lump sum of cash," said Katarina. Instantly Jana thought, The tunes! The one thousand pounds! It must be on its way.

Katarina continued: "But worries about money are over-shadowed by worries about love."

"They are? I'm *worried* about love?" Jana said, feeling dubious.

"Yes, you are," said Katarina. "The cards say that you're looking for simple contentment, companionship, someone to share this lovely house. Unfortunately, there are a number of spades here—too many for comfort, I think. The picture is not completely clear, but there may be some unwelcome events . . . a betrayal . . . hmm. Given that we're seeing two kings side by side, the cards are warning you about some visit by an officer of the law."

"Officer of the law?" said Jana. "Two years ago, Commissioner Bandhu Sharma threw me in the lockup overnight, and recently he came to do a bogus inspection." She was finding Katarina's card reading uncomfortably accurate.

"The timing might be ambiguous there," Katarina said. "Well. We've come to the end of the fan cards."

Disappointed, Jana wanted to say, But the part about love, how does that end? A reading concluding with a vague foreshadowing of bad luck—that didn't sound good.

Katarina, however, was spreading five more cards on the table. "These should clear up the uncertainties brought up by the fan," she said. "Turn over the first and the fifth."

Jana did as she was told, and Katarina said, "Two aces! Very auspicious! Now pick up the second and fourth."

Hearts—the friendliest of suits—appeared. "Delicious!" said Katarina. "The ten indicates a surprise and the nine that your wishes will come true. And now for the most determining card of all."

"Don't turn it over!" Jana cried. "Let's end on a good note. Really. I don't want to hear bad news at all."

"Shall I peek?" Katarina said.

"Oh, all right," said Jana, by this time feeling silly about being so fearful.

Katarina turned over the card and said triumphantly, "Nine of clubs! No need to worry at all. This reaffirms the other good things."

Jana was embarrassed by the wave of relief that came over her. Had she really been afraid to turn over a card? How absurd.

Meanwhile, Katarina was gathering up the cards and returning them to the box.

"Katarina, where did you learn to do this?" Jana asked.

"From a woman who came to the house to sell chickens, when I was little," Katarina said. "People in the village said she was a witch. I thought she was quite marvelous, if a bit scary."

Jana asked, "Did she ever tell you something that came true in your life?"

"Oh, yes, she told me I'd lose one whole life and gain another. She said that one day I would cross a frozen marsh, but not to be afraid."

Mesmerized by Katarina's story, Jana prompted, "And?"

"I *did* cross a frozen marsh," said Katarina. "The night I escaped from Hungary. On the Hungarian side, the searchlights were crisscrossing back and forth, and I had to crouch and crawl to not be seen. At one point, as I'd been told to do, I stood and ran, and I caught my leg in a rut and went down, hard. The pack I was carrying came off and split; all my things flew this way and that. I tried to stand up again, but I couldn't put any weight on my leg. So I started to roll. I rolled and rolled across the ground, until suddenly, these fellows speaking German had scooped me up and were carrying me to a jeep. 'Welcome to Austria,' they said."

"And you broke your leg," Jana said.

"Yes, rather badly. The Austrian students got me to a first-aid center, but the broken leg was more than the center could take care of. Oh, the leg got set, a few days later, in Vienna, but it never healed properly. They tell me that I could have it rebroken and reset, but so far, I haven't had quite the heart for that."

"I don't blame you," said Jana, with a shudder. She gathered up the cards. "The chicken seller—do you really think she could predict the future?"

Katarina said thoughtfully, "The frozen marsh surfaced in my mind only when I actually encountered it. Of course, the old lady may have told me dozens of things that *didn't* come to pass. One remembers selectively; it shapes a more poetic narrative of one's life." She paused and gave an impish little grin. "On the other hand—she may well have been prescient. I like keeping that possibility open."

"So does everyone, I think," Jana said. "We all want to think that *someone* can tell us what's going to happen. Thank you for the card reading. It was very artful."

"It was my pleasure," said Katarina.

A Letdown

Mary Goes to Church

Mary entered All-Saints Church and sank into her usual seat, in the back on the left. Usually, attending church put her in a good mood. She loved the building, with its high roof and exposed rafters, the arch above the altar, and the light filtering through the jewel-like stained-glass windows. It gave her a feeling of opulence.

On most Sundays, she sang the hymns with great enthusiasm, clapping along with the tambourines and tablas. Today, the first song was "Khushi Khushi Manao," which she often hummed while mixing cake batter. Yet this morning, singing such a cheerful song cost her considerable effort. "Rejoice, rejoice"? Not likely when she felt so pulled down.

She was tired, that was all, she told herself, tired from all that excitement in the house and Jack and Katarina's arrival. Could it have been just a few days before? That day had started before dawn, when Mary had put a fresh application of Goddess Tresses on her hair. Then she'd made the cake, whipping the icing until her arm ached. There'd been the walk to the taxi stand and all the greetings. Then serving tea. Then dinner. *Bapré bap,* what a day. She'd worked so hard to make it a success, but it had ended with an anticlimax.

For dinner, Mary, in consultation with Jana, had planned

the most European meal possible, as the safest thing to please Katarina. The menu was Mary's famous tomato soup, followed by roast chicken with roast potatoes and cooked carrots. She had given the salad greens an extra soak in disinfecting pinky water.

"Jack and Katarina don't have the immunities that we do," Jana had said. "We must protect them."

Mary had complied with these orders, although, truth to tell, she was skeptical about this germ idea. Should a Christian even believe in tiny evil invisible creatures? Nonetheless, just in case they *did* exist, Mary had boiled both the water *and* the milk for five minutes longer than usual.

This morning, trying to raise her voice in the gladness the hymn required, Mary felt a knot of resentment in her throat. After all her work to welcome them, couldn't Katarina have put in even a token appearance in the dining room that night? Couldn't she have eaten a few spoonfuls of Mary's soup at the table, rather than having Jack take a cup up to her bedroom?

Katarina, Jack had explained, was tired after the journey, and to Mary's disapproval, Jana had accepted this explanation without question. Jana herself had fussed around right up to eight o'clock. She was lighting the candles and giving a final readjustment to the fresh flowers—when Jack had appeared and asked if he could take just a little soup up to Katarina.

To be sure, Jack, on his return to the table, had praised the chicken lavishly, especially the crispy bits of skin. Still, there was a lot left over, and a mountain of glazed carrots, too. After Jack and Jana retired to the salon with snifters of brandy, what was Mary to do with the food they hadn't eaten? The tiny kerosene-powered refrigerator hardly had space for a small pitcher of milk, and in any case, Mary didn't think you should keep leftover food around.

Resignedly, Mary had eaten some of it herself, although she found European food bland. Then she'd asked Lal Bahadur Pun and Munar and Harmendra if they wanted some. Lalu ate the

chicken, and the other men the carrots, and Mary had barely
blinked before the last of Jack and Katarina's welcome dinner
had disappeared into their stomachs. The three men also polished off the remains of the chocolate cake.

The church service continued with a reading from the gos-
pel of Matthew translated into Hindi, and then another hymn,
"Raja Yeshu Aya"—Lord Jesus Has Come. Mary started to feel a
little better. Young Pastor Mitra, with his round, earnest face
and hair parted in the middle, was indeed a comforting soul,
which was only appropriate given his name: Pastor Friend. He
was just that. Today, when he read, "Well done, thou good and
faithful servant," he looked straight at Mary.

I hope Jesus knows how hard I worked this week, Mary
thought.

⁕ Time Is Ticking

After worship, she saw that Jacob John was waiting for her, standing against the whitewashed wall that separated the churchyard
from the wide expanse of the sky and hills. The breeze whistled
through the tall, straight deodars and carried the clean perfume
of the pines.

"*Vanakkam,* Mary," he said.

"*Vanakkam,* Jacob-*anna.*"

"What did you think of the sermon today?" Jacob John
asked.

"I liked it," Mary said glumly.

"And the singing?"

"Fine, also."

"Then what's wrong?" Jacob John asked. "Why are you looking pulled down?"

"*I* look pulled down?" Mary said. People rarely accused her
of that.

"No insult intended," Jacob John said. "I don't always feel completely tip-top myself. In fact, today I am on the borderline, one might say."

"Why are you on the borderline?" Mary asked.

"I have quite a few worries about the future," Jacob John said.

"Then you should come have your fortune told with Jana mem!" Mary joked. "She would tell you not to despair."

"I don't *despair*, exactly," Jacob John said. "But you know, time is ticking."

"Time is always ticking," Mary said. "Why does this fact distress you today only?"

Jacob John shook his head. "Mrs. Foster is so old. She is failing. . . . She is getting harder to take care of."

"I understand," said Mary. "She is almost ninety-three, no? I can see how the clock would be ticking especially loudly for her."

Jacob John nodded. "When I first worked for her—decades ago!—she was like a protector for me, almost a mother. Now, I am the protector for her. She's like a child, but a child going backward, daily getting weaker, not stronger."

"You take excellent care of her," Mary said.

"So far. But it can't last," said Jacob John. "The other day, she fell. I was able to get her to her feet again. But what if it happens again? And soon she will need someone to help her bathe and dress, and that will have to be a woman. Not me."

Mary said, "I, too, am feeling how time changes the ties between people."

"Oh?" Jacob John said.

Watching the last of the worshipers file by to say namasté to Pastor Mitra, Mary gathered her thoughts and tried to explain. "In the days of old, Jack sahib was like a son to me. When he was small, I bathed him, I dressed him, I played hide-and-seek around the mission compound. It seems like yesterday.

"Now? Now he has swept by me on the river of life. Suddenly, he's not even a *young* man. And then he brings this woman he wants to marry."

"But you were happy about that before, Mary," Jacob John said. "Don't you like the lady?"

Mary wiggled her head in a noncommittal way.

"*Not* good?" said Jacob John cautiously.

Mary took a deep breath. "This is how I see it. Just my idea, you understand. I think she is—a little *weak*. And maybe spoiled."

"How weak?" Jacob John asked.

"I don't know. . . . She has something wrong with one leg, I think. On the way back from the taxi stand, she kept stopping. She limps. She's not strong and perfect."

"Maybe Mr. Laird doesn't require someone strong and perfect," Jacob John said.

"Maybe not," said Mary, feeling that she'd been peevish and ungenerous. "But why would he want *spoiled*? Too tired to get dressed for dinner, she stays in bed and he takes her a cup of soup. What is he, her bearer?"

"Patience, Mary," said Jacob John. "Maybe you will like her better as the days go along."

"Like? Oh, I like her perfectly fine," Mary said. "I just don't know if she's good enough for Jack sahib, that's all I'm thinking. When European ladies are spoiled, they are *really* spoiled. Maharanis with white skin."

"Your Jana memsahib is not spoiled," Jacob John pointed out.

"She's not European anymore," Mary said. "She got her Indian passport many years back."

"When they live here a long time, some get less spoiled," Jacob John conceded. "But some get more so! One can't predict."

Mary pressed on with her misgivings: "One more thing. This woman, Katarina memsahib, has no family. She says they all died in some revolution. That sounds like an excuse to me. Something she's hiding—low-class background or whatever. Jack sahib, he comes from *very* good family, with a castle in the

U.K. and money and everything. How this will turn out, I don't know, I really don't know."

"Wait and see, Mary my friend, wait and see," said Jacob John.

They were now the only people left in the churchyard.

"Well," said Jacob John, "are you going back to the Jolly Grant House?"

Mary pulled a face. Go back and listen to Lal Bahadur Pun giving Jack sahib a bagpipe lesson?

"Come," said Jacob John, "we'll buy *idli* and *dosa* from Mr. and Mrs. Ramesh. And then go to the cinema. If you like Hindi films, that is. *Kabuliwala* is playing at the Bharat Mata. The story is about an Afghan who comes to work in India."

The invitation astonished Mary. Go and have food with Jacob John and then sit next to him in the dark, closed-in cinema? She thought it over briefly. Was there a law against it? No, there was not. Would it do any harm? No, it would not.

"Why not have some relaxation from work and worries?" Jacob John said.

Mary answered, "Yes, why not?"

Kind Invitations

⚘ At the Ramachandrans'

Jana and Katarina were puffing. Jack alone strode easily up the steep paths and stone staircases, even though laden with a backpack, Jana's handbag slung over one shoulder, Katarina's bag over the other, and a pair of heavy binoculars around his neck. They stopped for a moment to rest, and Jana removed a stone from her shoe.

Jana was wondering whether they should have taken this shortcut to the Ramachandrans' house, but Jack and Katarina had read in *The Globe-Trotter's Companion* that the view at the crest of the ridge was worth the effort, and Katarina had said her leg wasn't bothering her at all.

At the top, they looked back at the town. Jack handed the binoculars around, so that each in turn got a bird's-eye view of the people clustered in small groups to chat, the wandering cows sampling vegetables from stalls, the rickshaws rolling along at a faster clip. The surrounding hillside, with its stone staircases and winding paths, looked like a game of snakes and ladders. Jana found it strangely comforting to see the landscape as if in a silent movie. People might be squabbling below, but against the bigger panorama of rippling hills, life was serene.

Then they surveyed the north side of the mountain— Maharajah's Hill, which was dotted with villas of varied architectural styles. Large white houses surrounded by filigreed stone walls adjoined pastel bungalows with red tile roofs, and there was even a gray stone castle with parapets. In this vertical neighborhood, paths zigzagged between the houses, and in places, massive gray retaining walls held the mountain together. The wider road (the one they hadn't taken today but that was the more normal route) belted the lowest level of houses, and below that road, the hill dropped off in jagged chasms.

Having rested long enough, they took the series of paths and steps that led them to the cement wall circling Ramachandran's U-shaped single-story house. A red tile roof sat jauntily atop the yellow-washed walls. Through the ornamental grill of the gate, they saw a couple of women sitting cross-legged on the warm concrete of the courtyard, sifting rice. A moment later, the front door flew open, and Ramachandran stepped out and greeted them with folded hands. Asha and Bimla were close behind him.

"*Namaskar,* Laird family, we are honored to greet you! Mrs. Laird, *finally* you come to see my mountain aerie."

It was actually the first time she had been invited, because in her two years in town, Jana had socialized with Ramachandran and Rambir mostly at the Why Not? Tea Shop. After Jack and Katarina's arrival, however, both men had urged them all to come for tea at their respective homes.

"You're here!" Asha and Bimla cried, garlanding Jana, Jack, and Katarina with ropes of multicolored flowers, silver braid, and glittering paper rosettes.

"*Namaskar,*" said Jack and Katarina simultaneously.

Just inside, Padma was waiting with a round tray with little lamps on it, which she rotated slowly in the air in front of them, and then she put a dot of red powder on their foreheads. The whole family was in immaculate holiday dress: Ramachandran in a snow-white *mundu* and embroidered tunic, Padma in a peach-colored sari with a jeweled belt, and Asha and Bimla in brilliant blue-and-turquoise saris. Their younger sister, Nirmala, wore a smocked dress with a full skirt, and their older brother,

Vikram, was in his St. Bart's College jacket and striped tie. The two younger boys, T.K. and Sonny, were almost as formal in white shirts and bow ties, and the baby looked ready for the photographer in a sailor suit.

As a gift, Katarina and Jack had brought shortbread from Scotland, which Jack now took out of his backpack.

"Ripping!" said Asha. Bimla admired the plaid tin and the red ribbon.

"Come, come to the sitting room," Ramachandran said, leading them to an internal verandah and into a large room with blue walls sparsely decorated with framed family photos.

Every family member seemed to talk at once, in a swirl of English, Hindi, Tamil, and Malayalam. Jana did not speak or understand the South Indian languages; it seemed to her that people spoke a hundred miles an hour. They did not merely roll their r's but made them do strings of somersaults.

Ramachandran's nephew and his wife, Teddy and Twinkle, appeared with their three-year-old son and infant daughter. A few minutes later, Aunt Putli hobbled in and gave an amiable namasté. Then came a couple of young men, whose names Jana lost track of in the hubbub before they disappeared. Other people drifted in and out—doubtless the cousins and the hangers-on that Ramachandran was always complaining about to Jana and Rambir over lunch at the Why Not?

"Sit, sit," said Ramachandran, showing Jana and Jack and Katarina to the places of honor on the simple wooden-framed sofa. Padma and Ramachandran took their own seats in adjoining armchairs, Vikram drew up a small wooden chair with a low back, and Asha and Bimla got as close to Katarina as they could, on three-legged brass stools. There was still not enough seating, so Teddy went back to the verandah and shouted for more chairs, while the younger children found places on laps or the floor or leaning against their parents.

Jack, when he'd visited two years earlier, had met many of the Ramachandrans at the Treasure Emporium. Now they remembered everything he'd told them about himself and took up the interrogation where they'd left off.

"What is your position in your firm? Do you have a secretary? A driver to take you to work? No driver? You drive yourself? What kind of car do you drive? How much did you pay for it?"

In his earlier visit, the introverted Jack had been stunned by all this friendly interest. Today, Jana noted, he was fielding the questions and asking several of his own.

Katarina, for her part, was getting the adoring attention of Asha and Bimla. "How did you and Jack meet? Was it love at first sight? Let us see your engagement ring. Oh, how romantic."

"Come for a little tea" was the way Ramachandran had phrased the invitation. A little tea, however, did not begin to describe what was being offered now. First came brass bowls to wash their fingers in, followed by banana leaves to eat off, South Indian–style. The subsequent parade of *idlis, dosas, laddus,* coconut *barfi,* mango *barfi,* and several types of *halwa* was enough for three meals, if one chose to dine on sweets.

"Did you girls make all these wonderful things?" Katarina asked Asha and Bimla.

"We helped," they said. Jana pictured them crowding into the kitchen for a three-day orgy of chopping, mixing, kneading, and frying.

As the food disappeared from their banana leaves, other delicacies immediately appeared, as if to prove that nature abhorred a vacuum. Jana noticed that Katarina was growing pale and taking smaller and smaller bites, at longer and longer intervals.

"We only use purest ghee," Padma assured Katarina. "It's very healthy and safe, you can eat with no worries."

"It's all very delicious," Katarina said. "You've gone to so much trouble."

"No, no trouble at all," Padma said.

"Besides, Mums is trying to domesticate us," Asha broke in. "She's teaching us cooking as practice for when she and Dads bring in the grooms they want to foist on us."

"You see," Padma said to Jana and Katarina, "my girls are too modern and cheeky."

"I think they're quite wonderful," Katarina said, with a quick smile at the modern and cheeky girls, which made Ramachandran beam and even mollified Padma.

"Bring some more pistachio *halwa*," Padma said to the twins, "and more tea."

The visit went on for much longer than even Jana had expected. Once the flow of food had slowed down (if not exactly stopped), the family brought out photo albums and showed their relatives far away in Kerala. Nirmala ran and changed into her Bharatanatyam costume and did a demonstration of classical dancing.

"Uncle Jack," T.K. said, "do you know that poem 'I wandered lonely as a cloud'?"

At Jack's nod, T.K. recited it and they all applauded; then Sonny recited "The Charge of the Light Brigade," and everyone clapped for that, too.

"My children all do very well in school," Padma said, without false modesty.

It was dusk by the time Jana and Katarina climbed into the rickshaw that Ramachandran had sent a messenger to fetch. Jack ran beside, saying he needed the exercise. They reached the Central Bazaar as the lights were going on in the shops and the smell of cooking wafted through the alleys. At the house, Mary met them in the front hall, her face full of anticipation.

"Remember, I made a big mutton curry for tonight," Mary reminded Jana. "Eight o'clock?"

Jana felt a pang of stupidity. How could she not have predicted how stuffed they'd all be on returning from the Ramachandrans'?

"Oh dear," she said.

Mary's face fell, but Jack immediately said, "Don't worry, Mary. We'll rally by then."

Katarina, visibly exhausted, said nothing, but smiled wanly and went upstairs to lie down.

✎ Tea at Rambir's

The next morning, a note came from Rambir's wife, Ritu, with another tea invitation, this one for the following afternoon.

"Jana dear," Ritu had written, "I can't believe that you have never been to our apartment! I'm *making* Rambir take the afternoon off. It will be good for him to socialize with your family."

Having learned from her mistake, Jana warned Mary not to make dinner, although she doubted that Rambir and Ritu would put on as much of a spread as the Ramachandrans had. This visit, she predicted, would be simpler and more relaxed all around.

When the next day came, however, Katarina woke up with an upset stomach, which she attributed to the lunch she'd eaten at the Superior Tea Shop the day before. She didn't come down for breakfast. Jack took her some tea, and a couple of hours later, Jana tapped on her door and was relieved to find her up and dressed and smoothing over the covers on her bed.

"How are you feeling?" Jana asked.

"Approaching human," Katarina said. "Next time, I'll pass up that vegetable thing with the raw onions."

"Mr. Joshi of the Why Not? has a very low opinion of the Superior," Jana said. "He'll tell you, 'Why go *there* to get sick? Come *here*.' Do you feel up to the visit at Rambir's today?"

"Yes, of course," Katarina said gamely. "I wouldn't miss it."

At four o'clock, therefore, the contingent of three was standing in front of Rambir and Ritu's apartment, on the top floor of a four-story building built into the slope above the Central Bazaar.

Seconds after Jana's polite knock, the door swung open to

reveal Ritu, dressed in a pink salwar kameez and with her hair just cut in a fresh short bob. Although in her late thirties, she had the youthfully mischievous look of Asha and Bimla Ramachandran, who had been her physics students the year before. "Mrs. Vohra is *so* strict, but she's our best teacher," they'd told Jana.

Behind her stood Rambir, his V-necked pullover and windowpane-patterned shirt giving him a more casual demeanor than the jacket and tie he wore at the press. Jana attributed his relaxed smile to the presence of his adored—and adoring—wife. Ritu, in Jana's opinion, was a miracle worker. She could make Rambir stop worrying about the newspaper and civil war in the Congo long enough to listen to the hit parade on Radio Ceylon—and even to entertain out-of-town guests.

"Hello!" said Ritu, with a hug for Jana and a namasté for Jack and Katarina. "Welcome to the swallows' nest. That's how I think of this building. Our cliff dwelling!" She took the red plaid container Katarina held out and said, "Oh, lovely! Never enough shortbread, that's my motto."

Rambir and Ritu's living quarters were a fraction the size of the Ramachandrans', and completely different in atmosphere. In addition to family photos, the walls were crowded with group pictures of Rambir and Ritu and their college friends, framed university diplomas, a certificate extolling Ritu's excellence in teaching, and an announcement that Rambir's *Our Town, Our Times* had won first prize nationwide as best local newspaper. The sideboard boasted a radio, and the wooden couch was softened with cushions.

"It's very cozy," Katarina said.

"You have to see the verandah," Ritu insisted. "It's the best feature of the flat."

Accordingly, they stepped out onto the verandah and admired the long view of the mountains and Ritu's baskets of geraniums.

Then they came back inside, where Krishan, Rambir and

Ritu's cook-bearer, was moving platters onto the dining table. Samosas, marmalade sandwiches, éclairs, *pakoras*, petits fours, and *gulab jamuns* appeared—and shortbread.

"Oh dear, I see we brought coals to Newcastle," Jack said.

"They're always the best gift," said Rambir. "You know you've brought what people like."

"Ritu, what a spread!" Jana said. "You've outdone yourself."

"Here, take plates, all," Ritu said, "and then we'll settle over there." She waved in the direction of the sofa. She turned to Katarina. "Try one of these." She scooped up a syrup-laden *gulab jamun* with a spoon and put it on Katarina's plate.

"I understand you teach physics," Katarina said, accepting the plate. "And that you went to a national conference last year and gave a paper. That's so impressive."

"It was fun," said Ritu, "only I found it awfully hot traveling down there on the plains. We get spoiled living in the hills. Here, have an éclair."

Jana noticed a gray tinge creeping across Katarina's cheeks as Ritu added petits fours and a marmalade sandwich to Katarina's plate.

"Lovely, lovely," Katarina said hurriedly. "Ooh! That's plenty for me, thank you!"

"I'll just give you this *tiny* samosa with a minuscule amount of chutney," Ritu said, considerably stretching the meaning of "tiny."

As Katarina's plate got fuller and fuller, her lips got paler and paler; she poked at the refreshments with a fork, moved the food around her plate, and only occasionally took a truly minuscule bite.

Meanwhile, Rambir and Jack had ignored the directive to sit down. They stood by the table, attacked their own fully laden plates, and launched into a conversation ranging from population control to the United Nations Security Council.

Jana found it hard to relax. She worried that Katarina might suddenly have to make a dash for the loo—or the verandah.

She worried about Ritu, too; the seemingly carefree but hardworking teacher had certainly been obliged to rush home from
her day's classes to put on this tea party. Afraid that Ritu would
be hurt because Katarina wasn't eating much, Jana tried to com-
pensate by taking second helpings of everything.

"Ritu, it's all delicious!" she gushed.

When Jack finally seized the reins and said, "You've fed us
absolutely splendidly! But I think I should get these two back to
the Jolly Grant House," Jana was hugely grateful. Interesting,
she thought, that these social occasions can be simultaneously
a pleasure and a hurdle. She looked forward to walking off that
last *gulab jamun.*

Outside in the fresh air, Katarina's color improved, and the
three made their way through the early evening activity in the
bazaar. Most of this activity centered on food—people frying it,
grilling it, selling it, looking for it, eating it, carrying it away. A
street vendor yelled at them to try his kebabs.

"Another time," Jack called back cheerfully.

They skirted a man offering up maize roasted in the husk.
Jana was relieved to learn that despite lacking appetite for refreshments during the visit, Katarina had been captivated by Rambir
and Ritu. "What a lovely couple they are," Katarina said.

"They are indeed," agreed Jana. "And very unusual. They married against his parents' wishes. Rambir's dad wouldn't speak to
him for years, but Ritu managed to get everyone reconciled."

Jack thought this over for a moment. "Well, Mum," he said,
"I suppose Katya and I should be happy that you're the only
parent we have to worry about. In the sense of asking for your
blessing, of course."

Jana chuckled. "That you've got, in ample measure. I can't
imagine how anyone would oppose *your* marriage. *I* think it
was made in heaven."

Out of Sorts

⸎ Mary and Jacob John

In Mary's opinion, things were not quite proper at the Jolly Grant House. The day after the sahibs had gone to tea at the editor's flat, Jana mem told Mary that she wouldn't have to prepare dinner for that night, either. Jack sahib had offered to cook. Jack sahib himself! *Bapré bap*, what was this world coming to? Very well, Mary decided; if they don't want my food, I'm not forcing them to eat it.

Mr. Jack Laird had changed; that was very clear. He was dancing attendance on a woman who never ate anything and who napped all the time. Was he getting weak in the head?

All in all, Mary was beginning to feel like a stranger in the Jolly Grant House. Everyone had been taken in by Katarina's supposed charm—Jana mem, Lalu, Munar, even young Harmendra. Why did they not see things the way Mary did?

Knowing by now that Jacob John often took Thursday afternoon off, Mary took the chance of walking to Best Madras & Kerala Foods, where she was happy to find him buying his usual small packet of South Indian coffee. From the grocery store, they ambled over to the Municipal Garden. In the company of her friend, Mary felt her mood starting to improve.

Jacob John, for his part, seemed delighted to have the unexpected time with her. "Shall we go see *Kabuliwala* again?"

he suggested. "That film is so sad and beautiful. It makes you understand how a man feels when he is far from home."

Mary felt entirely differently than Jacob John did about being far from her place of origin; her home, she finally felt, was *here*. Moreover, she was of the opinion that, in the film, the man from Kabul had brought misery on himself by not keeping his temper. He'd stabbed someone. You can't go around stabbing people, she thought, insult or no insult to your honor. Better to turn the other cheek, even if you have to bite your lip while doing so.

"Spending money on a film we've already seen, I don't know about that," Mary said.

"But at least we know it would be spending money on something good," Jacob John said.

"We could go to the Europa." Mary proposed this alternative somewhat in jest, because the Europa was more expensive. By mutual agreement, Jacob John and Mary paid their own way on these excursions, and every movie ticket, Mary calculated, was worth a brick in the little white house she would build someday. Still, she continued: "They are showing *Anastasia*. That's about a woman who might be a princess—or might not."

"The Europa," Jacob John said slowly. "Okay, let's go see. If there are no cheap seats left, we can go back to the Bharat Mata."

Outside the Europa, there was a man hawking tickets to two balcony seats. "I'll give you the same price as for stalls," he said.

"You see?" said Mary. "We were destined to see this film."

In the balcony, Mary enjoyed the feeling of being in a high-class place, although she was worried about whom she might bump into. She reminded herself that she was not a boarding school student sneaking out to meet a boy at the cinema. She had a right to be there with whomever she pleased. A right to sit down comfortably in this padded chair, which she had paid for—although, granted, not at full price.

"Nice seats, right?" said Jacob John.

"Yes, they are very good," she said.

The next moment, she felt her stomach lurch. Scanning the rows below, she saw Jana mem's friend Ritu sitting with Asha and Bimla Ramachandran, and next to the twins, *bapré bap*, none other than Jana and Katarina memsahibs. Mary made a panicky glance at the stairs.

"What?" said Jacob John.

Mary gestured with her chin and a quick flick of her eyebrows.

"Never mind, let them be," said Jacob John. "They have a right to be there, no?"

Mary laughed nervously, still uneasy lest she be seen. She was grateful when the lights went down and the curtain went up, the whir from the projection room sounded, and the newsreel came on the screen.

After the film, they stood to sing the national anthem, then watched Jana and the others file out of the balcony. Mary had been sitting for a long time, even staying in her seat during the intermission, and she was stiff all over—knees, hips, and back. Jacob John appeared to feel the same way. They both stood and stretched.

"What did you think?" Mary said.

"The old duchess lady was like Sylvia memsahib," said Jacob John, which made Mary giggle.

"Did you think the heroine was a princess or not?" Mary asked. "I think she was just a refugee. So plain."

"She wasn't so bad," said Jacob John. "She looked like Katarina memsahib."

Mary said, "Yes, she did, but that's what I meant—both are quite plain indeed."

"I think the heroine in the film *was* the real princess," said Jacob John.

Mary felt annoyed—and even nervous—that he was disagreeing with her. She could well imagine having to pass herself off as something she wasn't, even as a princess. Had she not shed her old identity when she ran away from Madras? Surely that woman in the film was even more of an impostor than Mary herself.

◆ *Even Squirrels Run from It*

When Mary got home, Jack was getting the bagpipe lesson Lal Bahadur Pun had promised him. They were on the terrace on the basement level of the house, right outside Mary's window, and making a huge noise. First Lal Bahadur Pun would play a phrase, and then Jack would imitate him, on a long skinny tube called a chanter that he had brought with him from Scotland. You couldn't call that thing a bagpipe, thought Mary; it was a bag-*less* pipe. It looked like the flutes herd boys carried when they drove cows and horses, but the sound was raspier.

Lal Bahadur Pun was an exacting teacher, and the repetition of phrases, over and over, was almost more than Mary could bear. She reached up high and banged the window shut but still the sound was unacceptably loud. The picnic with Jacob John had long worn off, and she found herself getting hungrier by the minute. She went upstairs, crossed the dining room, and slipped out into the side yard.

Outside, the wailing noise hit her again. It was like a donkey trying to sing, Mary decided. She noticed a striped squirrel running across the paving stones and through a hole in the external wall. Every creature runs from that noise, Mary thought grumpily, except for human beings, and some of those run from it, too.

She went into the cookhouse, washed some rice and set it to boil, ground some spices, chopped onions, and made herself a simple sauce. By now the rice was done, and she scooped it onto a metal plate, poured the sauce over it, and carried it out to the side yard, where she sat cross-legged on the paving stones and ate her meal. It was growing dark; the wind was rustling through the trees and blowing cool on her arms.

After the sociability of church and the time with Jacob John, Mary felt very alone. With no one to interrupt her or talk to, she finished her food quickly. Then she washed her plate and cooking pots and returned to her own room.

The wool she had bought for matching scarves for Jack and Katarina was sitting in a bag in the corner, on the floor. Normally, Mary would use this empty time to knit. She picked Jack's scarf out of the bag and, sitting cross-legged on her charpoy, did one row of knit, another of purl. She contemplated doing a third row, but her heart was not in it. She put the knitting materials back in the bag, and lay down on her bed. Then she willed herself to go to sleep, but sleep didn't come.

Things to Digest

✦

✧ At Aunt Sylvia's

"We're actually feeling a bit visited out." Jack spoke politely, but a shadow of fatigue crossed his face.

"This one will be short, I promise you," said Jana. "And all you'll have to eat is Jacob John's cucumber sandwiches, or not even those if you don't want. Aunt Sylvia hasn't cooked anything for twenty years and doesn't give a fig whether people eat or not. Really, it will be easy. Aunt Sylvia will amuse you with her bons mots. Don't be taken in by her apparent slips of the tongue—they're all intentional. She calls the Elysian Fields the Illusion Fields, because, she fears, the afterlife may not be as heavenly as advertised. Anyway, after about twenty-five minutes, she'll threaten to keep Mr. Ganguly, and then we'll be dismissed. She'll say, 'Haven't we had a lovely visit!' and 'Do come back sometime before the century is out.'"

"Is she *your* aunt?" Katarina asked. "Jack didn't tell me about any aunts."

Jana laughed. "No, she's the aunt of an Anglo-Indian friend of mine who was a teacher at the Far Oaks School. Miriam—my friend—astonished everyone by marrying her pen pal and running off with him to manage a guesthouse in Australia. She still sends a money order every month to help support Sylvia. She and her bearer, Jacob John, live at my optometrist's house—Niel

Powell. Niel and Sylvia are among the very few Anglo-Indians left in town. A lot emigrated soon after independence—to Australia and Canada and the U.K."

On arrival at Mr. Powell's house, Jack looked at his watch. "I'm timing this visit," he said. "You promised it would be short. It is now . . . seven minutes after four."

They waited a few minutes at the closed gate before Jana cried, "Hullo?"

"Hullo?" Mr. Ganguly shrieked.

After a couple more minutes, Jacob John peeked out the front door. His puzzled look and workaday attire instantly revealed that he wasn't expecting visitors.

"Hello, Jacob John," Jana said, as he crossed the courtyard. "Is everything all right? Mrs. Foster told us to come today."

"She told me tomorrow, madam," said Jacob John.

Concerned, Jana said, "Oh dear, what a muddle. I know her note said Friday."

Jacob John hesitated a moment and said, "Come in anyway. I will tell her you are here. I think she needs visitors today. Please come."

He led them into the sitting room, then disappeared. After a few minutes, he returned to tell them, "Sylvia memsahib is coming in two-three minutes."

Two-three minutes turned into fifteen, during which Katarina and Jana made themselves comfortable in easy chairs and chatted about the view and the coziness of the room and the relative benefits of living right in the Central Bazaar versus at the more splendid remove of Maharajah's Hill. Jack walked around the room peering at the scientific tomes on the bookshelves and other evidence of Niel Powell's profession. The armchairs grouped around the fireplace, the heavy furniture, and the artifacts also betrayed Niel's preferences and interests: there was a telescope that matched the one Jana kept in her tower lookout room, a spyglass, a barometer, a ship in a bottle, a perpetual calendar, and some antique clocks.

Finally, striking a sudden feminine note in this masculine den, Sylvia made her entry. Walking with the aid of an elaborately carved stick, she looked festive in a pink floral dress, fuchsia clip-on earrings, and red pumps with little bows on them. Her cheeks were rosy with freshly applied rouge.

"My dears," she cried. "I must apologize for the mix-up. You have no one but me to blame! If I had a social secretary, I'd sack her! But I'm delighted to meet the famous Jack. And the lovely Katarina—you are *so* very kind to come visit." To Mr. Ganguly, she said, "Come here, sweetie, and give me a kiss."

"Kiss kiss!" said Mr. Ganguly, and brushed his beak against her mouth.

Then, spying the bottle of LPN10 that Jana had brought, Aunt Sylvia smiled brightly. "Ah! LPN10—Abinath's answer to aging and other horrors. How sweet of you. Let's drink to youth and crabby old age, too. Jana, *you* do the honors."

While Jana searched for cordial glasses in the sideboard, Aunt Sylvia settled herself in her favorite armchair with Mr. Ganguly on her wrist. Jacob John, unable to produce his usual cucumber sandwiches, was soon on the spot with a plate of Britannia biscuits.

"I must apologize for offering you such meager fare," Aunt Sylvia said.

"Not at all," said Katarina hastily; and Jack said, "Apricot centers, my favorite." Both looked comically relieved at not being obliged to eat.

"Well now, isn't the weather lovely?" Aunt Sylvia said. "We ordered it just for you."

"It is lovely," said Jack. "This is a delightful season. Balmy, actually."

"Yes," said Katarina, "the air is soft."

"And what do you think of our town?" Sylvia asked.

"Very welcoming," said Katarina.

"Almost to a fault," added Jack.

"There must be lots of tourists in the bazaars these days.

Our town is now famous, you know!" Sylvia turned to Jana and asked, "How is our good friend Rambir?"

"He's very well," said Jana, "and thinks it's about time that you and he sat down to concoct another think piece for the newspaper."

"I'll put my little gray cells to it," Sylvia said.

Jana turned to Jack and Katarina and explained, "Aunt Sylvia has strong opinions on world affairs."

"I should say I do!" Sylvia said. "This planet is not particularly well run, and it has to be pointed out from time to time. I *do* like your Prime Minister Macmillan, though. When you go home, please give him my best regards."

"How's the search for the fourth husband going?" Jana asked.

Sylvia's eyebrows went up. She smiled mysteriously, leaned forward, and said in a confiding tone, "I'm thinking of proposing to that French fellow—what's his name? Maurice Chevalier. Do you think he'd be interested?"

"He's crazy if he isn't!" Katarina said.

As the conversation progressed on the topic of romance, Katarina told the story of how she and Jack had met, while Aunt Sylvia, laughing in delight, egged her on.

The visit went swimmingly, Aunt Sylvia charming everyone. Then, suddenly, she straightened in her chair and looked up. "Well! Haven't we had a lovely visit? You *must* come see me again before the century is out."

Having been given the signal, Jana and Jack and Katarina bid their good-byes, and Mr. Ganguly told Aunt Sylvia that she was a cutie pie.

"Flattery will get you everywhere," said Aunt Sylvia.

On the way to the gate, Jack looked at his watch and announced, "four-forty-seven P.M. Bravo, Aunt Sylvia."

In the rickshaw on the way home, Katarina said to Jana, "What a delightful old lady!"

"Isn't she?" said Jana. "I was afraid, after what Niel Powell had told me, that we were going to find her out of sorts. But she didn't even make one joke about kicking the bucket, throwing in the towel, or heading off to the Illusion Fields. Anyway, thank you for accompanying me."

"It was a pleasure," said Katarina.

⚜ No Fever

The visit to Aunt Sylvia's was followed by a weekend during which Jack and Katarina took a bus down to Hardwar to see the holy places on the Ganges and Jana stayed home on duty in the fortune-telling salon. While Jack and Katarina were gone, Jana saw a constant stream of customers wanting advice on everything from renovating their houses to getting their children to study harder in school. Familiar problems, she said to herself, finding parallels to her own situation in every card she turned over.

Late Sunday night, Jack and Katarina staggered in, sunburned, dust-streaked, and exhausted. The heat at the lower altitudes had been, in Jack's words, "flattening," the bus crammed with people, including villagers with livestock; Katarina had practically had a goat in her lap. "It was all quite fascinating," Katarina said. "I wouldn't have missed it for the world." Neither, however, had energy for much more than a quick good night to Jana before going up to bathe and collapse.

Now, on Monday morning, Jana was finishing off her fried egg and toast alone in the dining room when Mary poked her head through the side door.

"More eggs, madam?"

"No thanks, Mary, this was lovely."

Mary removed Jana's empty plate and looked pointedly at the two unused place settings. "Where are Jack and Katarina sahibs?"

Jana said, "Jack went birding, but I think I heard him come in. He must be washing up. I'll go see in just a minute."

Mary's eyebrows crunched up in disapproval. She's in a funk, Jana decided, trying to remember when Mary had last acted like this. Ah, yes. With some embarrassment, Jana recalled that Mary had worn that same scowl during Jana's ill-fated romance in Bombay with an English businessman. Mary had not even been civil with the man. She'd told Jana he was "not a truth-telling person"—and it had turned out that she was right. The man, who'd acted interested in marriage, had disappeared and had not answered Jana's letters. In time, his picture, along-side that of his wife, had been published in the international edition of the *New York Herald Tribune;* it seemed that his interest in marriage had mainly been to escape his own for a while in a brief fling.

"Good riddance to bad rubbish," Mary had said. On seeing the picture and realizing that the man was out of Jana's life, Mary had instantly become more cheerful.

Come to think of it, Mary had also been grumpy around Jana's Bombay friends Cyrus and Lily King. In retrospect, Jana had to admit that, again, Mary had merely been acting justifi-ably protective toward her. Mary hadn't liked Jana partying with the Kings, either in Bombay or in Hamara Nagar, especially when Jana had grown starry-eyed over Cyrus's cousin and busi-ness partner, Max King. When Max had announced, to Jana's mortification, that he was marrying a young socialite, Mary's face had worn an "I told you so" expression for days.

So what on earth was Mary's gripe now, Jana asked herself. Was Mary overtired? Was the extra cooking getting to her? Had Jack or Katarina done something to offend? Maybe hiring that poor scared chap, Harmendra, had been a mistake. It was pos-sible that the fellow got on Mary's nerves more than he helped her.

"Mary," said Jana, "is everything all right?"

"Yes, madam," said Mary, confirming that it wasn't.

When she was done with breakfast, Jana went up and tapped on Katarina's door, surprised to hear Jack's voice say, "Yes?" After taking a hesitant peek, Jana entered the room to find that Katarina, gray-green in complexion, was sitting up against the pillows, with Jack seated on the side of the bed in his hiking shorts and a sweatshirt.

"Oh, so you *have* been out and back," Jana said.

"I did a quick three miles," Jack said. "It's a glorious morning out there."

"And how are you, Katarina?" Jana asked. "I'm starting to worry. You weren't feeling perfectly well even *before* going to Hardwar." She put her hand on Katarina's forehead and wondered if it was abnormally warm.

"I don't feel feverish," Katarina said.

"You can't always tell," said Jana. "I'm going for the thermometer."

Within moments, she was back, and handed Katarina the thermometer to put under her tongue. Her whole life, Jana had been a great respecter of illness, especially after influenza had killed both her parents and smallpox had carried off both her daughters and blinded her husband. One never knew when a seemingly trivial complaint could turn savage.

She asked, "Any tummy upsets in the night?" and Katarina shook her head.

After a couple of minutes, Jana carried the thermometer over to the window, where she was relieved to see that the silver line hadn't risen even to the normal mark.

"You were right," she said to Katarina. "You're cool as can be. Cool as a cucumber, as Jack's father used to say. Any runs?"

"A touch," said Katarina. "But mostly this feeling that I can't even face food without my stomach rising. The sight of grease is the worst."

"You'd better make a quick visit to Dr. Chawla's," Jana said. "He's got his own laboratory. He can figure out whether you've picked up some bug you can't shake. I'll walk you down to his clinic—or we can take a rickshaw. I'll send him a note to ask what time is best."

"Oh, thank you," said Katarina. "But I hate to bother you. If he can see me, I'll just pop down there by myself."

"Nonsense," said Jack. "I'll go with you. Actually, I should donate some bodily wastes to his laboratory, too."

"Oh, no! Your tum isn't quite right, either?" said Jana. "Did *you* pick up something over the weekend?"

"No, no," said Jack. "I'm just testing your house's new plumbing. It works fine, by the way."

"Abinath stocks paregoric," Jana said. "Although he'll probably tell you to take yogurt and chew on some fennel seeds."

Jack said, "Don't worry! Dr. Chawla will put us right in no time."

A Diagnosis

Later in the afternoon, Jana was tidying up in the salon when the front door opened and Jack's and Katarina's laughter sounded in the hall.

"Good, you're back," said Jana. "Sit down and tell me what Dr. Chawla said."

Sometimes, Jana had often thought, just going to the benevolent Sikh grandfather made you feel better instantly. "Nature will take its course!" Dr. Chawla would say. If nature needed some help, he might give you modern medicines from his own supply or send you down to Abinath's for something more Ayurvedic.

Katarina—and Jack, for that matter—were now the very picture of health and very smug about something.

"I take it the prognosis was good," Jana said.

"It was excellent," said Katarina.

She plopped onto the window seat and stretched her legs

out. Jack put a brown paper bag on the table and drew up a chair. Then the two of them glanced at each other, obviously trying not to grin.

"You two are looking awfully secretive," Jana said, her suspicion mounting. "Butter wouldn't melt in your mouths."

Jack said to Katarina, "Shall we tell her?"

Jana eyed Jack with mock severity, remembering the day, at age six, when he'd trimmed his sister Caroline's pigtails. Suddenly, their secret was obvious. My, I've been dense, she thought. Delhi belly, my foot.

"I know what it is!" she cried. *"When?"*

"Middle of December," they said together.

"He's sure?" Jana said. "Dr. Chawla, I mean."

"He's sure enough for our purposes," said Katarina. "He said all signs pointed in the same direction. He *could* prove it by testing on a rabbit." She squeezed up her face in abhorrence. "I said, Please spare the rabbit! Things will become obvious soon enough."

"They're not obvious now," Jana said. "You look perfectly slim and trim."

"Just as well," Katarina said. "When we get back, we can pop into the registry first thing and get married. That way, there will be less prevaricating to do at the agency where I work. They're a bit stuffy there."

"Stuffy? Not compared to the old duffers at *my* firm," Jack said. "Their eyebrows would shoot up to their hairlines. For those of them that still have hair, that is." He turned to Jana, suddenly serious. *"You* aren't shocked, are you, Mum?"

I should be, but I'm not, she thought, unable to keep from laughing.

"What's so funny?" said Jack.

"It's just comical," she said. "And wonderful."

I am soon to be a grandmother, she thought. Given her upbringing, she was amused at how uncomplicated—how purely joyous—her response to the news was. She was sure that if, unmarried, she'd told her own parents she was pregnant, there would have been an explosion heard ten miles away.

She went over to Jack and kissed the top of his head, then went over to the window seat and hugged Katarina.

"I am thrilled," she said.

Katarina smiled, too, but said, "I think, with all this excitement, I would like a little rest now."

"Go lie down for a bit," said Jack.

Jana heard their footsteps echoing in the stairwell and ending at the door to Katarina's room. Jack's footsteps did not continue up to the lookout room, and Jana heard the door to Katarina's room close softly.

·◌ *Stew in Three Colors*

To Jana's relief, over the next few days both Jack's and Katarina's digestive systems stabilized, and Katarina's appetite and energy started to return. Much as she loved taking meals in the new dining room, Jana felt ready for a change, and she proposed dinner at the Victory Hotel. Jack and Katarina were enthusiastic about this idea. Jana thought Mary would be happy to have yet another night off; Mary, however, acknowledged the news with a cursory flick of her head and a grumpy curl to her mouth.

When Jack and Katarina came back down again at seven, Jana was ready in the salon, dressed in a green raw silk salwar kameez. Jack was relaxed but natty in a sports coat and open collar, and Katarina elegant in a fluid dress that changed from teal to gray, depending on how the light hit it.

"Do I need a necktie?" Jack said.

"No, you both look very nice," said Jana. "You will earn Mr. Dass's stamp of approval. These days, some people try to eat dinner in their hiking clothes, and he gets most distressed."

As they set out through the Central Bazaar, the bigger stores were open and brightly lit with electricity, while the small vegetable vendors sat on the street with their baskets, selling onions and radishes by kerosene lantern.

At the far end of town, they walked alongside the wrought-iron fence that enclosed the Municipal Garden, glancing over at the tourists strolling along the paths inside. An open-air puppet show was in progress. As the characters hit each other with sticks, children buried their faces in their mothers' saris, a few moments later to be coaxed out to watch the puppets reconcile and dance.

Katarina stopped for a moment, entranced. "It's a storybook scene. And yet—it's just another evening in the park. A bit of garden-variety magic. Something one takes for granted—until it disappears." She smiled at Jack and then at Jana.

They edged the wall to the Victory Hotel, exchanged salaams with the *chokidar* at the gate, and went down the red gravel driveway lined with white triangular bricks.

In the foyer, Jack's eyes widened at all the changes that had occurred since he'd been there two years ago. The new owners had taken out the moth-eaten tiger that had posed in the center of the floor and removed the antelope heads from the walls. Huge mirrors now reflected the sleek modern furniture. Mr. Dass, however, had not changed; he scurried out from behind the new counter to greet them.

"Mrs. Laird, it has been far too long since you dined with us!" he cried. "Mr. Laird, we have been waiting to see you!"

"Mr. Dass," Jack said, "I'd like to have you meet my fiancée, Miss Esterhazy."

Katarina wished Mr. Dass namasté, making him beam. "You are already speaking Hindi, I see, Miss Esterhazy," he said. "You are enjoying yourself, I hope?"

"Oh, I am," Katarina said. "We're having a perfectly grand time."

Mr. Dass smiled as if he were responsible for this happy

situation. "I am giving you the best table in the house," he said, and led them through French doors into the dining room.

"What a beautiful room," Katarina said.

"I feel the same way," Jana said.

She'd always loved this room, even as a ten-year-old, on holiday with her parents in 1912. Its wood-paneled walls and high ceiling hadn't changed, perhaps because the new owners just hadn't gotten around to tinkering with them yet. As before, the oval tables were set with white linens, the butter balls were sculpted into rosebuds, and the serviettes folded into swans.

"Here you are," said Mr. Dass, seating first Jana and then Katarina. He telegraphed a quick signal to one of the bearers standing alongside the wall, then retreated back into the lobby.

"Are you at all hungry?" Jana asked Katarina.

"I could eat something bland," Katarina said, studying the menu in front of her.

Reflecting the heritage of the new owners, the menu listed an ambitious assortment of French and Parsi dishes. They scanned it carefully, discussing the merits of *coq au vin* versus chicken *dhansak*, while their bearer waited, tolerant, knowing, and a bit bored.

Jana asked him, "What's available tonight?"

"Chicken stew," the man said.

Katarina said, "Where does it say that on the menu? I only see *coq au vin* and chicken *dhansak*."

"Chicken stew is always available," said the bearer.

"How is it cooked?" Katarina asked. "Is it very spicy?"

"Spicy? No, not to worry, memsahib, no taste at all. It's made especially for English sahibs and memsahibs. And Americans," he added.

"Sounds like just the ticket," said Katarina. "I'll have that. With a tiny bit of bread, if I may."

"As much bread as you want," said the bearer.

Jack ordered *coq au vin* and Jana, chicken *dhansak*. When the dishes arrived, they all looked suspiciously like the same stew, except that one was white, one was yellow, and one was red.

"I think they boil the chicken in a big pot," Jack guessed, "then stick some of it in a second pot with a splash of red wine, and some more in a third, with a dollop of masala sauce."

Jana took a bite. "Mine's quite delicious. Try yours."

Jack did as he was told, and his eyebrows went up in surprise. "Very passable. Katya?"

"Not much taste, as promised," said Katarina, adding a little salt. "It will be bland and tolerable, just as Dr. Chawla ordered."

Jana and Jack washed their food down with the local Ophrysia beer, and Katarina had some club soda, which she said kept her stomach settled. Halfway through, the string band started playing waltzes: "The Merry Widow," "Tales from the Vienna Woods," "Skaters' Waltz." Jana knew their repertoire by heart but could always happily hear it again.

Jack and Katarina got up to dance, Jana watching them fondly from the table. Her thoughts turned to the Puritanism of her husband, William; for him, dancing and drinking and going to the movies had been a sin. What a burden such an attitude puts on the work of marriage, she thought. Thank goodness Jack and Katarina weren't shackled by *that* kind of morality.

Finally, after Jack and Katarina had returned, a cart arrived with a selection of toffee baskets, mango fool with ladyfingers, and little porringers of *kheer* with almonds on top.

"You know, I think the food *is* better under the new ownership," Jack said.

"The meal was exactly right for me," Katarina agreed.

"Have one of these nice sweets," Jana said to her. "That *kheer* would slip down easily."

Katarina nodded and accepted one of the little bowls. Jack took a toffee basket with ice cream, and Jana, a mango fool. She ate the dessert slowly, savoring the tangy-sweet taste, and the music of the band, and the sight of Jack and Katarina having a good time.

Leaning back in her chair, Jana said, "You know, instead of waiting until you get home to go to the registry, you could have a very simple wedding at the house. We could have a very nice party, actually. I think people in town would love to come help you celebrate."

"Would they, really?" said Jack. "They wouldn't be coming just to avoid hurting your feelings?"

"I wouldn't want people to feel they had to bring a gift," said Katarina.

Jana said, "We can spread the word via the grapevine that a gift is not necessary. Let's see, how many people would we have?" She started counting on her fingers. "Rambir and Ritu. The Ramachandrans. Oh! The girls will be ecstatic."

"Lovely old Dr. Chawla might come," Katarina said thoughtfully.

"Your friend Mr. Powell and his aunt Sylvia," Jack said.

"Might I invite my friend Kenneth and his daughter, Sandra?" Jana asked.

"By all means, invite them!" Jack said.

They continued, surprised to find themselves up to a guest list of forty-odd people without even trying.

"If we can't seat everyone inside, we could set up a *shamiana* in the courtyard," Jana said. "It's completely doable. But don't worry, we don't have to decide right this minute. Sleep on it."

❧ *Just Dash Off a Letter*

Jack and Katarina slept on the idea, and then, making Jana swear that the wedding would be modest and quiet, they said that they would extend their visit through late June.

Katarina said gleefully, "I'll be able to tell my grandchildren about my romantic wedding in the Himalayas."

Jana was amazed that Jack seemed so favorable to the idea;

perhaps the possibility of getting additional bagpipe lessons from Lal Bahadur Pun had tipped the scales.

"And your stuffy employers?" Jana asked.

"Oh, they're in favor of marriage," Jack said. "Some of them have been telling me for years that I should try it. What's more, they approve of filial piety. I'll say that my mother insists on having the festivities here."

With Jack and Katarina's decision to stay, Jana got a burst of resolve to make decisions in her *own* life as well. The currents of love and talk of marriage floating around the house felt contagious. Maybe Jana had been wrong that romance with Kenneth was out of the question. In the past, when she'd thought about making an overture to him, she'd drawn back, but now she would be brave. Gentlemen, she had been taught, should make the first move in matters of the heart, but if she resigned herself to that approach, her tombstone would surely read, "She waited in vain."

She thought, too, of the card reading Katarina had given her, in which Katarina had implied that Jana should take one small step in the direction she wanted to go. Jana had told young Deepak the same thing, and it was time to heed her own advice.

That afternoon, when there was a quiet interlude, Jana gathered pen and paper and settled herself at the table in the salon. Mr. Ganguly, perhaps thinking she was going to do music transcriptions, whistled a few bars from a tune of old Ian's.

"No," Jana said, with a chuckle. "I'm just writing a letter. Give me inspiration."

"I love you," said Mr. Ganguly.

"Too strong," said Jana. "Not quite yet."

Then she wrote, "Dear Stu, Much excitement! Jack and Katarina's wedding is going to be *here*! You *must* come. Bring Sandra, too."

So far so good, but what now? Suddenly, she had what struck her as a brilliant idea. She'd suggest a holiday later that year—

say, to Goa, where the beaches were lovely. What could be more romantic than swimming in the sparkling warm salt water by day, having a sundowner on the verandah while watching the last light play on the waves, and visiting old Portuguese cathe-drals, hand in hand? Moreover, as of last year, Goa was now a part of India, with no formalities at the border.

An hour later, the table and floor were littered with crum-pled-up drafts of the letter. "Planning a little trip . . . might it coincide with your in-country leave? It would be so nice to get to know each other a little better." She'd thought a long time before coming up with the question "Shall I book a suite?" The suite part, she felt, was perfect, since it left the issue of bed-rooms ambiguous. Finally, she was satisfied with her carefully chosen phrases. The door was open, and she'd just see if Ken-neth would walk through.

Putting the letter in the envelope, she felt her stomach flip-flop. Be brave! She steeled herself. Jack and Katarina were brave, *they* weren't cynical and fearful about finding love, *they* went ahead and seized it. (And propriety be damned, Jana added.) She got a stamp from the sideboard, hesitated for a few more seconds, then licked it and pressed it down on the envelope with her thumb.

"Walk?" said Mr. Ganguly.

"Yes," said Jana decisively. "Let's take a quick stroll to the PTT."

Then, with Mr. Ganguly on her shoulder, she hurtled through town and, at the PTT, thrust the letter at the startled clerk before she could change her mind. The loud *whomp* as the clerk canceled the stamp sounded like an affirmation to her, an excla-mation point to a sentence. There, done!

Look at My Happy Face

◦§ Marriage, Pah

"Jack sahib and that Katarina person are getting married in our house," Mary said to Jacob John as they walked to Mr. and Mrs. Ramesh's stall after church. "Now we have nothing but talk about weddings. You'd think no one had ever gotten married before."

"You're not happy?" said Jacob John.

"Yes, yes, I'm very happy," Mary said. "Look at my happy face."

Jacob John said, "If that's happy, I don't want to see you sad."

She met his deadpan gaze and they both burst into laughter.

Jacob John said, "Of course they're talking about it! They are young, looking forward to life. You don't remember that time?"

Mary shuddered. Why would she want to remember feeling powerless and afraid? Would one *choose* to call up nightmares? "I prefer *this* time," she said.

"A wedding is very exciting," Jacob John mused. "Everyone dressed in their best, and music playing . . ."

"Pah, music. We already have that in our house, all day long, and now it's worse than ever. Lal Bahadur Pun acts as if he is going to play for the prime minister and the queen of England. Practice, practice. Wah, wah, wah."

"When Jack and Katarina sahibs have all gone home, you will miss them," Jacob John said. "You'll say it's too quiet."

"I will welcome the quiet," said Mary, unwilling to be talked out of her bad mood.

"Come, come, what's the problem?" Jacob John asked.

Mary burst out, "This woman, she thinks she is some sort of maharani. And Jack sahib is her *chaprassi*. Little more than a peon! *Oh, I don't feel well.* Don't worry, darling, I'll take you to the doctor. *Oh, I'm feeling so tired.* You lie down, my love, I'll bring you a cup of tea."

"So, he's a nice man, Mr. Laird," Jacob John pointed out.

"Soft in the head," Mary said.

At the Best Madras & Kerala Foods, Mr. and Mrs. Ramesh were debating whether taking over this little, not very lucrative stall had been wise, and whether they should go back to South India.

"We should all go back Madras-side," Mrs. Ramesh said. "Mr. Jacob John and you, Mrs. Mary Thomas, why stay here? Your families would be happy to see you, wouldn't they?"

"I have duties here," Mary said, brusquely.

Mr. Ramesh pulled out a Tamil newspaper he had been saving and flipped to the back pages. "Mary, here is a picture of a Mr. Thomas Thomas. He must be a relative of yours, no? Cousin, maybe?"

Mary squinted hard at the picture. Could it possibly be? How could her husband have lived that long? He would be—oh, sixty-six years of age, more or less, by now. But with his habits, she would have thought he'd be long dead. Yet—that scar in the shape of a frown, just above the right eyebrow . . . how many people would have that?

"I don't think it's any relation," she said.

"Read the story, Mr. Jacob John," Mr. Ramesh said. "It's quite miraculous."

The story was actually an obituary. When Jacob John read aloud, " 'Mr. Thomas Thomas was laid to rest in the churchyard

of St. Thomas Church . . .'" Mary felt such a rush of emotions
that she had to sit down on the cement ledge in front of the
Rameshes' shop. Shock, relief, surprise, and curiosity came over
her in quick succession. She could hardly catch her breath.

"Mrs. Thomas, what is wrong?" Mrs. Ramesh said. "You are
looking quite sickly."

"No, no, nothing is wrong," Mary said. "Jacob-*anna*, please
continue the story."

"'Twenty years ago, Mr. Thomas Thomas was in prison for
robbing an elderly couple . . .'"

That's not surprising, Mary said to herself. It sounds just like
him.

Jacob John continued: "'Suddenly, Thomas Thomas received
a vision. He said that both Jesus and the Virgin Mary and the
apostle Thomas appeared to him and told him to mend his
ways.'"

Any story to get out of jail, Mary thought.

"'The priest of St. Thomas Church, believing what Thomas
Thomas said, offered to give him food and shelter if he swept
the church daily and spent the rest of his time in prayer. So, for
the next twenty years, this is what happened.'"

Thomas Thomas praying? Mary couldn't picture *that*.

"'When Thomas Thomas was on his deathbed,'" read Jacob
John, "'a very bright light shone above his head, in the presence of witnesses. The local people proclaimed it a miracle. A
brass plaque in his honor now hangs on the wall of the church.
Mr. Thomas was predeceased by his wife and had no children,
but his memory will live in the hearts of all men.'"

Jacob John looked up. "Such a touching story, no? It shows
that even a bad person can mend his ways."

Mary couldn't help herself: the image of her degenerate husband bathed in celestial light was so improbable that she started
giggling.

"You find the story amusing," Mrs. Ramesh said.

"No, no," said Mary, forcing herself to stop laughing. "It's very inspiring."

"You're *sure* that man was not your relative?" Mr. Ramesh pressed.

"We didn't have saints and criminals in our family," Mary said, stretching the truth about the criminals. "Just ordinary folks. Remember, many people are named Thomas."

Mr. Ramesh turned to his wife. "I told you there was no connection."

Mary and Jacob John ate some *idlis* and then they each bought a measure of South Indian coffee, which Mrs. Ramesh wrapped up in some brown paper. With their packages in hand, they strolled over to the Municipal Garden and sat on a bench, watching young couples play with their children.

"Was that true?" Jacob John asked Mary.

"Was what true?" Mary said.

Jacob John spoke gently, but his tone was knowing. His steady brown eyes were fixed on her face. "That man, Thomas Thomas, he was truly no relation of yours?"

Mary took a deep breath. Could she trust him with her secret? She had long since sized up Jacob John as a sober and tolerant and forgiving man—a Christian gentleman who would live by the maxim "He who is without sin, let him cast the first stone." Jacob John, she was sure, would not cast stones at her.

"You can't always tell from a newspaper photo," she said. "But he *does* in fact look like my husband."

"Aha," said Jacob John. "So—now you really *are* a widow."

Mary had passed herself off as such for three decades. If you wait long enough, she reflected, sometimes a lie becomes the truth.

"Are you giving me your condolences?" she said.

"I'm offering my sincere sympathy," he said.

She scrutinized his face and saw one corner of his mouth

lifting by a millimeter, which sent her, for the second time that day, into a bout of giggling.

"Now you are free to marry," Jacob John observed.

Mary instantly stopped laughing. "Why would a free person enter a prison?" She hadn't meant to sound so vehement, but the question had popped out like firecracker.

"Do you see it that way?" Jacob John said, appalled. "Marriage is the normal state of human beings."

"Were *you* happy with your wife?" Mary said.

"Why, yes, I was," Jacob John said. "When she died, I didn't think I would ever be happy again."

"You didn't fight?" Mary said incredulously.

"We fought," said Jacob John. "Who doesn't fight?"

Mary persisted: "You didn't beat her?"

"No, never," said Jacob John. "Why would I have beaten her?"

Instantly, Mary felt ashamed to be saying such things. She could not picture Jacob John raising his hand against anyone. She turned to him apologetically. "Jacob-*anna*," she said, "I am so sorry. I know you would never do such a thing. But—such a thing was done to me."

"That will never happen again," said Jacob John. "Not as long as I am your friend. And especially not if you allow me to be more than your friend."

All the way home, Jacob John's phrase "more than your friend" resounded in Mary's head.

I'll Get Myself a New Job

At lunchtime the next day, as she was heading from the kitchen to the dining room, Mary heard laughter and then, popping out suddenly from the conversation, her own name. "Don't you think that . . . Mary . . . Yes, but it would be better . . . We'll tell her . . ." When she entered the dining room, Jana and Jack and Katarina looked up at her, suddenly falling silent.

Once again, Katarina had eaten only a small amount, even though Mary had made rice and cooked vegetables just as Jana had instructed, very mild, because Katarina, it seemed, was still adapting to the food. Why would adults want to eat such mush? That on top of breakfast, which had been *suji*—white porridge— with a tiny bit of Lyle's golden syrup.

Jack, to be sure, had cleaned his plate. "Good lunch, Mary!" he said.

"Thank you, sahib," she said, clearing the table.

Back in the kitchen, Mary stacked the dishes beside the sink. "Wash up carefully and put everything back exactly where it belongs," she snapped at Harmendra.

"Yes, Mary-ji," he said, but not quite meekly enough for Mary's taste.

"What's the matter with you?" she said. "Why are you looking at me that way? Have some respect! Now, do your work! I don't know why I hired you."

Feeling better for having chewed out Harmendra, she went down to the terrace and sat on the wall with her back to the mountains, looking up at the house. She had a terrible feeling in her gut that she knew what Jana and Jack and Katarina had planned to tell her. It was this: Jack and Katarina were going to take Jana back to Scotland with them, and she, Mary, after thirty-some years of working for Jana, would be dismissed.

"Thank you for your service," Mary imagined Jana saying. "We'll write, of course."

Dismissed after toiling at the dusty mission, Mary fumed. After going where Jana mem wanted to go, and picking up just like that whenever Jana mem wanted to leave a place.

I will not be dismissed, Mary decided, now in a state of righteous indignation. I will give notice, of my own accord. I will seize my own future.

What's more, she thought, there is an opportunity in this situation. After I quit, I will talk to Jacob John. I will tell him that I have changed my attitude toward marriage, that now I think, if you have the right person, it could work.

She continued painting this picture of her future. Pastor Mitra will marry us, right in All-Saints Church, with the light filtering through the stained-glass windows. I will wear a nine-yard sari of the highest-quality silk, and new gold ornaments. Jacob John will wear an embroidered *sherwani*—or maybe a suit and tie.

Children, of course, are not possible. My sainted first husband deprived me of that joy for all time, thanks to the diseases he gave me. But Jacob John has a son with three children; he'll provide the family, ready-made. When the son and the daughter-in-law and the grandchildren visit us, Jacob John will make sure that they treat me with utmost respect.

✑ *A Long-Ago Arrival*

Mary's plans for the future, however, soon mingled in her mind with her memories of the past. Retiring late to her room, she lay awake, recalling the blistering-hot day when she'd arrived at William and Jana's mission station.

How tired she'd been then, and scared, and hungry, and how dusty her feet were from the ten-mile walk on the dirt road. At the railway station, a man had told her about how the American sahib and his English wife at the Children of the Cross Mission were looking for a girl to help with the three children. "Go quickly," he said, "before someone else gets that job."

And so, at high noon, Mary had arrived at a walled compound and stood at the open gate looking across a bare patch of ground at the mission building. The main house, combining office and living quarters, was long and low, with a verandah and a thatched roof. The sunlight was blindingly white, and Mary was dizzy from having walked so far in the heat.

A white family was having lunch on the verandah—a man, a woman holding an infant, a boy of about five years of age, and a girl of about two. Mary didn't know whether to call out to them, or what to say. Then, suddenly, the little boy saw her and turned to tell his parents. Next, the man was beckoning to her to come forward. Mary came up onto the verandah, grateful for the shade, and stood a few feet from the table, her heart pounding.

The family didn't look like the exotic Europeans Mary had seen in Madras, fancy people who rode in automobiles and sat for hours having drinks in the gardens of their beautiful houses. These mission people seemed more humble. For Europeans, they were dressed simply, the man in a short-sleeved shirt and half-pants, the woman in a plain cotton dress. The man was tall and muscular, with very bright blue eyes. His wife, with her hazel eyes and dark curly hair plaited down her back, hardly looked British at all; she might even have passed for Kashmiri. She is thin and tired, Mary decided, almost as much as I am.

The man spoke first, in some language Mary later realized he considered Hindi; then, when Mary stared blankly at him, the woman took over, speaking a more intelligible mixture of Hindi and English. Mary's knowledge of either language had been minimal. She'd known she would need them, however, and even back home had seized on every opportunity to learn as much as possible. On her way north, she'd quizzed other train and bus passengers on how to say common things: greetings, where do you live, what is your name. Not yet knowing how to write, she'd locked everything in her head with fierce determination.

"What work can you do?" Jana mem had asked her.

"Everything," she said firmly, in English, with an adamant wiggle of her head.

"And your chits?"

Oh, oh, she had feared that she would be asked for letters of recommendation, and now that was happening. She'd considered buying some chits, or having a professional letter writer tailor some particularly fine ones for her. But during her escape, it had been a choice between paying for chits and paying for food. Now she took a deep breath and said, "Sorry, no chits, madam."

Jana turned to William and said, "I don't think that makes much difference. You can't really trust the chits anyway." She spoke again to Mary. "How old are you?"

"Fifteen years, madam," Mary said.

"She's awfully young," Jana had said to William. "But . . . she seems keen to do the job."

The infant in her lap—baby Fiona—was getting fretful. The little girl—Caroline—got out of her chair and leaned up against Jana, and the little boy—Jack—also stood up. Mary saw that his knees were dirty and scuffed, and that his half-trousers were too short. His gaze, however, was observant for one so young.

By now, both William and Jana were looking more relaxed and receptive, and Mary sensed that her goal was within her grasp.

"Sir, madam," she said, "I am a Christian."

There were many situations in which this was not an advantage, but Mary had been told that at the mission, it would tip the scales in her favor.

"Honey," William said to Jana, "it seems like the work of God. I think we should be thankful and hire her."

Meanwhile, Mary had come a little closer and smiled at Caroline, who had smiled back and then hid her face in her mother's dress.

"Mummy," Jack said, "that woman looks nice."

"I agree, darling," Jana said.

"Is she going to be our ayah?" Jack's small face was hopeful.

"Yes, darling," said Jana, "I believe she is."

Predictions

⁓ *Divination by Pendulum*

Jana came in from her afternoon errands in the bazaar to find Katarina lying on her back in the window seat in the salon, with her knees jackknifed. Jack stood over her dangling a ring on a string over her abdomen.

"It's going in a circle," Jack said.

"Yesterday it went in a straight line," said Katarina.

"Physics lesson?" Jana asked. She put Mr. Ganguly on his perch, from which he watched the sway of the homemade pendulum, his head going back and forth.

Jack turned and said, "Just doing a bit of divination. This room seemed to be the best venue."

"And the results?" Jana said.

"Ambiguous," Jack admitted.

"A circle is a girl, an oval is a boy," Katarina said. "I have this feeling that it's a girl."

"Have you a preference?" Jana asked.

"One of each," said Katarina.

"You think it's *twins*?" Jana asked.

"No, no, I mean *eventually*," said Katarina.

"There would be a certain efficiency in twins," Jack said, "don't you think?"

Katarina made a grimace of mock horror. "One at a time

will be ample." She swung her legs back down, sat up on the
window seat, and plumped the cushions.

"You've told Mary, right?" Jana said.

"No, we're going to do that today." Jack looked at Katarina.
"Should I tell her or should you, or should we do it together?"

Katarina thought for a moment. "She's so attached to you.
You're still her little Jack baba, needing to be scrubbed behind
the ears and wanting extra helpings of whipped cream."

Jack said, "It might embarrass her, though. It's rather an
intimate thing to be talking about. I think it would be better if
you did it, woman to woman."

"I'm willing to, but—I feel awkward in her presence," Katarina said. "She's distant with me. I don't think she likes me."

Jana said, "Of course she likes you! Why ever wouldn't she?"
Jana spoke with far more confidence than she felt; she was
loath to admit that Mary had not taken to Katarina as warmly
as everyone else had. However, deep down, Jana recognized
that the signs of Mary's dislike had been there all along: the use
of "madam," the unsmiling expression, the conversational
exchanges kept to the barest minimum. What was bothering
Mary, anyway? Could it be simple—jealousy? Resentment of a
newcomer who had captured the limelight?

Jack turned to Jana. "What do you think, Mum? Do *you* want
to tell Mary?"

Jana said, "I think you're right. It would be a special kind of
confidence, coming from Katarina."

"Very well," Katarina said. "I'll go tell her right now. Where
is she?"

"In the kitchen," Jana said.

Katarina put on her shoes and headed across the hall, and
Jack went upstairs to read, leaving Jana in the salon by herself.
She shook her head in amusement at the thought of Jack swing-
ing a ring over his pregnant fiancée's abdomen.

What were those old wives' tales about predicting the sex of a baby? Carrying low was a boy, carrying high was a girl? Or food cravings—salt for a boy, sweet for a girl?

It was all a good guessing game, Jana thought, and whichever the baby's sex, she'd be delighted. She pictured her grandchild growing up and excelling at sports—a boy walloping a ball with a cricket bat, a girl charging around the field with her hockey stick.

Or perhaps he—or she—would be a violinist and would reach much higher levels of skill than she had. One day in the future, maybe Jana would be sitting next to Jack and Katarina in a concert hall in, oh, say, Vienna and listening to internationally renowned child prodigy young Master Laird or little Miss Laird play Paganini variations at blistering speed.

↞ Mary Learns a Secret

Meanwhile, Mary was busying herself in the kitchen—or at least making sure that Harmendra kept busy.

"Peel just the skin. Don't be wasteful," she said to him. Really, did she have to tell this boy *everything*? She watched carefully as Harmendra, seated cross-legged on the floor with the basket of potatoes by his side, sulkily followed her instructions. Then, after he seemed to be satisfactorily launched on the task, Mary looked on the shelves for a tinned ham. Cold ham with mashed potatoes—stupid dinner, she thought, but at least it didn't take much work. She turned and observed Harmendra again.

"Cut off that green bit," she said, gesturing to the potato the young man was now working on.

"But that's not skin," Harmendra pointed out. "You said cut off only skin."

"Yes, but if it's green, it's not good to eat," Mary said. She added silently, It will give our delicate maharani Katarina a stomachache, and we certainly don't want to do *that*.

"Are you going to make fried potatoes?" Harmendra asked hopefully.

"No," said Mary. "Mashed."

"Oh," said Harmendra. "A lot of work, mashing."

"The young memsahib doesn't want fried things," Mary said.

Lunch had been a sorry affair, she thought, what with the rice lacking seasoning, and plain bread as accompaniment. Everything had looked white and boring to her. And now here was something else white and bland—plain potatoes. Well, she thought, as soon as I quit this job, I won't have to cook *this* kind of food anymore.

A figure in the doorway startled her; she looked up, realized it was Katarina, and felt a rush of embarrassment. Had the young memsahib read her mind?

"Oh, I'm sorry," Katarina said. "I didn't mean to make you jump."

"No problem," muttered Mary. For the life of her, she could think of no reason why Her Highness should be hanging around in the kitchen.

"Mary, might I talk to you just a moment?" Katarina asked.

"We are just now preparing dinner, madam," Mary said, not meeting Katarina's eyes.

"I could help," offered Katarina. "I could peel some potatoes."

"No, madam, not necessary," Mary said. "Harmendra is here to peel the potatoes."

"Well, then," Katarina pressed on, "might you take a little break, and we could chat outside? Maybe down below, on the terrace?"

Mary took a deep breath and bowed to the inevitable: this lady was not going to be talked out of talking. After washing her hands and wiping them on her sari, she followed Katarina outside and down the stairs to the terrace.

"Let's sit," said Katarina.

Mary perched on one of the terrace chairs, uneasy and distrustful, and Katarina drew up another chair and sat, closer than Mary would have preferred. It was quiet here, behind the house, protected from the street noises. In the trees beyond the wall, a few monkeys leapt from branch to branch and came to rest, among them a mother with a tiny baby clinging to her underside. Above the rippling brown-and-purple ridges, high in the hazy June sky, huge birds with fringed wingtips wheeled and soared.

Katarina smiled at the scene. "It's so lovely," she said, "and the breeze feels so nice and mild." She was wearing her hair loose and seemed relaxed and at peace, in no hurry to go anywhere or do anything. She had just had her thirtieth birthday, Jana had told Mary. At the time, Mary had thought, That's quite old for a bride—couldn't Jack sahib have found someone who hadn't wasted her best childbearing years? Today, however, Katarina looked younger than her years to Mary.

The resident squirrel ran up close to them and then turned around and scampered off, as if wanting to deliver news but finding, on closer examination, that it had mistaken them for someone else. At a distance, it turned once to observe them, then disappeared.

As the moments ticked by, Mary began to wonder why she had been summoned to sit outside and admire the view. Was it merely because Katarina wanted company while taking the air? Jana mem would have done *that* with her. As Mary grew increasingly mystified—and eager to go do just about anything else but sit there—Katarina spoke.

"Mary, you've been so kind to Jack and me," she said.

Well, that's nice talk, Mary thought, but if someone starts out with a compliment, watch out for a complaint—or a request for another service. Some people gave a gift with one hand, then took it back with the other.

"I know I've put you to extra trouble in the kitchen," Katarina went on, "and I do want to say that I appreciate how much bother it is to change all your routines and make food you didn't plan to make."

"No bother, madam," said Mary, still wondering what the considerate tone was all about.

"The problem was," Katarina said, "I've been having trouble keeping food down. But that's getting a little better every day, now."

"That's good, madam," Mary said.

"The reason is a bit of a secret," Katarina said. "No one knows about it yet but Jack and Jana memsahib—and Dr. Chawla."

On the alert and now much more interested, Mary glanced up into Katarina's face. A smile was playing around Katarina's mouth.

"I don't think we'll tell the men in the household just yet," Katarina said. "But we decided that it wasn't fair not to tell *you*. You've been with Jana a long, long time. You've really seen her through thick and thin. You took care of Jack when he was a little boy. And his sisters, I understand."

"I did that," said Mary. At least this woman appreciated those facts, and had heard about Mary's early service with Jana and the tragedy of the two little girls dying. A lump started to form in Mary's throat as she said to herself, Perhaps Katarina is a more understanding person than I thought.

"So, what I wanted to tell you," said Katarina, "was that now *I* am going to be a mother myself."

"Yes, madam," said Mary, "of course. I wish you all happiness and many children in your marriage." She was aware of the stiffness and formality of her own words.

Katarina, though, did not seem put off and said, laughing, "No, what I meant was, *soon*. I'm having a baby. I mean—I'm pregnant."

Mary let out a long, low *"Bapré bap!"* The pieces of the puzzle—Katarina's fatigue and lack of appetite, Jack's extra attentiveness and concern—started falling into place. Mary looked up, straight into Katarina's shining face. "This is the truth?"

"Why, yes," Katarina said. "This is the truth."

"Jana mem knows? And Jack sahib, too, you said."

Katarina pealed with laughter. "Jack most of all!"

As the eavesdropping squirrel made another foray onto the terrace and back, Mary sat and digested what she'd heard. The story unfolding was not the progression of events that Mary would have predicted for Jack and his bride. The normal way to do things was to get married and then have children, and if you didn't do it the normal way, usually there was drama, often dismay and temper tantrums and a sense of emergency. But here was Katarina, her eyes bright, her skin glowing, looking the way expectant mothers should look when all was well in their world.

So much for Katarina, but what was Mary to think of Jack sahib? Jack, no village lout or movie villain, had made Katarina pregnant before they were married. The idea was a lot for Mary to absorb. Normally, she would consider a man who took advantage of innocent women as a bandit and *badmash*. Sometimes such men got off scot-free for their vile deeds; other times, at least in films, they made the man marry the girl, or else she did away with herself by various gruesome methods.

Yet Jack, apparently, had not forced himself on anyone, and certainly not on this lady who was sitting here gently talking with Mary and enjoying a beautiful June day.

"So, Mary, what do you think?" Katarina said.

What *did* she think? Mary gave Katarina a long, amazed look. Now Jack's maharani no longer seemed to her a spoiled brat or a delicate invalid. Katarina was human, decided Mary, that's what she was. Not perfect, not high and mighty, but happy and open and human. Moreover, she was asking Mary to be on her side. Her heart full, her arms wanting to cradle the child that very minute, Mary felt a rush of protectiveness both for Katarina and for her baby.

"I think," she said slowly, "I think this is a very good thing. The baby will be very strong and beautiful. Just like you— Katarina mem."

She considered the situation for a moment before adding, "And I think you should get married. *Now*, even. Straightaway."

"Don't worry, it will happen!" Katarina laughed and rose from her chair. "We won't let him off the hook." Mary, understanding that it was a joke, but thinking it really wasn't, also stood.

There was a moment of the slightest awkwardness, and then Katarina gave Mary a shy hug. Mary, feeling Katarina's slender arms around her, had the sense that a wall had come down. Jana and Jack had already taken Katarina into the family; now she, Mary, would too.

Mary Ayah

The next afternoon, Jack and Katarina were out for a walk and Jana was in the salon, reading another short, dismal letter from Tilku. It was dated the third of June. Three months at that place he'd spent, and things *still* weren't getting better for him.

"Boys here steal," it said. Jana's heart sank. Had some of those brand-new clothes and books they'd bought disappeared? She'd given Tilku a padlock for his trunk, but had he been careless and left some of his things about? Or had he lost things but now was making excuses to her, in advance?

"Jana mem?" Mary's voice from the archway startled her.

"Yes, Mary?"

"I'm going to the bazaar."

This is a very odd time of day for Mary to do errands, Jana thought. "Is there something you need in a hurry?" she asked.

Mary said, "I'm going to that little spice shop in the Upper

Bazaar. They have the best ginger root and fennel. For herbal tea."

"Oh," Jana said. "Are you not feeling well?"

"It's not for me," Mary said. "It's for Katarina mem. I'm going to make her some tea that will settle her stomach. Ginger and fennel."

Jana smiled. "That's kind of you, Mary."

"Also, we have no Britannia biscuits in the house. She should keep a packet of them by her bed," said Mary. "And eat one slowly when she wakes up."

"Ah, yes, that's a good old trick," said Jana, who had used it herself.

Mary wobbled her head slowly, her eyes tense with apprehension. "Jana mem, you know, I am thinking something."

"What are you thinking, Mary?"

Mary said firmly, "I'm thinking we must have this wedding *soon*. That way, Katarina memsahib will be safer."

The word "safer" interested Jana. Did Mary think that Katarina had better get that wedding band on, *ekdum*, before some terrible twist of fate occurred?

"Mary," Jana said, "it's going to be all right. On the twenty-sixth of June, right here in the house, under our very noses, Jack and Katarina will be safely married. And after that, they'll live happily ever after."

"You think?" said Mary.

"I do," said Jana firmly. "Now, you're not to worry."

"All right," said Mary. "Is there anything in the bazaar that you need this afternoon?"

"No, thank you, Mary," Jana said.

"Then I'm going now." And off she went, looking determined and protective. When Jack was small, Jana remembered, Mary had often worn that very same expression.

Taking One's Lumps

*⋖∘ **What Can You Expect from Duffers?***

Jana was in the courtyard, pulling an occasional weed from between the paving stones, when the postman arrived at the gate. He was a cheerful soul and very well informed about everyone's business, often commenting on the items he was delivering: "*Finally*, your son writes you!" or "This looks like a wedding invitation; I guess they found a bride for that useless boy" or "Your pension has come, thanks be to God."

Today, his expression was proud as he handed a large, battered envelope to Jana. "From U.K.," he said.

One glance at the return address told Jana what it contained. Her heart sank with disappointment. "Oh, blast!" she said.

"Madam?" said the postman, puzzled and hurt.

"Nothing you did." She sighed. "Thank you."

Inside, in the salon, she tossed the packet on the table without opening it. Jack and Katarina looked up from their newspapers.

"What's that?" Jack asked. "Why the long face?"

"It's the tunes." Jana shook her head. "Old Ian's dance tunes. When you were a little boy, didn't he play them for you?"

"He did," said Jack, "all the time, but I didn't think they were on paper anywhere."

"They weren't," said Jana. "I wrote them down. From memory. I thought I had a good chance of getting them published, but it looks as if they've come back like a homing pigeon."

By now, Mary had arrived in the room, and Lal Bahadur Pun, too, questioning looks all over their faces. Jana deduced that they had been chatting with the postman.

Katarina said hopefully, "Perhaps the publisher copied them and sent back the originals."

"Fat chance," said Jana.

"Well, you can't tell until you *look*," Jack said. "Do you want *me* to open it?"

"I can open it, Jana mem," Mary said.

"I, also," added Lal Bahadur Pun.

Jana let out a resigned breath. "No. I'd better face the music. So to speak."

She got a letter opener out of the sideboard drawer, slit open the envelope, and withdrew a sheaf of papers. Seeing that the top sheet was a cover letter, she started to read. After a couple of lines, she let out a helpless laugh, having immediately seen that the writer was not one to dispense false hope.

"Well?" asked Jack.

"Oh, all right," Jana said and, taking a deep breath, read aloud:

"Dear Mrs. Laird,

"Thank you for sending us your submission, all the way from northern India. I'm afraid you should have spared yourself the postage.

"You have obviously put a great deal of time and effort into transcribing these tunes. Yet, I fear I must tell you that because of their narrowly personal value and old-fashioned nature, they probably would find a prohibitively small audience. You might consider donating them to a family archive or a repository of that nature. Perhaps a local music lovers' society would be more interested. I am sorry to disappoint you, but I feel it would be doing neither of us any good to give you false encouragement. Publishing is an uncertain and expensive business, and I regret that we cannot afford to take on projects for sentimental reasons.

"Yours very truly, Ian Duff."

"What!" Katarina cried. "Duff? More like *duffer,* I would say."

"Who *is* he?" Jack said, picking up the envelope. "Hmm. Duff and Ferguson. Never heard of them. Second-raters, *I* would say."

"This man has no brains," Lal Bahadur Pun said darkly. "He doesn't know good music."

"Badmash!" cried Mr. Ganguly. *"Buddhu!"*

"Give that paper to Mr. Ganguly to tear apart," Mary said.

"Oh, you all are very sweet, but . . ." Jana shook her head helplessly.

Silence fell upon the group. Well, that's that, Jana thought. "Maybe this Mr. Duff is right." She sighed. "Maybe a family archive *is* the right place for the tunes. Jack, when you go home, you could take the packet with you. Put it in the vault with the family correspondence."

"Now, just a minute," Jack said. "You are going to send it straight out to another publisher. It's like falling off a horse. You must get back on, immediately. You can't give up after one attempt."

"I don't even *know* another publisher," Jana cried. "The postage alone is very expensive. Look how much it cost to send this off."

"Mother," Jack said, in exasperation, "for God's sake, don't worry about *postage.*"

Katarina, who had been musing, suddenly suggested, "Write another cover letter. And why don't you include a photo of your whole household? People like photos."

"We've got a photo we had taken the first year," Jana said. "Lalu in his tartans and Mary and Tilku and Mr. Ganguly and I, in front of the Jolly Grant House."

"Just the ticket," Katarina said. "Also, don't put the manuscript in a ragged old envelope. Put it in a nice new cardboard box."

"Put a title page on the collection," Jack said.

Mary offered, "*Jana Mem's Family Tunes.*"

Lal Bahadur Pun said, "*Tunes from the Olden Days, Written Down Now.*"

"Call it *The Jolly Grant House Collection,*" Jack said. "What do you think of that?"

"I suppose it's all right," said Jana. "In fact, it's rather nice."

"Shakespeare was wrong, you know," said Jack. "A rose by any other name might smell as sweet, but a pile of paper needs a moniker. Hold on while I fetch something from upstairs."

While he was gone, Jana reflected that putting a name to a collection really *did* make it sound more important. After a moment, Jack returned with a copy of the *Scotsman* he'd bought at Muktinanda's a few days previously. Flipping through the advertisements, he finally came across one for a music publisher. "Here you are. Your next target."

"You make it sound as if I'm doing archery practice," Jana said.

"You can look at it that way," said Jack. "Now run up to Muktinanda's and get a fresh new cardboard box to mail it in. Or do you want me to?"

"I will go to Muktinanda's, Jana mem," Mary said.

"Or I," Lal Bahadur Pun said.

Jana looked around at the circle of determined faces, amazed that they were not letting her slip the manuscript into the almirah and forget about it.

"Start writing that letter," Jack said. "We can get the thing in the post by the end of the day."

"But we have a *wedding* to plan!" Jana cried.

"All the more reason to get this out of the way this afternoon," said Katarina.

"All right, then, I'll do it," said Jana, and, with the help of the entire household, she had the packet back at the PTT two minutes before closing time.

⚭ A Phone Call to the Headmaster

The next day, the postman stopped briefly at the gate with a worried look on his face.

"Madam," he said to Jana. "I know you are expecting one letter. From young Tilku at boarding school. Always on Tuesday you get this letter."

"Right you are," said Jana. "It *is* Tuesday."

"But, Madam, down at PTT, they gave me no letter to deliver. So all I am bringing to you today is my sad apologies."

"Not your fault, brother," Jana said. "If there's no letter, there's no letter. Although I agree that it's worrisome. Tilku gets punished if he doesn't write his weekly report, such as it is."

She went back in the house and mulled over this small event—or nonevent, the dog that didn't bark in the night. Come to think of it, she hadn't heard from Headmaster Chopra yet, either. Wouldn't both he and Tilku have responded to the news about the wedding by now?

The matter preyed on her, and by late afternoon she decided to go down to the PTT and call St. Regis Pre-Military Academy.

"I told you to get a phone," Jack said.

"I know," said Jana. "I will, one of these days."

Arriving out of breath at the PTT, she gave the school's telephone number to the clerk, then took her place in the queue, where she had time to study her fellow customers. There were obviously many, many stories behind the calls that were about to be made. A girl of perhaps fifteen had her arm around a middle-aged woman who kept wiping her eyes on the end of her sari. A young man in a beige shirt and trousers read a telegram, folded it, unfolded it, and read it again. If you want to see portraits in emotion, thought Jana, come to the telephone queue—it's less expensive than the cinema, and one hundred percent authentic.

When it was finally Jana's turn, she gratefully squeezed into the booth, closed the door, and waited for the tumbling ring of the phone.

"We have your party on the line," the operator said, and next Jana heard a smooth female voice: "St. Regis Pre-Military Academy. This is the office of the headmaster. Miss Rastogi speaking."

"It's Mrs. Laird," Jana said. "Young Tilku's sponsor."

During a long pause, the line crackled with static, until Miss Rastogi finally said, "I see."

"I would like to speak to Mr. Chopra," Jana continued.

"I am sorry, he is busy," Miss Rastogi said quickly.

Not expecting such short treatment, Jana said, "Then perhaps you can take the message. We're having a wedding at my house in Hamara Nagar in a couple of weeks, and we wondered if Tilku could be excused from class in order to attend."

"Tilku."

My word, wondered Jana, how dense can the woman be?

"I—I will pass the line to the headmaster," Miss Rastogi said.

A couple of minutes went by, during which Jana glanced frequently at her watch and grimly imagined how much the call was going to cost. Finally an officious but wary voice said, "Headmaster Chopra here."

Still worried about the phone charges, Jana stated her request as quickly and precisely as possible

"But, Mrs. Laird," Mr. Chopra said. "Is Tilku not already at your house?"

"No," Jana said, "he's in school. In *your* school."

"We sent him home last Friday," said Mr. Chopra, "by the regular bus."

"Friday?" cried Jana. "This is Tuesday. Where *is* he?"

"That's something you should know, not I," said Mr. Chopra.

❧ Rusticated

After she'd hung up and paid for the call, Jana practically sprinted home from the PTT, arriving disheveled and still disbelieving what she'd heard. Running down to the terrace, she interrupted a piping lesson Jack was getting from Lal Bahadur Pun and had them follow her up to the kitchen, where Mary was showing Katarina how to make chapattis.

"I got through to the school," Jana said.

"But what happened?" Jack said. "Has something happened to Tilku?"

"I should say it has!" Jana said. "He's been rusticated. He was sent home from school on Friday, which means he's been Lord knows where for the past five days."

"Rusticated?" Katarina said. "What does that mean?"

Jana shook her head in frustration. "It means he's been suspended. Booted out until the end of term. The headmaster—Mr. Chopra—said he'd been caught stealing. Then he added that since Tilku's marks were so terrible anyway, there was no chance he'd pass his final exams. Chopra says they'll give him one more chance next term. Apparently the so-called Disciplinary Board deliberated for hours."

"He was stealing?" said Lal Bahadur Pun. "What did he steal?"

"I have no idea," said Jana.

Mary removed her cooking pot from the hearth. "We all told him to behave himself," she said heatedly. "Myself, I told him many times. Many."

"I can't believe he was caught stealing," Jana said. "Why would he need to steal? He had plenty of pocket money."

"Boys steal," said Mary matter-of-factly.

Jack said, "I wonder what really happened. It's not always clear with groups of kids."

Jana said, "The question is, where is he *now*? I wonder if he went to the hotel. That's where he used to live, after all, out back in the servants' quarters."

"If you had a telephone, you could call Mr. Dass," Jack said.

"But I don't. Don't rub it in," Jana said.

Dashing inside, she scribbled a quick note, then asked Lal Bahadur Pun to find a messenger in the bazaar and have him run down to the hotel as fast as he could. An anxious hour and a half went by before the messenger returned, panting, with the reply.

Jana seized the note and read, "Dear Mrs. Laird, We have searched our premises from head to toe, without success."

"Oh, damn," she said. "He might not even be in town."

"We should look in the streets," Lal Bahadur Pun said.

"The subedar-major and I can go," Jack said to Jana. "You stay here."

"What nonsense!" Jana said. "I'm coming, too. Mary and Katarina, you stay here. Don't wait for us to eat. We don't know when we'll be back."

Jana went to her bedroom and got a cardigan out of the almirah. Her mind was racing. Why had Tilku not come home? Was he just too embarrassed? Had he had anything to eat for the last several days? Where had he slept these last few nights? She prayed that he had not been kidnapped or fallen over one of the steep *khuds* in the neighborhood, to die a gruesome death at the bottom of a ravine.

At the gate, Jack and Lal Bahadur Pun were waiting for her with flashlights. With determination, they set off through the darkening town, ducking into the shops to ask if anyone had seen the small messenger boy who lived at the Jolly Grant House.

At the very top of the Upper Bazaar, under a three-walled shelter, a team of four rickshaw wallahs had parked their vehicle and were celebrating the end of the day's work with home brew. On learning that Tilku was missing, they immediately all said, "The hotel, the hotel," then, when Jana shook her head, started arguing among themselves.

One, after convincing the others that he had the answer, turned to Jana. "Look in that small deserted house on the top of Maharajah's Hill. They call it the haunted house—the *bhoot bangla*. That's were the boys go. To smoke *biris*."

"And ganja," the second said.

"And drink home brew," noted the third.

"And teach each other how to pick pockets," added the fourth, increasing Jana's despair.

"Thank you, we'll try there," she said, quickly.

"This is the absolute limit," she fumed, as she headed back downhill with Jack and Lal Bahadur Pun.

"What's the limit?" Jack asked.

"That the rascal may have been in town for days. Really, it makes me annoyed! What is he *thinking*?"

"Chances are he's *not* thinking," Jack said. "That's the problem. Thinking is not the long suit of twelve-year-old boys."

"He needs a good talking-to!" Jana found herself outpacing the two men as the three of them hurtled through the Central Bazaar.

"He needs a good beating" was Lal Bahadur Pun's opinion.

"Let's not plan his welcoming reception until we see him," Jack said.

They took the sharp right onto the shortcut that went over Maharajah's Hill, climbed the stone staircases and steep paths at a relentless clip, reached the crest, and started downhill, beaming the flashlights on the path through the forest. Around a clump of pine trees, the *bhoot bangla* came into view, and a few seconds later, they could see through the door of the small detached kitchen.

It was clogged with *biri* smoke. Inside, Tilku held a bottle of something above his face, letting a small stream fall into his mouth without touching the rim. He was dressed in his school uniform, but his jacket had charcoal smudges on it, the shirt was stained, and his shoes were scuffed. With him were three boys Jana had often seen in town as they ran back and forth on messenger duty. They were barefoot, dressed in khaki shorts and shirts that had surely belonged to several people before them.

"Hey, Tilku sahib, don't drink it all yourself," one of the other boys said.

"Tell again how they promoted you in school," another prompted.

Lal Bahadur Pun stepped forward, his muscular frame filling the front door. All four boys looked up suddenly.

"You! Tilku!" Lal Bahadur Pun lunged forward and grabbed the boy by the ear, which caused him to drop the bottle. As the contents spilled onto the cement floor, the three other boys leapt to their feet, terrified.

"You, hoodlums!" cried Lal Bahadur Pun. "Get lost!"

The three squeezed around the doorway and made a dash down the path. Meanwhile, Tilku was screeching, "Lalu, stop! My ear! You're paining me!"

"You'll get a lot more paining before I'm through. Madam," Lal Bahadur Pun said to Jana, "shall I beat this boy?"

A flash of terror shot across Tilku's face.

"No," Jana said quickly, "no beating. We'll take him home now. Tilku, where are your things? Did you bring your suitcase home? Your bedding?"

Tilku shook his head. Now that Lal Bahadur Pun had let go of his ear, he could stand upright. When he met Jana's eyes, his face crumpled like that of a six-year-old child. Sobbing, he allowed himself to be led back over the hill and down the stairs and paths to the street, and on arrival at the Jolly Grant House, he was still unable to give an account of himself. On seeing him, Mary told him he stank and ordered him to go downstairs and scrub himself with soap and hot water. "Then go to your room," she said.

"He's got no clothes or bedding or anything," Jana said.

"So, he will be cold," said Mary unsympathetically.

Jack broke in: "Tilku, I'll bring you some clothes and a blanket. Go, do as Mary tells you."

"You and I will talk in the morning," Jana added.

✑ *Jana Talks to Tilku*

Jana had learned that it was often easier to have a heart-to-heart talk with someone outdoors, where the wide sky and the moving clouds could remind you that your concern was perhaps not so earthshaking after all. Accordingly, the next morning she took a seat on the low wall of the terrace behind the house and beckoned to Tilku to join her. She didn't know whether to laugh or cry at his waifish appearance—he swam in Jack's pullover, and he'd rolled up the legs of Jack's trousers several times. Jana studied his walled-off, expressionless face, wondering where the irrepressibly cheerful boy she knew had gone.

"So, Tilku. What happened at school?" Jana said.

Tilku, avoiding her gaze, merely shook his head.

"I telephoned the headmaster yesterday by sheerest coincidence," Jana said. "He said they had sent you home for the rest of the term. Now, why was that?"

Tilku looked up; his eyes flashed and he said hotly, "No reason, Jana mem."

"But the headmaster said there was a reason. Two reasons. He said that you were failing and that you stole money. Were you failing? Did you steal money?"

Tilku grimaced. "I was not yet passing, Jana mem. I was trying, really I was. They make you learn such strange things. Memorizing things with no sense! Just streams of words. 'I wandered lonely as a cloud.'"

Jana drew a breath. She could well believe that Tilku had been required to absorb reams of material he didn't understand.

At the Why Not? a while back, hadn't Rambir and Ramachandran been arguing about that very issue? Rambir had said that education should not be a matter of rote learning. Ramachandran had quoted lines of Alfred, Lord Tennyson and pronounced himself grateful for having committed them to memory at a tender age. Rambir had retorted, "If our kids have to memorize, at least they should be memorizing Rabindranath Tagore."

"All right, let that pass for the moment," Jana now said to Tilku. "Did you steal money? How much? From whom?"

Tilku burst out passionately: "None! From no one! It was another boy who stole ten rupees. But the dormitory master didn't believe me. He said, 'Don't tell lies. You deserve a good caning.' He made me hold out my hand and get six cuts with a ruler."

Jana felt a stone in the pit of her stomach. She knew that cuts meant strokes of a ruler, not slices with a knife, but it still brought an image of bloodshed to her mind.

"Let me see your palm, Tilku," Jana said.

Tilku turned his right palm up, and, wincing, Jana saw two or three scabby lines where the ruler had broken the skin.

"You swear you didn't steal," she said firmly.

"I told you that, Jana mem, and it was the truth."

Jana sighed. How could she get to the bottom of this story? It was Tilku's word against everyone else's.

Meanwhile, Tilku was growing increasingly fidgety. He pushed the sleeves of Jack's sweater farther up on his forearms, reminding Jana of how they had found him luggageless the night before.

"Oh, by the way," she said. "Your things. Did you leave everything back at school? Clothes and books, and so forth?"

Tilku didn't answer immediately.

"What happened to them?" Jana insisted.

"Some I left in my trunk under my bed," Tilku said sulkily. "Padlocked. Others I took on the bus."

"And? Where are they?"

"I . . . I sold them in the bazaar," Tilku admitted, look-ing away. "To a *kabariwalla*. I needed money for food, Jana mem."

Jana let out an exasperated breath. "Tilku, really, I am vexed. Why did you not come straight to the Jolly Grant House, the minute the bus arrived, and tell us everything?"

Tilku didn't answer immediately, but finally he spoke in a subdued voice that twisted Jana's heart. "I was too ashamed, Jana mem. I couldn't face any of you in the house. Jack sahib wouldn't think I was a good boarding school student. And Lalu and Mary ayah would say I had dishonored the whole household. And you, Jana mem? Last year, you said, 'The skies are yours, Captain Tilku.' And now you are only disappointed. I can tell by the look on your face."

Like a lake beginning to force its way through a crack in a dam, a tear trickled down Tilku's face. "Are you going to send me away?" he asked.

With a lump in her throat, Jana shook her head.

"I am *not* going to send you away, Tilku," she said. "But we will have to figure out what to do next. Apparently, the school will give you one more chance next term. Do you want to go back?"

At the words "one more chance," Tilku startled and his eyes darted to Jana's. What was going on in his head? she wondered. Could he possibly want to go back? *She* certainly wouldn't have, in his situation, but then again, she wasn't a twelve-year-old Nepali boy without too many other choices in life.

❧ Jack Weighs In

Back in the salon, Jana told the little she had learned of Tilku's story to Jack and Katarina. Jack listened intently, his eyes narrowing. When Jana had finished, he walked over to the window and stared out, his hands in his pockets.

"Jack?" Jana asked. "What are you thinking about?"

Jack turned and breathed out audibly. "I was thinking that it sounded all too familiar."

"What sounded familiar? Being blamed for something you didn't do?" Jana asked.

"Yes, that kind of thing was always happening in school. Boys kept the truth from the adults. The students who snitched weren't necessarily the biggest truth-tellers."

"So, you think Tilku *is* telling the truth," Jana said.

"I do, actually," Jack said. "At least, it's completely possible. I got punished once or twice for things I hadn't done."

"With cuts of a ruler?" Katarina said.

"Good Lord, yes," said Jack. "And worse. I got my share of canings at school."

"Canings?" Jana asked, astonished. "*You?* Whatever for?"

Jack shrugged. "Pranks. Idiotic things."

"What, for example?" Jana said.

"Oh—throwing eggs, making apple-pie beds, hanging chaps' underwear from the school gate . . . that sort of thing."

"You never told *me,*" Jana said to Jack.

"You didn't need to know," Jack said. "What could you do about it, weeks later, from India? In any case, Great-grandfather MacPherson was in charge. He generally added a few more swipes of the cane, on occasions when he got a report of some dire deed I'd committed."

"Grandfather caned you?" Jana had indeed thought of Grandfather MacPherson as a severe man, but he'd never used any kind of corporal punishment with *her.* Apparently being a girl offered some advantages in life, although she hadn't thought so at the time.

"Did other boys play tricks on you?" she asked.

A flash of distaste crossed Jack's face. "I got my head flushed down the toilet once."

Jana felt outraged. "You could have *drowned*," she said.

"Well, I didn't, did I? I wouldn't make too much of it, Mother."

Jana stared at Jack in disbelief. Back in those days, now more than twenty years past, she'd pictured him triumphing on the tennis courts and winning the hundred-yard dash. She hadn't considered that school might have a darker side.

"So you don't think Tilku's school is unnaturally harsh," she asked now.

"I didn't say that," said Jack. "It may well be. But—all things considered, it may still be the best place for him at the moment."

"I'm not convinced of that at all," Jana said. "I'm still worried about him."

Jack asked in a quiet tone, "Were you worried about me when you sent me off—a lot farther away?"

Jana said heatedly, "Of course I was! The reason I sent you back to Scotland in the first place was that I was *dreadfully* worried. Would you have preferred to stay and get smallpox like your sisters? Do you think I blithely shipped you off like a parcel?"

Jack paused for a couple of seconds before answering, while the image sprang to Jana's mind of a tearstained little boy saying good-bye on the railway platform, his figure slight and vulnerable as the chaperones helped him up into the train.

Finally, Jack said, "I know you didn't send me off like a parcel."

Jana got up and put her hand on his shoulder, her heart aching at having been the cause of those childhood tears. Quietly, she said, "Sometimes it felt like it, I suppose."

He smiled. "As you see, I survived."

With grateful relief, Jana felt the lump in her throat dissolving.

"You did, thank goodness," she said.

"I'll go talk to Tilku," said Jack. "If you don't mind my meddling. Maybe I can get to the bottom of all this."

❦ A Man-to-Man Conversation

The rest of the morning got gobbled up with shopping. Jana and Katarina spent a good two hours at All-India Saree Jubilee, picking out a sari that would make up nicely into a wedding dress. The shopkeeper recommended a length of traditional red silk with gold designs, but Katarina hovered between a cool blue-green sari and a shimmering honey that brought out the gold flecks in her hazel eyes.

Superstitious rhymes passed through Jana's mind. *Marry in red, better off dead.* (That would come as a surprise to brides in Asia, she thought.) *Marry in blue, your love will be true.* As for gold—Jana could remember no associations with that color. "Marry in gold, never grow old?" she mused aloud.

"Is that a Scottish saying?" Katarina said. "Or an Indian one?"

"Neither, that I know of," said Jana. "I made it up."

"It sounds lucky to me," Katarina said.

That clinched the decision in favor of the pale gold sari. Then came unglamorous but necessary purchases: light bulbs at Pahari Provisioners and white cotton thread at This and That Dry Goods. After that, driven home by hunger pangs, they headed for the Jolly Grant House, stopping only briefly at Royal Tailors to ask Feroze if he'd come over later that day and talk about the style of the wedding outfit.

The house was quiet when they arrived. Jack and Tilku were nowhere in sight, and Jana and Katarina went into the dining room to find just two places set. Crossing the side yard to the kitchen, they finally came upon Mary, who announced that Jack had taken Tilku out to lunch.

"Well, that was a nice idea," said Jana, although she was prickling with impatience to know how the man-to-man chat had gone. "Tilku didn't have much in the way of clothes, though."

"He looked *jungli*," Mary said disapprovingly, "but Jack sahib said, Never mind, come along, just act like it's a new style."

"Lesson Number One, apparently," Jana said.

Lunch was a chicken salad, simple but nicely flavored with fresh basil and mint leaves from plants Mary grew just off the kitchen. Katarina and Jana had just peeled and eaten the dessert of fresh Dehra Dun lychees, when they heard voices at the front door.

"Now, remember what I told you," Jack was saying. *"Illegitimi non Carborundum!"*

"Yes, sahib!" Tilku answered. "Down with sons of bitches!"

"That's the ticket," Jack said.

Next, Tilku could be heard scampering down the back stairs, and Jack came into the dining room, chuckling.

"From the look on your face, things seem to have gone well with Tilku," Jana said. "Have a seat and tell us what happened. Where did you eat lunch, by the way?"

"Kwality," said Jack. "We had Chinese. We each had a big tubful of noodles with some squiggles of pork on top." He pulled up a chair, took a lychee off Katarina's plate, peeled, and ate it. "Mmm! Lychee! There's no taste quite like it."

"Come on, tell us what happened," Jana said.

"Actually," said Jack, "I listened more than I talked. Tilku was reticent at first, but once the floodgates were open, I got quite an earful."

"And?" said Jana.

"Regarding the theft—he was definitely framed," said Jack. "The son of a friend of the headmaster's was the guilty party."

Jana let out an exasperated breath. "How infuriating!"

"It was, rather. Also, what he didn't tell you was that the older boys in his dormitory were doing a lot of hazing. It's worst when someone just arrives, as Tilku had. He was naive enough to tell a teacher, which got him a double dose of abuse." Jack shrugged.

"So, what did you say?" Jana asked.

"Among other things, I told him about getting my head flushed down the toilet. You should have seen his face. *You,*

Jack sahib? And then he laughed so hard I thought he was going to fall off his chair."

Jana winced, hearing about this episode again.

"The interesting thing is," said Jack, "Tilku's mortified about being suspended, but mostly, he feels responsible for it. He thinks he was stupid and brought things on himself. That he should have been wilier. But—here's the outcome—he wants to go back."

Jana stared at Jack. "What! He *does*?"

Jack said, "Yes, he wants a chance to put things right. He can't bear quitting a school having been branded a thief and a liar—and a dunce. It's a question of honor. He's got guts, that little scrapper. I admire that."

"Still," said Jana, "the school sounds quite horrible. The headmaster was so unctuous when he first met me—and so curt on the phone later. I wish there were room at Far Oaks or St. Bart's. You don't think St. Regis is going to do him irreparable harm?"

"I don't think so," said Jack. "And, as you've seen, it's hard to get one of those slots in a boarding school. If he makes it through, a lot of other things after that will seem easy. It will open doors for him."

Jana paused to let this sink in.

"Will he pass his courses, though?" she said.

"We'll see," said Jack. "I have a feeling that he will."

"And what is that feeling based on?" Jana asked, interested that her engineer son was now making a prediction based on intuition that contradicted the facts to date of the case.

"I've seen boys come from behind before," said Jack. "They had a certain look in their eye. He's got that look."

Things and More Things

✑ Aunt Sylvia's Worldly Goods

Shortly before breakfast the next morning, Mary tapped on Jana's bedroom door and handed her a note that had just arrived by messenger. The enormous handwriting sprawling across the page announced that it was from Aunt Sylvia, who had written, "Jana my dear, please forgive this presumptuous request. I know you were just here with Jack and Katarina, but might you come by this afternoon?"

Thinking of her busy day ahead, Jana's heart sank. Mr. Joshi was coming to talk about the vegetarian part of the wedding dinner, Mr. Dass about the meat dishes. Feroze was bringing Katarina's wedding dress for a fitting. He was also going to discuss an outfit to make for Jana, and she hadn't even bought the cloth yet. Moreover, when was she ever going to find time to practice several of Ian's tunes, to play during the reception? Still, it was better not to delay meeting her fragile old friend's request, so with a sigh, she penned a quick affirmative answer.

She'd take Tilku, too, which would get him out of Mary's hair and help entertain Sylvia. And Mr. Ganguly—he was always good medicine.

At Aunt Sylvia's, Jacob John met them at the gate as soon as the rickshaw pulled up, and this time, there was no question that they were expected. In the living room, Aunt Sylvia was alert and regally upright in her usual chair. Seeing her expertly coiffed hair, Jana deduced that little Julie from Hair Mahal had made her rounds. A bright blue necklace provided a cheerful accent to Aunt Sylvia's blue floral dress.

"Jana my dear," said Sylvia, "you are a love to come on short notice. And who is this?" She peered through her bottle-thick glasses.

"This is Tilku, Aunt Sylvia," Jana said, drawing the boy forward. "I told you about him last year."

"Oh, yes," cried Sylvia. "*Captain* Tilku! You're the one who's going to be a pilot. I see they've let you out of school for the famous wedding."

Tilku looked as if he wanted to make a quick dash for the door, but Jana fixed him with a steely glance and said to Sylvia, "We are *very* glad to have him home for a few days. Tilku, show Aunt Sylvia some of the new tricks you taught Mr. Ganguly."

Tilku told Mr. Ganguly to be a dead bird, which he did, frighteningly convincingly, his eyes closed and his body stiff and horizontal.

Aunt Sylvia gave a half-amused, half-horrified cry. "Oh my, he is the very picture of mortality. I wonder if *I* will look as dead as that when I'm dead."

"Good bird, Mr. Ganguly," Tilku said, and Mr. Ganguly righted himself and said to Aunt Sylvia, "Hello! I love you."

"Ah! A resurrection! Would that it were always that easy. Come here, sweetie," she said, offering her arm to the parrot. "I love you, too. And I'm glad you're not really dead." She kissed the top of the bird's head, then handed him back to Tilku and turned to Jana. "The reason I asked you to come is—I started thinking about what I could give your Jack and Katarina as a wedding gift."

"You don't need to give them anything, Aunt Sylvia," Jana said. "They're not expecting a gift, I assure you."

"Oh, but I *want* to," Sylvia said. "And I think I have just the ticket. Would you open that trunk for me?"

Jana bent down and opened the old-fashioned wooden foot-locker to reveal a jumble of pasteboard boxes, bundles tied up with string, bags of various sizes, and a feathered hat that made Mr. Ganguly cry out in alarm.

"Hand that hat to me, please," said Sylvia, and put it upside down on the side table. "Don't worry, Mr. G! No one's going to make you into a hat. Very well, Jana, please open that wooden box."

Jana did as instructed. Inside the box, on a flattened red velvet lining, were a few shiny coin-silver serving pieces: a small fork with curved tines, a fluted jam spoon, sugar tongs, a gravy ladle, and a baby spoon.

"Do you think Jack and Katarina will like them?" Sylvia asked. "The box isn't very big, so they should be able to fit it into their luggage. That's a pickle fork, by the way. I hope they eat pickles."

Jana laughed. "I'm sure they do."

Jana held the baby spoon in her hand for a moment, an image flashing through her head of a small dimpled hand dipping the spoon into a bowl and splattering porridge all over the place.

"Now the child can be born with a silver spoon in its mouth," Sylvia said.

Child? Jana couldn't remember mentioning anything about the baby to Sylvia, who now had a blandly innocent look on her wrinkled face.

"I mean, when the time comes," said Aunt Sylvia.

As Jana put the spoon back in the box, Aunt Sylvia continued: "Once I'd gotten started with the gift idea, I kept going. I said to myself, why keep things locked away in a trunk? That's stupid."

"Stupid," cried Mr. Ganguly. *"Buddhu!"*

"Glad you agree." Sylvia turned to Jana. "You see those three small boxes? Open them, please."

Each box, Jana discovered, contained a large old-fashioned gold pocket watch.

"I inherited one from each of my husbands," Sylvia said. "Two army officers and a businessman. I'm giving one of these watches to my long-suffering benefactor, Niel, and one to Jacob John. My guardian angels." She pointed to the third watch. "Would Lal Bahadur Pun like that one?"

"I should think he would be delighted," Jana said.

Next, Aunt Sylvia decided that a heavy white tablecloth should go to Jana. "For your new dining room," she said. "I'm not giving many dinner parties these days."

Last came a narrow, leather-covered box containing a gold fountain pen and matching mechanical pencil. "I know the perfect person to give *this* to." Aunt Sylvia turned to Tilku. "Our young scholar here. Well, my boy, would you like this?"

Tilku turned to Jana, a spasm of anxiety crossing his face.

"Shall I take it, Jana mem?" he asked.

"Of course, Tilku. Mrs. Foster is giving it to you."

Thrown into confusion, Tilku said, "Thank you, Jana mem."

"Don't thank *me*," Jana said. "Thank Mrs. Foster."

Tilku stood up and put his hands together and stammered, "Thank you very much, madam."

"That's quite all right, my dear."

On the way home in the rickshaw, Tilku and Jana and even Mr. Ganguly seemed tired out by the visit.

Tilku said, "Jana mem, when I go back to school, will you keep this gold pen and pencil at the house? I don't want to take them with me."

"Of course," Jana said. "I understand. They might get stolen at school."

Tilku's face twisted. "No, Jana mem. That's not it. Other people might say *I* stole it. They'll never believe an old lady gave it to me. Even if it's the truth, that sounds like a fairy story."

The wheels of the rickshaw turning on the gravel sounded their rhythm in Jana's ear. How sad, she thought, to assume that you won't be believed. They rode along with no further conversation, Tilku holding the pen and pencil set in his lap and taking an occasional peep into the box. Back at the Jolly Grant House, he handed it to Jana.

"When you're ready to take these back," Jana said, "just tell me. Okay?"

"Okay, Jana mem," he said.

Where Are the Emeralds?

As Jack and Jana and Katarina settled down at the dinner table, Jack said to Katarina, "This is your initiation rite, you know. Mary told me that she's preparing some *really* good food."

The door from the side yard opened, Harmendra held it open, and Mary swept in bearing a tray loaded with dishes. As she placed them on the table, she explained: "This is spicy; this is sweet. This is fruit; this is vegetable. This chutney is made with mango and green chilies. That one, with tomatoes and onions. The lime pickle is somewhat hot. Take small amounts. Taste, taste."

Each took a tentative bite of something different. Jana brought the slightest bit of lime pickle to her mouth just as Jack was saying, "I'd dilute that if I were you."

"Too late," said Jana, her eyes already streaming.

"Take papadum in between spicy things," Mary suggested.

Jana thought she knew Mary's repertoire by heart, but even for Jana, this meal was a new experience. Mary had outdone herself. Each dish, Jana understood, was a labor of love every step of the way—from zealous shopping to careful dicing to precise mixing and frying and proud presentation.

"What do you think, Katarina mem?" Mary asked. "If it's too spicy, use more rice."

Katarina swallowed a mouthful and looked up at Mary.

"Mary," she said, "it's too wonderful for words." Then, words having indeed failed her, she jumped up from her chair and gave Mary a hug.

Mary, laughing but flustered, said, "Sit, sit, Katarina mem! Try the other dishes, too. Jana mem? Jack sahib? Food is satisfactory?"

"It's more than satisfactory," Jana said.

"Mary," Jack said. "This is better than any hotel."

"I hope so," said Mary, and left the room with a look of victory on her face.

No one could resist the temptation to overeat that night. Jana washed down Mary's fiery specialties with the local Ophrysia beer, and then, in a state of relaxation verging on silliness, she found herself telling the story of how, the year before last, the ladies of the American Women's Club had descended on Ramachandran's Treasure Emporium like a swarm of locusts, discovering first editions signed by Rudyard Kipling and a cigarette case that had belonged to Mohammed Ali Jinnah.

"And it was all because one of the ladies asked me where I got my necklace," Jana said.

Jack said, "That reminds me, Mother, did you ever rent a safe-deposit box to put them in?"

"Put what in?" said Jana.

"The emeralds."

Jana felt her pulse quicken. *This* was a part of the story she didn't want to get into. "I didn't, actually," she said. "It seemed like such a bother. I'd never wear them if I had to run down to the bank each time."

"So you *do* wear them," Katarina said.

"Of course," said Jana. "They're my most festive accessory."

"Oh, I want to see them." Katarina clasped her hands. "Would you show them to me?"

Jana paused. "I would love to," she said, "but I can't. Not tonight."

"Why not?" said Jack. "You're making things sound so mysterious."

Damn Jack! He has a streak of the old man in him, Jana thought, as Jack gazed at her, sternly waiting. She remembered squirming as Grandfather MacPherson interrogated her on some small mishap—a missed train, a lost book, a bill not paid the minute it arrived.

"I don't have them here," Jana said.

"But you just said you *didn't* rent a box," Jack pointed out. "Are they out being cleaned? Or repaired?"

"All right, I'll tell you where they are." Jana admitted reluctantly, "They're down at Priceless Gems, in *their* vault."

"Because?" Jack said.

"If you must know," said Jana, steeling herself for his reaction, "I used them as collateral for a small loan."

"A loan? You borrowed *money*?" The muscles around Jack's eyes tightened.

"Now, don't fret, Jack," said Jana, looking him straight in the eye and trying to keep her voice even. "I'll have them back in no time flat."

"Why did you have to borrow money?" he persisted.

"*Really,* Jack. You *are* being a nosey parker." Why did Jack choose engineering, she asked herself. He could have done well in law or police work.

Jack insisted, undeterred: "I want to know."

"It wasn't for some silly whim," said Jana. "I had several unusual expenses. Such as the improvements to this house and Tilku's school fees. All very worthwhile things."

Jack's face softened a little, but his expression was still intent, as if he wanted to put things right that very minute. He said, "First thing tomorrow, I'll go to Precious Jewels or whatever it's called and get back the emeralds."

"Priceless Gems," said Jana. "I'll have to go with you, to sign for them. But, Jack, darling, you don't have to *rescue* me."

"I won't try to do *that*," said Jack. "But I'm happy to rescue the emeralds."

"I will pay you back," Jana said firmly.

"Charge her double interest," joked Katarina, breaking the tension that had fallen on the room.

✑ Deepak Minding the Store

The next morning, Jack and Jana walked down to Priceless Gems, Jana with the paperwork from the loan in her shoulder bag. It struck her as comical to be taking orders from Jack on the issue of the emeralds, and although she was happy to be getting them back, she felt vaguely like a schoolgirl being marched to the principal's office. They reached the store at about ten A.M., finding Mr. Shah's son, Deepak, on duty in the anteroom. When he saw Jana, he gave a visible start and blushed deeply. For her part, she felt almost as embarrassed as Deepak, for surely his father had told him that she was one of those ladies who pawned their jewels to pay their bills. Thus exposed as at least vulnerable (if not incompetent) in the financial sphere, she wondered whether her credentials as an adviser on career and personal matters had been called into question.

Nonetheless, she squared her shoulders, smiled brightly, and made the introductions; Deepak, following her lead, regained his composure and offered Jack his hand.

"How are you liking it here in town, Mr. Laird?" he asked, with more poise than Jana would have expected.

Jack having said that he found Hamara Nagar very pleasant and the shop most impressive, he and Deepak agreed that the weather at this time of year was far preferable to that of the plains. Deepak then offered tea, coffee, Coca-Cola, pineapple juice, and *nimbu pani,* all of which Jack and Jana politely refused.

Once it was established that even water was not necessary, Deepak asked, "What can I show you today? You are here looking for a special piece of jewelry, perhaps?"

"We're here to *collect* some pieces, actually," Jack said. "And to pay off a loan against them."

Jana fished in her bag for the receipt and the loan agreement, and handed them to Deepak.

Deepak glanced through the contents, a muscle in his eyelid twitching. Apologetically, he murmured, "Yes, yes, of course, I see. You have some emeralds here." His demeanor suggested that it had all been a big mistake, as if one day, in a fit of absent-mindedness, Jana had left the jewelry on the counter and ambled off.

"Your father was here the day I brought the emeralds in," Jana said. "He signed the paperwork, I believe."

Deepak looked down at the papers again and nodded. "Yes," he said, "that is indeed his signature."

"And where *is* your father?" Jack asked. "May we have the pleasure of seeing him?"

Deepak hesitated, then said, "He—he's actually out of station. An emergency came up in our Dehra Dun branch. He left *me* in charge. *Me.*" His mouth drew back in the expression of appalled anxiety that Jana had seen in their earlier meetings.

"I'm sure he had full confidence in you," Jana said sympathetically.

"I would imagine that it's a straightforward matter to pay off a loan," Jack said.

Deepak's unhappy head gesture could be equally interpreted as yes or no. He confessed, "It's just—I've never handled the early repayment of a loan. More people pay late than early."

"It's all spelled out, I believe," Jana said evenly. "You take the money and we take the goods. May I show you?" She held out her hand; Deepak handed back the document and Jana pointed to the right clause.

"Yes, yes, you are right," Deepak said.

"Might you get the emeralds out of the vault now, please?" Jana asked.

Taking a deep breath, with the air of a man who has finally pulled himself together, Deepak said, "Yes, yes. I will return, immediately."

After a long fifteen minutes, Deepak was back, now looking as if he might cry.

"Is there a problem?" Jack asked, with more than a trace of Grandfather MacPherson in his voice.

"The—the emeralds are not there," Deepak said. "At least, I didn't see them. Everything is organized with a number on it, but none of the pieces left in the vault as collateral had your number on it."

Jack's face was now ominously stern, and he drew a deep breath; Jana wondered whether he might be counting to ten to control his temper. Finally, he asked, "And—what is the explanation for that?"

"I—I don't know!" Deepak's voice rose to a wail. "I don't know at all!"

"Deepak," said Jana gently, "you could certainly get in touch with your dad and find out, couldn't you?"

"I—yes, yes, that's what I will do, I will telephone straightaway to his office in Dehra Dun. We have telephone service now, you see. I will—just one moment, don't go away."

"Never fear, we won't go anywhere," said Jack, as Deepak's back disappeared through the inner sanctum door.

Another fifteen minutes passed, and Deepak returned, finger marks making a mess of his previously well-combed hair.

"He's not in the office," Deepak said, with a note of desperation that couldn't have been worse if his father had been kidnapped and taken to Argentina.

"All right," said Jack, his voice flat. "Kindly keep trying and send a note up to the Jolly Grant House the minute you know what the situation is."

"Of course! Of course! Don't worry, Mr. Laird, you'll know in no time flat."

Deepak looked so pathetic that Jana said, "Don't worry, I have full confidence that everything is under control."

She spent a few more minutes calming Deepak down before Jack said, "Let's get along, then. I don't think we're spending our time productively here."

As they stepped from the dim light of the shop into the bright sunshine, Jack said, "Your friend Mr. Shah could be in Dehra Dun having imitation pieces made up as we speak."

"Jack, for heaven's sake!" Jana said. "My friend Mr. Shah, as you call him, is a highly esteemed jeweler with a reputation to defend. There's not a chance in a hundred that he's trying to pull off some shady scheme. Have you been reading too many crime novels?"

"I haven't been reading crime novels at all," Jack said. "I'm just trying to defend your interests, Mother."

"Give me a little credit for having some intuition about people," Jana said.

Jack stopped and gave her a long look. "Of course," he said. "I'm sorry. I was a bit on edge."

Jana accepted Jack's apology with a shrug and a pat on the arm, but when no note from Deepak had come by nightfall, she started to wonder if Jack's suspicions were justified. Had her trust in Mr. Shah been misplaced? Thinking that a distraction would help to diminish this worry, she suggested that they listen to the news on All India Radio before dinner, and carried the radio down from her bedroom into the salon.

Usually the silvery tones of Roshan Menon soothed Jana, but tonight a substitute was reading the news, and both her voice and the stories were disturbing. A demographer looked ahead to the days when there would be standing room only on the earth—why, the long-suffering planet was already home to more than three billion people! The peace treaty of 1954 between India and China had expired—not a good sign.

Worst of all, both Delhi and Dehra Dun had been rocked by a phony jewel heist, in which the store owners had been in collusion with the thieves in order to get a large insurance settlement.

"The guilty parties were both diamantaires," said the announcer, "whose names will be revealed by the police at a later time."

Jack put down his whisky, leaned back in his chair, and fixed Jana with his gaze. "Dehra Dun, eh?" he said. "Your Mr. Shah has a branch there, doesn't he? And he deals in diamonds."

Jana said, feeling a mix of irritation and anxiety, "Oh, Jack, really! Turn that radio off."

"Tomorrow, we're going down to Priceless Gems again and getting to the bottom of this," Jack said. "Or maybe our first stop should be the police station."

"Not the police!" Jana said. "Have some patience, please."

❧ Double Indemnity

Early the next morning, while on his customary walk, Jack picked up a copy of the *Times of India*. Alone with Jana at the breakfast table, he read aloud: " 'Police in three states widen net on diamantaire scandal.' "

"That has nothing to do with us," Jana said, hoping that she was right. "We are to carry on, and a note from Deepak will soon be here. If not Deepak himself."

That morning, she attempted to act as if nothing were amiss, taking Katarina to the *mochi* to have her feet traced and to pick out the leather for her wedding slippers. By lunchtime, Jack was saying that it was time for another visit to Priceless Gems; reluctantly, she agreed, but when they got there in midafternoon, the store was closed, with no explanation on the door.

Back at the Jolly Grant House, and neither in a good mood, they heard voices in the salon: the deep tones of a male, the musical laughter of Katarina, and the higher pitch of Mr. Ganguly. Mary, meeting Jack and Jana at the door, whispered, "Shah sahib is here in the salon, Jana mem. I gave him *nimbu pani*."

"See?" Jana hissed under her breath to Jack.

In the salon, Mr. Shah was standing at the window with Mr. Ganguly on his arm, with Katarina next to them.

"Ah, Mrs. Laird!" said Mr. Shah. "You see, your future daughter-in-law and your parrot and I have already introduced one another."

If Jana had intended to greet Mr. Shah frostily, the sight of Mr. Ganguly and Katarina obviously putting their stamp of approval on the visitor completely disarmed her.

"You got my telegram, I presume," Mr. Shah said, moving Mr. Ganguly to his perch.

Jana was taken aback. "No, what telegram? When did you send it?"

Jack, meanwhile, had spied a buff-colored envelope on the sideboard, and now he quickly ripped it open. Scanning it in a few seconds, he handed it to Jana, who read silently, "APOLOGIES DELAY STOP NO-FAIL DELIVERY EVEN TODAY JOLLY GRANT HOUSE STOP KIND REGARDS MLSHAH."

"I understand you visited my shop to collect your pieces," Mr. Shah said, opening his briefcase and taking out a familiar long rectangular box.

"Oh!" said Katarina, as he opened it and laid it on the table. Freshly cleaned and polished and twinkling up at them were the necklace of emeralds with its large central pendant and the clustered emerald earrings.

"Beautiful! Marvelous!" said Mr. Ganguly, flapping his wings and casting a covetous beady eye on the glittering gems.

"I'm sorry I had to remove them to Dehra Dun," Mr. Shah said. "Last week, I had to buy a new insurance policy for jewelers and diamantaires, and my coverage was not good unless I had the latest kind of safe and two armed guards! I don't have that kind of safe in Hamara Nagar yet, but I do in Dehra. So, I took my most important pieces to Dehra and stored them there. I also had yours cleaned and reappraised, by the way. They're worth at least three times what you thought they were. I have a customer in Paris who would give a hundred thousand new francs for them in an instant. Are you interested?"

Jack and Jana and Katarina exchanged astonished glances.

"Er—not at the moment," Jack said slowly. "We'll just enjoy them ourselves for a little while."

"Of course," said Mr. Shah.

Jack went upstairs to get the cash he would need to pay off Jana's loan, while Mr. Shah amused Jana and Katarina with stories of life in the jeweler's trade.

"But, Mr. Shah," Jana said, "why didn't you tell your son, Deepak, what you'd done with the emeralds? He was in such a state!"

"Oh," Mr. Shah sighed. "I did. I gave him detailed instructions on minding the store, and in any case, he knew he could get me on the phone. He's just been so distracted these days that anything I say goes in one ear and out the other. It will be a while before he's ready to take over the family business."

Jack returned from upstairs with the cash, Jana retrieved the paperwork from her satchel, and Mr. Shah and she signed papers certifying that the loan was discharged and the collateral goods delivered.

With Mr. Shah gone, Jack and Jana and Katarina looked at one another and burst into laughter, and Mr. Ganguly made two or three turns on his perch.

"Jack, thank you," Jana said. "I *am* happy to get the confounded things back. Funny why people make such a fuss about gems, though. After all, these are merely a bit of beryl colored with some chromium and vanadium."

Jack's eyebrows went up in surprise. "I'm impressed that you're spouting geology at me."

"A few facts I learned from Mr. Shah," Jana said. She handed the box to Katarina and said, "Try them on."

Katarina went over to the mirror and held the necklace up to her neck, Jana following her to fasten the clasp.

"Stunning," said Jack. "They go well with your coloring."

Katarina turned and smiled at Jack, then inserted the ear-rings. Perfect, thought Jana. Aloud, she said to Katarina, "Why don't you wear them for the wedding? You said you needed something borrowed."

"Oh, no, that's too much," Katarina said. "What will *you* wear?"

"I'll find something," Jana said. "Wear these, do. Emeralds are said to bring faithfulness in love. And easy childbirths. I'm a bit beyond needing that."

"In that case," said Katarina, "I will. With thanks."

✁ Completely Valueless

Later that afternoon, Jana went up to the Treasure Emporium to find some costume jewelry to wear at the wedding. Stepping inside the familiar, incense-scented depot, she was startled by some new acquisitions of Ramachandran's: a statue of the leg-endary rani of Jhansi on one side of the door and a statue of Joan of Arc on the other. Both lady warriors were on horseback, with swords at their belts.

Jana threaded her way through tables full of hookahs, brass finger bowls, paperweights, bronze figurines of Hindu gods, and perpetual calendars, finally finding Ramachandran's aunt Putli on duty at the far end of the room. Aunt Putli could not always be counted on to recognize Jana, but now, hobbling out from behind the stand-up desk and peering through thick glasses with tortoiseshell frames, she gave a smile and said, "Hello, Jana sweetie."

"Auntie-ji, you've got new specs!" Jana said. "They look very nice on you."

"Mr. Powell fitted me," Aunt Putli said. "For years, everything looked so blurry. But now the world is once more sharp and clear. I am younger! I am reborn!"

"That's wonderful, Auntie-ji," said Jana.

"Now I know, even, exactly what *you* look like," Aunt Putli said. Her face dropped in perceptible disappointment. "Somewhat older than I thought. But not to worry—you are still fairly good-looking for one of your age. What do you want to buy?"

"Auntie-ji," Jana said, "I need a set of jewelry. Something inexpensive. I don't want to worry about losing it or having it stolen or whatever."

"What color?" Aunt Putli demanded.

"Oh, any color. I haven't even bought the cloth for my outfit yet." Jana thought, This will be like a man buying a necktie first and then getting a suit to go with it.

Aunt Putli wiggled her head confidently and turned to search in a drawer. Finally, she said, "Try this" and held up a necklace of red and purple stones.

Jana took the necklace, fastened it around her neck, and studied herself in the blotchy old hand mirror Aunt Putli held up for her. Cheerful little impostors, she thought. You might even take them for rubies and amethysts—from a distance.

Aunt Putli next fished in another drawer for earrings, finding only a single one to her satisfaction and going to a second drawer to look for a mate. Finally, she seemed satisfied and handed two dangly clusters to Jana, announcing, "These earrings match each other, almost. They are *very* valueless."

"Rather sweet," Jana said. Yes, the earrings were fraternal twins rather than identical ones, but the differences were not important from a few feet away. However, one earring lacked a clasp. "I see a small problem here."

"That problem is so small that you shouldn't even call it a

problem," said Aunt Putli, quickly taking a clasp from another box.

With the earrings in place, Jana examined the total effect, squinting a bit to see in the cloudy mirror.

"Not to worry, the stones in theses pieces are genuine fake," Aunt Putli said. "This time you can be assured. First-class rubbish, cent percent guaranteed. No possibility of mistaking for Mughal this and that. Take, take, you will be happy. Three rupees for all."

The same as four large Cadbury chocolate bars, Jana said to herself, and handed over the cash without bargaining.

Aunt Putli beamed as she wrapped up Jana's purchases in a sheet of already wrinkled tissue paper and tied it with a bit of string. "Wear them for local duty!" she instructed.

"Thank you, Auntie dear," Jana said.

"Bye-bye, my child," said Aunt Putli.

With her accessories in hand, Jana then dashed to All-India Saree Jubilee, where she found a purple sari that went well with the stones. On the way home, she surprised Feroze Ali Khan by dropping in at Royal Tailors. Feroze was just about to close up shop, but he turned on the electric light overhead, chasing the dusk from the storefront.

"You have bought *purple* cloth?" Feroze asked, knowing her preference for green.

"I'm adapting to new circumstances, Feroze sahib," she said.

"Wisdom requires," agreed Feroze, then took a pencil and envelope and artfully sketched a festive long-skirted dress.

"Perfect!" said Jana. "You have my measurements. Can you make it in time for the wedding, Feroze sahib?"

"Have I ever failed you?" Feroze asked.

"Never," said Jana.

It's a Sin

❧ Jacob John's Vigil

Each week since the first of April, the All-Saints congregation
had grown bigger, as more and more tourists and summer resi-
dents arrived in town. On the third Sunday in June, as she
arrived at the worship service, Mary heard one woman telling
another about her trip from Delhi. "When I got here and opened
my suitcase," the woman said, "the clothes were still warm. As
if they had been in the oven. Baked clothes, just like bread."

Luxuriating in her day off, Mary settled herself in her customary pew. As usual, they sang "Khushi Khushi Manao," and
today, Mary's mood matched the cheerful words. She was looking forward to Jack and Katarina sahib's wedding, now only
nine days off. With noise, lights, people dressed in their best—it
would be a bright, shining event that would make everyone
happy. The Jolly Grant House would be lit up, with flowers everywhere and a big *shamiana* in the courtyard to protect guests
from an unseasonal shower.

We are holding a celebration, Mary thought. Our first! In
Bombay and at the nawab's house, Jana had been the guest at
plenty of big parties, but Mary had not attended those. This
time, Mary would be close to the center of things.

Out of the corner of her eye, as the first song finished, Mary saw Jacob John slip into the pew across the aisle. Instantly, she felt a jolt of concern: her friend's usually pristine uniform was rumpled, as if he'd slept in it. As the service continued, Mary's concern grew. Jacob John sang the hymns in a distracted way, sometimes lapsing into silence. During Pastor Mitra's sermon, he even nodded off. When the last hymn began, Jacob John's head jerked up suddenly, and he sat upright with his eyes opened extra wide, trying to look as if he had been awake the whole time.

After the service, Mary threaded her way through the crowd in the sunny courtyard and found Jacob John standing apart, against the wall.

"Is everything all right, Jacob-*anna*?" Mary asked.

Jacob John said, "Sylvia memsahib had another fall yesterday. She tripped over her own shoes and banged her head against the corner of the almirah. I heard something and came running from the kitchen and saw her passed out on the floor."

"*Bapré bap!*" Mary exclaimed.

Jacob John continued. "Dr. Chawla came to the house and took a look at her. He said that we must watch her eyes and make sure one pupil is not bigger than the other. Also, he gave orders to me to check in the night to see if she can be awakened. So. I didn't sleep much."

Mary said, "It's more work to be the nurse than the patient."

Jacob John nodded his head in agreement. "That is the truth."

Poor Jacob-*anna*, Mary thought. He looks as if he himself needs tending, rather than tending others.

"Then this morning," Jacob John went on, "Powell sahib took Sylvia mem to the hospital anyway."

"Oh," said Mary. "If he had taken her last night, you would have had a good night's sleep."

"Such is life," said Jacob John.

"Let's have a nice walk," she suggested, gesturing toward the gate. "Maybe to Mr. and Mrs. Ramesh's grocery?"

"Yes, let's go there," Jacob John said. "I am in desperate need of coffee. I didn't have time to make any for myself this morning."

"Aré," said Mary, practically feeling Jacob John's headache.

They walked across town to the grocery, where the smell of freshly ground and brewed coffee greeted them. Mr. and Mrs. Ramesh, who were drinking out of large metal tumblers, sold a small tumbler each to Mary and Jacob John.

"Mr. Jacob John! Mrs. Mary Thomas!" they said, bubbling all over with eagerness to tell their news. "We are going home!"

"Have you a buyer for the shop?" Mary asked.

"Yes, yes, buyer will take possession in three weeks," Mr. Ramesh said. "And the day afterward, we will be on the train. Bag and baggage!"

Good news for one person isn't necessarily good news for the next, Mary said to herself. "Will the new people carry the spices I need for my food?" she asked.

"Maybe," Mrs. Ramesh said cheerfully. "But one can never tell if they will keep up the quality."

Mary frowned at this lack of concern. These people were leaving Mary and Jacob John and their other South Indian customers in the lurch, without even a trace of apology.

"You have a problem, Mary-ji?" said Mrs. Ramesh. When Mary shook her head, Mrs. Ramesh turned to Jacob John. "You, too, should think about going home, brother," she said. "Mrs. Foster will not live forever. You won't be chained to her any longer."

Mary said to Mrs. Ramesh in a stern tone, "It's a sin to wish for someone's death."

Mrs. Ramesh scratched her scalp. "Who is wishing for anyone's death? Did I say that? No. I'm merely saying that easier days are ahead for our friend Jacob John. I am wishing him best of luck."

"We all wish him that," said Mary dourly.

She was glad when they finished the coffee and left the Rameshes gloating over their impending journey home.

"How about the cinema?" Mary said to Jacob John. "*Boot Polish* is playing at the Bharat Mata. It's about two orphans trying to survive on their own."

"No orphans for me today," said Jacob John. "I'm thinking I need to go sleep. Will you forgive me?"

"Of course," she said, swallowing her disappointment. "I will go do some knitting. I have many articles to finish."

They walked together to the turnoff to Maharajah's Hill.

It was time for them to exchange *namaskars* and take their separate routes home.

"I will see you next Sunday," said Mary. Then, because she couldn't stop herself, she asked, "Would you really go to Madras after—when you are no longer needed with Mrs. Foster?"

"I don't really know," he said. "My son is there; I could live with him. But, on the other hand, *you* are here."

She stood there with her cheeks getting all hot. "Yes, I am here," she finally said, feeling foolish to be repeating the obvious. Her disappointment that she was not going to have his company any more that day was now replaced by a cautious happiness. For a moment, she watched his back disappear on the road toward Maharajah's Hill, then she made her way home through the Central Bazaar.

She remembered their earlier conversation about marriage. She'd been rude that day, calling marriage a prison that she didn't want to enter again. But maybe, she hoped, he hadn't taken those words too seriously.

Perhaps, Mary mused, Jacob John's imagination would be captured by the idea of the whitewashed brick house that she was going to build one day. The house would be a sort of dowry. But it would be much better than a dowry paid out by parents—it would be an independent woman's part of a wedding bargain. This time, if Mary got married, there would be no parents fussing around, no one going into debt to get a son-in-law. The groom would be a known quantity, not some stranger who would turn out to be a horrible man.

It would be, thought Mary, just Jacob John and me. With our knowledge about life and our savings and the fact that we like to joke and talk and go to the cinema—and simply be together.

A Silver Lining

On learning from Mary that Aunt Sylvia had been hospitalized, Jana had gone to visit her in the community hospital and returned feeling depressed. Her elderly friend had been lying flat and listless, the bruise on her forehead a lurid purple and her conversation reduced to a muttered reference to "going west."

"Aunt Sylvia!" Jana had scolded. "You are not heading off into the sunset anytime soon."

Two days later, entering the courtyard of the two-story community hospital, Jana noted that somebody had garlanded the statue of Jesus. Things were looking up for *someone*, she supposed that meant. As always at the hospital, a group of dandy wallahs hunkered in a ring, smoking and gossiping, and behind them, against the wall, the sedan chairs in which they had transported patients were lined up like beached boats.

Jana exchanged salaams with the wallahs and passed through the arched entryway to the building, her nose wrinkling as the pine fragrance from the surrounding woods gave way to the smell of rubbing alcohol. She took the staircase up to the second floor and went down the plain, bare hall, her footsteps echoing off the cement floor. In the women's ward, followed by the curious gazes of the patients, she made her way between two long rows of beds until she got to Aunt Sylvia's. It was in the far corner, with easy access to a window.

"'Hail to thee, blithe spirit,'" chirped Aunt Sylvia. My, thought Jana, what an improvement! Sylvia was propped up against a couple of pillows and dressed in a colorful embroidered bed jacket. There was a ribbon in her freshly shampooed hair. She'd been talking to Niel Powell, who now rose from the bedside chair to greet Jana; in a suit and tie, he seemed overly dressed for a hospital visit.

"My goodness, this is a veritable party!" Sylvia said.

"You *are* better," said Jana. "Thank heavens. How are you, Niel?"

"Very well, thank you," said Niel, pulling up an empty chair from another patient's bedside.

Sylvia said, "I'm champing at the bit to get out," which made Jana look inquiringly at Niel.

"We're not going to risk a relapse by too early a release," he said sternly.

"Oh, Niel, you hover so!" said Sylvia. "Jana, he acts like a mother with a sick child."

"That sounds rather lovely to me," Jana said. "Not the sick child part, but the fact that he takes care of you."

"I know, I know," said Aunt Sylvia. "He *is* sweet." She adjusted her covers, making a book that had been on the bed tumble to the floor. Jana picked it up and put it on the side table. "*Great Expectations*, I see."

Aunt Sylvia said, "We've been having a dose of Dickens. Niel's been reading, dear lamb."

"Good medicine, I should think," Jana said.

"Excellent," said Aunt Sylvia. "Better than those *injections* they insist on giving me. Who would think that poking *needles* into people makes them feel better?"

A young woman in a sari and white nurse's cap brought a tray in and set it down on the bedside table.

"*Dinner* at this hour?" said Aunt Sylvia. "Totally uncivilized, and I haven't any appetite. Niel and Jana, do you want my dinner?"

Jana and Niel exchanged amused grimaces.

"I take it you don't," said Aunt Sylvia. "Is there any ice cream on the tray? Give that to me first."

There was no ice cream, just a dish of *kheer,* which Aunt Sylvia said she would eat. After that, she took one bite of mashed potato, pronouncing herself done just as the nurse arrived and told Niel and Jana that they were welcome to leave.

"Bye-bye, dear kiddies," Sylvia said. "Very, very soon, I'm going to get out of this bed and walk home. I'm not missing the wedding! I'm going to wear a dress I bought in 1925—it's back in style, thanks to the swings and arrows of outlandish fashion. Mark my words, I'll be there."

"That's the spirit," Niel said.

"Good night, Aunt Sylvia," Jana said. "It's wonderful to see you so much better."

As Jana and Niel descended to the front hall, Niel said, "If she walked home, it would be the first time she's walked any distance in ten years. Ah well, refusing to acknowledge infirmity is her way of dealing with life—and who's to say it isn't the best way?"

Jana, again wondering about the suit and tie, asked Niel, "Are you on your way to a special occasion?"

"I am, actually," Niel said. "A Rotary club awards dinner." He turned to her suddenly. "Would you like to come, too? I have an extra ticket. The meal's usually quite edible. And it would be nice for me to have good company."

Jana's mind turned quickly to the household. They could get along without her tonight, she decided. "What a kind invitation," she said. "Have I enough time to change my clothes?"

Niel said, "I'll do a couple of errands and swing by for you in an hour."

At home, happy for the speed of the hot water that gushed into the tub, she took a quick bath, put on a full-skirted dress, and twisted her hair into an ornate clip. When she came down to the salon, Jack and Katarina and Mr. Ganguly were entertaining Niel.

"Beautiful, marvelous," cried Mr. Ganguly, flapping his wings.

"My sentiments exactly," Niel said. "That's an intelligent bird."

"Can you children get along while I'm gone?" Jana asked Jack and Katarina.

"I believe so," said Jack.

"Have a lovely time," said Katarina.

"Have a lovely time," Mr. Ganguly echoed.

❧ A Ceremony at the Giant Skating Rink

The dinner, Niel explained as they walked down the street, was always held at the Giant Skating Rink.

"It's less outlandish than it sounds," he said. "In British times, the rink was used for fancy dress balls, formal dinners, and theatrical performances—as well as roller skating. It's still one of the most convenient places to hold a big event. They carry in a few dozen tables and lots of chairs and put the speakers at the head table on the stage, and there you go."

"You sound as if you'd been to many events there," Jana said.

"Quite a few," admitted Niel.

They went through a front hall, past the sign where prices for admission and skate rentals were painted in wobbly letters, and through swinging doors into an immense hall so high-ceilinged that it felt like an aviary. On the wooden floor, the dinner tables were already filling up with the business and community leaders of the town.

"We've got assigned seats," he said and led her up to the stage, to what turned out to be the table of honor. Examining the place cards, they found "Niel G. Powell, Sharp Eyes Vision Care" and, next to it, "Guest of Niel G. Powell."

"I've never brought anyone to a Rotary club dinner before," Niel said. "But they always provide for the possibility. At last, it has come true." He was interrupted by a portly man in a three-piece suit who had come rushing across the stage.

"Niel, my friend, welcome, welcome, welcome! Everyone is so excited about tonight's function. So appropriate! And long overdue!"

While Jana wondered exactly what was appropriate and overdue, Niel did the introductions. "Jana, this is Mr. Banerjee, president of our chapter. Mr. Banerjee, Mrs. Laird."

"The lady with the famous parrot!" said Mr. Banerjee, apparently overjoyed. "Well, well, well! I do hope you enjoy the evening. We're all very proud of Niel and grateful to him." With that, he descended to the skating rink floor to greet Mr. Shah, who was making a dignified entrance with a lavishly bejeweled woman at his side.

Still mystified by Mr. Banerjee's remarks, Jana took the chair that Niel offered and glanced out at the crowd as Niel seated himself. She spied Ramachandran and Rambir, established at a distant table and, from the look of things, already talking politics. Then she peeked at the printed menu and program. Oh dear, what a lot of speeches! Her heart sank until she saw "Keynote Address" and "Special Award."

"Niel!" she exclaimed. "Why didn't you tell me this dinner was in honor of *you*?"

"I didn't want to frighten you," he said with a chuckle.

"Have you had time to prepare a speech?" she asked. "What with going back and forth to the hospital to see Aunt Sylvia?"

He reached into his pocket and took out a few note cards. "I jotted down a few thoughts here and there," he said.

A platter of appetizers appeared, and Jana bit into a crispy chickpea patty and then some excellent cauliflower fritters. Creamy *palak paneer* with fresh greens followed, and then more vegetable dishes and several types of bread and spicy condiments. Meanwhile, Niel was entertaining her with stories of growing up in Calcutta.

"And so, why did you choose to come and set up shop in Hamara Nagar?" Jana asked. "It's rather off the beaten track."

Niel said, "Oh, childhood nostalgia, I suppose. I went to St. Bart's College and always remembered my time there very fondly."

"I wish we could get Tilku into St. Bart's," said Jana, and told Niel the whole sorry saga. "He's going back to St. Regis for at least one more term, even though it's quite horrible."

"Perhaps he could transfer," said Niel thoughtfully.

"There's no space at St. Bart's," Jana said. "Or at Far Oaks. I already asked."

Niel lifted an eyebrow, implying that the issue might be resolved in another way.

Their talk about how families always presented new challenges was interrupted by the arrival of pistachio ice cream and éclairs. Jana was stirring sugar into her tea when President Banerjee took the microphone and introduced the first of the long roster of speakers.

Then followed an avalanche of words, during which Jana found herself fighting to stay awake, finally hitting on a strategy for keeping her eyes open, which was to watch *other* people nodding off. Catching Niel's eye, she realized that he was doing the same thing, and they exchanged half-suppressed grins.

Everyone woke up, however, when Mr. Banerjee boomed into the microphone, "And now for the moment we've all been waiting for" and turned the podium over to Niel.

Niel's speech was entitled "Optics and Options," and, mercifully, it turned out to be pithy, witty, and short.

"Niel, you are an inspiration to us all," Mr. Banerjee said. "And now, for your contribution to the community, for your work among schoolchildren, and for your free eye care to the indigent, we offer you a small token of our appreciation."

He handed Niel a large silver cup inscribed with the words "Eyesight and Insight" while the audience stood and applauded. Jana, too, rose to her feet, followed by the other guests at the table of honor. Looking bemused but appreciative, Niel nodded his thanks and gestured namasté to the crowd.

"What a lovely evening," Jana said as the rickshaw they'd taken from the rink pulled up to the gate of the Jolly Grant House. "And congratulations on a well-deserved award."

"Oh," said Niel. "I merely did a little here and there. It was never very difficult for me to see one more patient at the end of the day. It would have been mean-spirited to turn them away because they couldn't pay. The secret is to tuck these moments in."

"These moments?" Jana said.

"Of philanthropy," said Niel. "Sometimes one thinks, Oh, I must do something really dramatic—give my entire life to a cause, or whatever. And the other approach is to make a small bit of effort here and a small bit of effort there."

"Those bits added up," Jana said. "You are perhaps too modest a man."

Niel shrugged. "It doesn't really matter what the rest of the world thinks of you, does it now?"

"Perhaps not," said Jana.

Niel got out of the rickshaw, went around, and helped her down on the other side. "Well. That was delightful. Thank you for the company."

"It was my pleasure," said Jana. "And the food was, as you promised, quite edible. More than edible, in fact."

Taking his outstretched hand, she pressed it for a moment between her own.

"See you at the wedding?" she said.

"God willing," he said. "We're taking things one day at a time, but I will do my best. Good night. Good night, Subedar-

Major," he added to Lal Bahadur Pun, who, from his guard's post, had been watching the exchange between Jana and Niel.

As the rickshaw rolled off, the Gurkha asked, "Nice evening, Jana mem?"

"Very nice, thank you, Subedar-Major," she said, as he gave her a pleased look. Then she added, less formally, "Good night, Lalu."

Counting Down

Padma Concerned

Settled in her now established favorite armchair in Jana's salon, Padma took a sip of *nimbu pani* and put her glass down on the copy of *Filmfare* lying on the side table.

"You wouldn't let my astrologer set the date for the wedding," she scolded. "And now you're vulnerable, you know. Katarina and Jack are at risk, and you are, and the house is. And now we've also got Mrs. Foster lying there in the hospital. You don't find it alarming that a possible death will occur just before the marriage?"

Jana said, "Padma dear, when does one *ever* know for certain that a death will not occur? I do indeed find it distressing that Aunt Sylvia is laid up. But I very strongly hope that she'll rally and even be able to attend."

"You ask for miracles," Padma said dismissively.

"'Ask and it will be given to you,'" Jana said. She practiced no particular religion, having been influenced by so many of them. Occasionally, her late husband's favorite Bible verses popped out of her mouth, as this one did now.

Back to the question of the astrologer, Padma said, "At the very least, allow my pundit-ji to come bless your house just before the ceremony. He did when you moved in; he should also do so on a momentous occasion like this. You need extra protection, with everything in your house being so irregular."

The tension on Padma's beautiful face was palpable and impressed on Jana the intensity of her concern. *She's not just being a busybody,* Jana realized. *She wants the best for everyone.*

"Of course, Padma darling," Jana said. "Thank you very much for suggesting it."

Padma's face brightened. "There's no point in tempting fate, now, is there? The road of life is full of potholes and shaky bridges. You should try to get God on your side. Any God at all."

Jana smiled. "It wouldn't hurt, I'm sure."

ᘓ *An Illegal* Shamiana

The next morning at breakfast, Mary had just brought a plate of rumble-tumble eggs to the table when Lal Bahadur Pun appeared in the doorway of the dining room.

"Sorry to disturb, madam," he said. "A messenger from the police department just delivered this notice."

"Oh, Lord," groaned Jana, taking the envelope. *"Bandhu."*

"Bandhu?" said Katarina.

"Police Commissioner Bandhu Sharma," Jana said. "First thing in the morning. No doubt telling me I've done something wrong."

Lal Bahadur Pun said, "The messenger has been instructed to wait for a reply."

Jana picked up a clean knife, slit open the envelope, and read aloud:

"To: Mrs. William Laird
"Subject: Violation of municipal code 876-A2

"Dear Mrs. Laird:
    "It has been brought to our attention that you have erected a *shamiana* on the premises of your residence at 108

Central Bazaar, known by its vulgar name as the Jolly Grant
House."

"Its vulgar name, eh?" Jack said. "That puts you in your place."
Jana continued reading:

"Temporary structures are covered by Hamara Nagar
municipal code 876-A2. You are required to file an application for such a structure six weeks ahead of commencement
of construction. To date, we have received no such application in our office from you.
    "You are therefore classified as causing a disturbance
within city limits."

"Well!" said Jack, spreading marmalade on his toast. "You
certainly are a scofflaw, aren't you, Mum."
Ignoring her son's impertinence, Jana kept on reading:

"Minimum penalty for said disturbance is Rs. 500, payable immediately. You must also deconstruct said structure.
    "Said structure may be reerected upon payment of acceler-
ated construction permit, Rs. 1,000."

"He's certainly trying to get your attention," Jack said.
Jana snorted. "He's got that. Oh, blast. What shall I do, send
him fifteen hundred rupees and tell him he's a jolly good fellow? I don't happen to have that amount lying around waiting
to be spent. I must say, this so-called penalty is a bit steep even
by Bandhu's standards."
Mary put a fresh pot of coffee next to Katarina and then
turned to Jana. "If you pay, he will think of another thing you
must pay for."
"And if she doesn't pay?" Katarina asked.
Mary said, "The same thing will happen."

Lips pressed together, Jack had been musing. "Let me deal with Bandhu," he said.

"*How?*" Jana asked.

"I've got an idea." Jack turned to Lal Bahadur Pun. "Lalu-ji, would you tell the *chaprassi* that I would like a meeting—no, an *audience*—with Commissioner Sharma."

Jana turned to Jack, puzzled. "You don't intend to give Bandhu what he wants, do you?"

Jack said, "The first thing is to figure out exactly what he *does* want."

"So," Lal Bahadur Pun said, "I am to convey the message that Laird Sahib will come to the police office, right?"

"That's right," said Jack.

"When?" said Lal Bahadur Pun.

"At the commissioner's convenience," said Jack.

Lal Bahadur Pun gave a nonchalant half salute. "Okay, sir, if that's what you say." Then he paused and turned to Katarina. "Madam, one thing."

"Yes, Subedar-Major?" Katarina said.

A slight pink rose to the Gurkha's cheeks. "You remember the young woman selling textiles in the Upper Bazaar?"

"Yes, I remember her," Katarina said. "I bought a couple of scarves at her stall, and we got to chatting. She talked about escaping from Tibet. I told her about getting across the Austrian border from Hungary."

"She is *so* eager to see your wedding," Lal Bahadur Pun said. "But she is too shy to ask."

Katarina said quickly, "Invite her, then! Or, better yet, I'll go to her shop and do it myself."

Lal Bahadur Pun looked pleased. "I'll tell her to stay in the background and not make any trouble."

"She can stand in the *foreground*," Katarina said. "We'd be delighted to have her."

When Lal Bahadur Pun had left, Jana asked, "How many wedding guests are we up to today? I've lost count."

Jack and Katarina each pulled a face and shrugged.

"Two hundred? Three?" Jana asked. "Well, *think,* please. Whom have you invited?"

Jack spoke slowly, trying to remember: "I invited Mr. Shah. I felt bad about misjudging him, and this seemed like a good way to put things right. And then I bumped into Rambir in the street and learned that his parents will be visiting, so I said, Bring them along, too."

Katarina said sheepishly, "I've also invited a few other people I've met in the bazaar besides the scarf seller. One gets talking, you know. And Asha and Bimla begged to bring some of their school friends."

An hour later, the messenger returned from the police office to say that Commissioner Sharma would see Mr. Laird at eleven A.M., and half an hour in advance of the meeting, Jack strode off, telling Jana not to wait lunch for him. He arrived back just as Katarina was modeling the party slippers the *mochi* had made.

"What happened between you and Bandhu?" Jana asked. "You were gone an awfully long time."

"We had a nice leisurely chat," said Jack. "He's not a bad fellow, really."

"Not a bad fellow?" Jana exclaimed. "He stuck me and Mr. Ganguly overnight in his lockup."

"Ah, yes, he joked about that," Jack said. "'A bit hasty of me' was the way he put it. 'Live and learn! A minor misunderstanding between friends.'"

Jana stared at him in disbelief. A misunderstanding among friends—that was rich. "Did you pay him the fifteen hundred rupees?"

"Oh, never you mind about that," Jack said cryptically. "He'll be attending the wedding, by the way. I thought I should tell you so you don't faint on seeing him."

"What!" cried Jana. "You invited Bandhu Sharma to the *wedding*?"

"It will all work out, my dear mother," said Jack breezily. *"Sub theek ho jayega.* Everything will go fine."

"Where'd you learn that?" Jana said. "Jack, what kind of wheeling and dealing have you been up to?"

Jack said, "We discussed—oh, architecture and logistics and this and that. He's quite a creative thinker."

"It sounds as if you buttered him up," Jana said. "Really, Jack, have you no shame?"

"Some," admitted Jack. "But not a crippling amount. And a little less every year, as I grow older."

A Telegram

"Telegram, Jana mem," said Tilku.

Oh, thought Jana, another one of those many telegrams arriving at all hours, sending Jack and Katarina best wishes. Then she noticed that it was addressed to her. She tore it out of its cover, quickly glancing down at the sender. K S-S. Kenneth Stuart-Smith.

Finally, an answer to her letter! After almost three weeks had gone by with no response, Jana was regretting proposing that holiday to Goa. She was certain that she had put Kenneth on the spot and made herself look silly in the bargain. So much for being brave and resolute and taking action, she told herself.

"WAS ABSENT ON TOUR STOP," she now read with relief. "JUST RECEIVED YOUR LETTER STOP APOLOGIES DELAYED REPLY STOP ARRIVING JUNE 25 WITH SANDRA SHARE CELEBRATIONS STOP DON'T BUY CHAMPAGNE STOP LETTER FOLLOWS STOP CHEERS KSS."

Well. He hadn't mentioned the Goa idea. Never mind, she thought. If he hadn't yet accepted it, nor had he given her an outright rejection. As for him bringing the champagne, she was delighted. It was wonderful to have a friend with access to duty-free liquor.

The next day, the promised letter from Kenneth filled in all the details. The idea of a trip to Goa, he said, was wonderful but . . . Oh dear, she thought, here comes the but, and the but, though not insulting, was unwelcome news.

"I've been transferred," Kenneth wrote. "The State Department has decided to stick me in an office for a couple of years in Washington, D.C. So it's farewell, India, for a while and hello, Foggy Bottom. They're sweetening the deal by hinting at a possible ambassadorship after that. Who knows? They'll probably send me to some obscure post where the ambassador doubles as the janitor."

A reference to a vague future softened the blow: "When the dust settles, maybe I can get some leave and then we can take that holiday to some exotic place."

Closing the letter, she put her hands in her pockets and went over to the bay window and stared out. You had to give him credit; the man had tact. She remembered a phrase Kenneth had used in a much earlier conversation about his work. With delicate diplomatic situations, he'd said, you don't have to say no, but you don't have to say when, either.

In his letter, he'd phrased things in such a way that, when he came to the wedding, they could face each other without embarrassment. She hadn't lost a friend—at least, she didn't think so—and for that, she was grateful. She also felt that she'd learned a lesson. With a free spirit like Kenneth, a globe-trotter who didn't need a regular companion, it was probably better not to pursue him.

·⚬ Parrots in Hospitals

Late that afternoon, she decided to squeeze in a quick visit to Aunt Sylvia, with Tilku and Mr. Ganguly as additional company. Jana was sure that pets would not be welcome in the wards, but she figured that Tilku could take him up on the second-floor verandah and amuse Aunt Sylvia through the window.

"Is Foster memsahib dying?" Tilku asked Jana as they trudged up the steep road to the community hospital.

Jana said firmly, "No, she decided against it."

Tilku thought that one over, obviously not sure about how such a decision might be implemented. "How old is she?" he asked. "She looks as old as the Himalayas."

"Not quite," said Jana. "She's ninety-two."

Tilku calculated aloud: "Her age is ninety-two. My age is twelve. If I divide ninety-two by twelve, that makes . . . seven. With remainder of eight. So she has lived almost eight of my lifetimes. That's a lot of lifetimes."

"It is," said Jana, impressed that despite his failing grade, he seemed to have learned *some* mathematics at St. Regis Pre-Military Academy.

"I don't like hospitals, Jana mem," Tilku said. "People say that if you go there, you die."

"For heaven's sake, Tilku," Jana said. "People die if they wait until the last minute before going there. If they went in earlier, before they were *very* sick, they'd have a better chance."

At the community hospital, Tilku headed off past the gossiping dandy teams around the back of the building while Jana went inside and up to the women's ward, where she found Aunt Sylvia sitting up, propped up against several pillows and on the lookout for entertainment. The arrival of Tilku and Mr. Ganguly at the window made Aunt Sylvia's cloudy old eyes widen through her thick glasses.

"Hello, beautiful," Mr. Ganguly called, craning his neck forward from Tilku's shoulder.

"Oh, pass that bird through to me," Aunt Sylvia said. "The nurses will never know. Besides, what will they do if they catch me? Throw me out? That would be quite fine with me."

Tilku hesitated for a second, but at a wink from Aunt Sylvia, he leaned through the window and deposited Mr. Ganguly on the metal footrail of her bed.

"Excellent!" said Aunt Sylvia. "How are you, sweetie?"

"Excellent!" repeated Mr. Ganguly, which made the other patients in the room turn instantly and stare in his direction.

"Quiet, please," Jana whispered to Mr. Ganguly.

"I love you," Mr. Ganguly pealed out to Sylvia, completely ignoring Jana.

"I love you, too, sweetie," Aunt Sylvia said. Then, even more loudly, she cried through the window, "Captain Tilku! Have you used that pen and pencil yet?"

"No, madam," Tilku said.

"Why not?" Aunt Sylvia asked.

Tilku replied happily, "I'm on holiday, madam. No school-work to do."

Aunt Sylvia leaned back against the pillows. "Aha. I see. Well, how are the wedding preparations?" she asked Jana.

"Coming along nicely," said Jana. "With the help of diplomats, engineers, astrologers, and half the Central Bazaar."

"I still plan to attend," Sylvia said, with complete conviction.

"I certainly hope you will, too," Jana said.

Sylvia said, "You see—I marched up to the gateway of the Illusion Fields and thought better of it. Besides, dying just as you're about to get Katarina and Jack safely married off would have been inconsiderate and in poor taste."

"Aunt Sylvia, I have no fear that *you* are going to do anything in poor taste," Jana said.

"Manners count, don't they," Aunt Sylvia was saying when footsteps sounded in the hall, putting the whole ward on alert. Jana quickly scooped up Mr. Ganguly and was about to hand him through the window to Tilku when the nurse arrived in the doorway, a tray in both hands. Mr. Ganguly, freeing himself from Jana's grasp with a loud screech, flapped his wings vigorously and flew to the foot of another patient's bed.

"What on earth?" cried the nurse, losing her grip on the tray, which fell to the floor with a loud crash. Jana gasped in dismay as syringes and saucers and pills and little cups of liquid went flying in all directions.

"Catch that creature!" the nurse shrieked, as Mr. Ganguly, panicked, moved on to the footboard of the next patient, and the next.

"Come along, Mr. G," coaxed Jana, but the parrot dived for the floor and waddled under one of the beds.

"I can get him," Tilku called from the window.

"Stay out, you," yelled the nurse, but it was too late; Tilku had clambered up over the windowsill and was on his hands and knees, chasing Mr. Ganguly from under one bed to another.

Welcoming this break in the hospital routine, the patients took sides, some egging Mr. Ganguly on to escape, others encouraging Tilku to catch him.

"Go, *tota sahib!*"

"Here, here, come around this side and you'll get him."

By now, several patients from the men's ward had heard the commotion and were in the doorway, some wrapped in blankets and others in their undershorts. Shrieking, "Bye-bye, bye-bye," Mr. Ganguly continued to escape his pursuers, scuttling through the crowd and landing in the hall. Jana and Tilku chased after him, but every time they got close, he flapped his wings and took off, flying, landing, hopping, and dodging. Down the staircase he went, into the main hall, around the waiting room, and then, finally, out the door. When Jana and Tilku arrived in the courtyard, he was perched on the shoulder of the statue of Jesus.

"Come down, you dreadful bird," Jana ordered.

She stood there, alternately commanding and entreating the parrot without success. Finally, one of the dandy wallahs, who'd all been watching in delight, strolled over and took a groundnut out of his pocket and handed it to Tilku, who held it

up tantalizingly to Mr. Ganguly. Suddenly the picture of docil-
ity, the parrot fluttered down to Tilku's shoulder.

"Thank you very much," said Jana to the dandy wallah, as
his fellow carriers guffawed and applauded.

"Off we go," she said, with dignity, to Tilku.

Halfway down the street, Tilku told Jana, "I changed my
mind about hospitals, Jana mem."

"How's that?" said Jana.

"I thought they were very sad and dangerous places, but
they can be very funny," Tilku said.

"I doubt we'll be allowed to enter that one anytime soon,
though," said Jana.

They continued on home, Mr. Ganguly riding along in
demure silence.

Mary's Gifts

⁓ Mary Knits

Mary's eyes were burning. Her head ached, and with every stitch she took, she felt a nasty pinch in her forearms. What time could it be? She'd served the dessert at about ten in the evening; then, not staying to supervise Harmendra in the cleaning up, she'd retired to her room and gotten out the wool for the baby sweater. Jack and Katarina's scarves were finished and folded neatly on a recessed shelf in her wall.

One dozen more rows and the baby sweater would be done, too. Mary was getting excited as it took shape. With its pattern of cables and little pom-poms, it was the most intricate and beautiful garment she'd ever made. The wool—a pale yellow—was brand-new, purchased retail at Knitter's Paradise, with no reduction in price.

The pains were now shooting from wrist to elbow. She'd hurt herself this same way a few years before, from spending too many hours knitting Christmas gifts. She knew that there was only one cure for the ailment: put the knitting needles down. She'd considered waiting and sending the scarves by parcel post after Jack and Katarina had left. But that was *so* expensive and slow, she'd decided. And what if someone stole the parcel?

Outside, owls called to each other on the wooded hillside;

inside, down the hall, old Munar was snoring. Mary looked up suddenly to see Tilku in her doorway and stopped knitting.

"Why aren't you sleeping, boy?" she asked. "It must be one o'clock in the morning!"

"I can't sleep, ayah-ji," Tilku said pathetically.

"Why not?" Mary said, not even trying to keep the irritation out of her voice.

Tilku's face twisted. "Thinking about school," he said.

"So? You're a lucky boy to go to school," Mary said. "Now you won't have to be like me, learning some little thing here and there when I have time. You'll be moving about among sahibs. You'll *be* one, yourself. Don't act like a spoiled child. Go to bed."

She picked up her knitting again, slowly tucking the yarn around the needle. Tilku, however, remained standing in the door.

Mary snapped, "I said, go to bed! Oh, what now?"

Tilku's eyes filled. "I have just five more days of happiness: good food, Mr. Ganguly, freedom. And then—finished. Done."

"So, don't think about it," Mary said. "Don't spoil the five days for yourself. This is life, you have to learn. Go to bed, I tell you. If you don't have good sleep, you'll feel even worse."

Tilku hesitated for one more second, and Mary said, "Go!" A few seconds later, Mary heard his door click shut.

She resumed knitting, trying to go slowly and make the least amount of effort possible, so the pain would be less. She did one row that way, but it took so long that she gave up in impatience and again took up her usual blindingly fast pace. Pain will not kill, she said sternly to herself, whipping through the eleventh-to-last row, and the tenth-to-last, all the way down to the very end. She cast off the beautiful little yellow stitches with a sigh of triumph, attached the front and the back and the sleeves of the garment, and held up her handiwork. Though practically nauseated with fatigue and pain, she felt exultant. "My best work," she said, laying the little sweater on top of the two scarves. Then she rubbed her arms and said her prayers and went to sleep.

Even I Can Be Beautiful

The next day was a long day, made even longer by the soreness in Mary's arms. She felt as if she had a sunburn *inside* her skin. She struggled through breakfast and lunch, picking things up stiffly with both hands and keeping her arms as straight as possible.

"Mary, what's wrong?" Katarina asked at lunch.

Mary could hardly say, "I was knitting a sweater for your baby," but she went as far as to admit, "Using the arms too much."

"Take aspirin immediately," Jana said. "And put some ice on it."

After swallowing the two aspirin Jana gave her, Mary took the few ice cubes that could be made at a time in the tiny refrigerator, wrapped them in a dish towel, and placed the bundle first on one arm and then on the other, keeping it there until the discomfort from the cold overcame the pain from the inflamed tendons. Then, grateful that Jack and Katarina and Jana were planning to have Chinese food at Kwality Restaurant for dinner, she spent the rest of the afternoon quietly, icing her arms at frequent intervals.

By five o'clock, she was very bored of this routine, and her arms had stopped shrieking. I shall go take the air, she decided.

She extricated her keychain from the drawstring of her sari and unlocked the padlock to the footlocker under her bed, reaching in for her cloth purse. The purse was thick with bills, and she remembered that she had been too busy for weeks to make a deposit at the bank.

"All-India Saree Jubilee is still open," said a coaxing little voice in her head.

"What an extravagance!" she said aloud. "That sari would pay for two windows and a door in my house."

The coaxing voice continued: "But you've already got the money for the two windows and the door. And think of how that silk feels in your hand. Like cooling water when your skin hurts from the sun."

Oh, thought Mary. The deep yellow of that nine-yard sari was so rich. Even I—pockmarked, plain-faced, stocky old Mary—would look beautiful in that sari. And why not look beautiful? Why not dress in richest silk, like a queen?

"You work and work and even hurt yourself for others," said the small voice. "But what about doing something for yourself? Go!"

"Now?" she asked aloud.

"Now!" said the voice.

She felt a surge of energy, which suddenly and mysteriously even lessened the pain in her forearms. Grabbing her cloth purse, she headed out the door.

W–Day Minus One

✑ Special Delivery

Early in the morning on the day before the wedding, a line of porters trudged through the front gate of the Jolly Grant House, some with crates on their heads, others with tables and chairs strapped to their backs. Lal Bahadur Pun, in his khaki military uniform, directed traffic: large tables to the dining room, to be used for the buffet; chairs and small tables to the salon and courtyard for dinner seating. Jana watched from the courtyard, Mr. Ganguly on her forearm.

Getting the tables and chairs had been something of a triumph, and Jana drew a sigh of relief when they were in place. At first she'd thought the hotel could lend them some furniture, but Mr. Dass had apologetically told her that the Victory was overflowing with guests and couldn't spare so much as a board and trestle. The Far Oaks School, closed for semester break, had come to the rescue, with tables and chairs from the student dining rooms. Inspecting the dark varnished tables, Jana saw carvings memorializing youthful romances of who knows how long ago. On one table, the initials "CA+WT" were enclosed in a heart. On another, bold capitals proclaimed, "LAKSHMAN LOVES ANNA!"

Then she and Mary spread the tablecloths—yards and yards

of heavy cotton from Fabulous Fabrics, hemmed the week before in an orgy of stitching at Royal Tailors.

They barely stopped for the most minimal lunch, samosas that Jack brought back from the Why Not?, and then they started to unpack the cutlery, also borrowed from the Far Oaks School.

In early afternoon, the rarely heard sound of an automobile in the street took them by surprise. An American station wagon had drawn up to the gate, where it was attracting a growing crowd of onlookers. When Jana realized who it was, her stomach lurched with sudden mortification. In spite of the tactful letter Kenneth Stuart-Smith had written her, could she really look him straight in the face?

"Special delivery," called Kenneth through the driver's window. With his golf shirt, tanned arms, and wind-tossed hair, he looked casual, on vacation, and utterly relaxed. Jana felt her own tension begin to disappear.

"Hi, Jana," called Sandra from the passenger seat.

"You're here!" cried Jana. "How did you get a permit to drive inside town?"

"Applied directly to God," said Kenneth. "By phone."

"God has a telephone?" Jana asked.

"Bandhu Sharma has one," said Kenneth. "He was very accommodating. I told him I had to get the champagne to the Jolly Grant House."

"He's no doubt planning to drink half of it," Jana said.

"No problem—I brought extra," said Kenneth, getting out of the car and giving her a hug, while Sandra hopped out and came around from the passenger side. Even in faded jeans and a man's sweatshirt, with her blond hair in two ponytails, she still looked to Jana like Princess Grace of Monaco. The year before last, Jana had worried considerably about the girl, when breaking the Far Oaks School curfew had seemed a matter of honor with Sandra and she'd even fallen over the *khud* one night on her way home from an unauthorized outing. Now, no longer a boarding school student, Sandra looked much happier, the sullen stoniness gone from her face. Unexpectedly delighted to see her, Jana welcomed her with open arms.

"Hi, Jana!" said Sandra. "Dad told me I have to be on my best behavior. Is that really true? It will be an awful strain."

"Do the best you can," Jana said.

"Aw! And here's Mr. Ganguly." Sandra tickled the bird's neck and got told that she was beautiful.

Meanwhile, Kenneth went to the back of the car and lifted the tailgate, revealing a dozen large canvas-wrapped bundles.

"Packed in ice," he said, "with sawdust and several layers of burlap, just the way they used to pack ice for shipping from Boston to Bombay, a hundred and fifty years ago. If Lal Bahadur Pun will give me a hand, we can carry this stuff down to the basement to keep it as cool as possible."

When the champagne was safely stored, Kenneth returned to the courtyard.

"I'm blocking the street," he said. "I'll have to move the car down to the hotel and check in. But maybe I can leave Sandra here with you."

"Of course," said Jana. "Go on upstairs, Sandra. You can help the girls and Katarina."

As Jana watched the station wagon disappear through the crowds on the narrow street, she felt a mix of affection and relief. Kenneth's arrival had occurred just as naturally as in the days before she'd written that letter. Now, there was a gentleman and a friend, she said to herself, even if the term "gentleman friend" did not apply.

Henna Designs

Back in the front hall, Jana heard a squeal coming from upstairs in the guest room, followed by a burst of high-pitched laughter.

Her curiosity aroused, she climbed the stairs to the second floor and tapped lightly on Katarina's door.

"Who is it?" one of the Ramachandran twins called.

"No boys allowed!" the other twin called.

"Password!" came Sandra Stuart-Smith's voice.

"It's me," Jana called.

The door opened a crack and Sandra peered through. She cried to the others, "Shall we let her in?"

"She can come in," came Katarina's voice.

Inside the room, Katarina, dressed in a lace slip, was leaning against the headboard of her bed, her arms and legs resting on towels. She was flanked by Asha and Bimla, who were painting her arms and legs with black swirls and flowers and lozenge designs. A scent of eucalyptus hung in the air, and flattened foil cones littered the table.

"Look, Auntie Jana, what do you think?" Bimla cried.

"My arms are cramping!" Asha cried.

"Here, let me do some more." Sandra grabbed a cone. "How about I make some runes? Hungarian *mehndi*. Katarina, have you got any leg left?"

Katarina was already covered with designs up to the knees and elbows.

"Turn around," said Sandra. "I'll put some on your back."

Asha bumped against one of the bedside tables, overturning a bottle of Coca-Cola.

"Now look what you've done," Bimla said.

Jana dashed for the bathroom, grabbed a towel and wetted a corner of it, and rushed back to blot up the brown puddle on the rug.

"Don't let Mary know you spilled," she said. "But speaking of Mary, I know she'd love to see the designs. May I send her up?"

"Ask her if she wants *mehndi*," Sandra said. "We've got lots more! Jana, do you want some?"

"Not this time," said Jana, heading for the door.

❀ A Time-out with Jack

After sending Mary up to witness the *mehndi* painting, Jana climbed the two flights of stairs to the lookout room, where Jack was lying on his cot, reading. The tranquil atmosphere in this room was so different from the excitement in the one below that she couldn't help smiling.

"Come in," said Jack. "Have a seat." He put an envelope in his book to save his place and started to get up off the cot.

"Stay where you are," Jana said, settling herself in an armchair, and Jack stretched out again with his hands clasped behind his head.

"I take it you've been with the vestal virgins," he said.

"I have." Jana laughed. "They're out of their minds. You seem frightfully calm, however. By the way, are you sure you don't mind being banished to the hotel tomorrow?"

"Not at all," said Jack. "By then I may welcome a bit of banishment."

Jana laughed again. "You're a good sport."

My son has been transformed, thought Jana. He never used to be this flexible, or to think that noise and confusion and people were enjoyable. On the other hand, perhaps *he* hasn't really changed so much; maybe I didn't know him as well as I thought. Aloud, she said, "This visit has all been so different from the way you usually like things. Or used to like them. Ever since you've arrived, you've had a constant stream of visits and errands and having to sort out muddles."

"Do I look any the worse for it?" Jack said.

"No, you don't," Jana said quickly. "You've done very well indeed, for someone who likes society in small doses."

"I've been mending my misanthropic ways," Jack said. "In any case, *you're* the one whose house has been invaded."

Through the open windows, a burst of laughter from the bedroom below broke into their conversation. Yes, the house has been invaded, but that is the way it should be, Jana thought. People in every nook and cranny, preparations for celebrations going on—but, she admitted, it was also nice to have quiet places to which people could retreat, such as this room.

She said, "You know, I think Grandfather Jolly would be tickled by all this activity in his house."

Jack said, "Oh, his ghost is definitely flitting about. In fact, I think I heard him last night."

"Owls," said Jana. "But you never know. He might have come back as one of them."

"Just make sure he doesn't get into the champagne," said Jack.

Jana sat for a while, enjoying the island of calm and the quiet company of her son. She realized that there might not be so many of these moments in the future; as a family man, he would soon have other people clamoring for his attention all the time. The distance between Scotland and India wouldn't help, either; how was she going to see that grandchild growing up?

She wished she could stretch out this brief passage, capture permanently the sunlight streaming through the window, the laughter floating up from the *mehndi* painters downstairs, the relaxed way Jack lay there on his back with his legs crossed.

Finally, she rose reluctantly and said, "I'm off to arrange flowers. But, Jack—I just wanted to tell you—"

He looked up questioningly.

"You're a brick."

Haste to the Wedding

❦ Sound Check

Two hours before the wedding guests were to arrive, Jana went into the courtyard to find the newly expanded dance band from the Victory Hotel. The musicians were talking with Tilku and trying to get Mr. Ganguly to imitate the notes they whistled.

"Madam, we are here!" the men announced. "Where shall we set up?"

That was a good question. She'd pictured three or four string players bowing their instruments in the corner of the salon, but now they seemed to have added a clarinet, a saxophone, a trumpet, and drums, so that plan was clearly not going to work.

"Jana mem, put them on the verandah," Tilku suggested. "The sound can come through the window."

Finding that a good solution, Jana led the musicians around the verandah to the side of the house. The drummer required special attention, accompanied as he was by five porters. They unpacked drums and cymbals and triangles and brushes and wooden blocks, the drummer testing one component and then another, to the intense interest of Mr. Ganguly, who flapped exuberantly and gave an imitation of each new clang, buzz, and thump.

"Sound check!" announced the trumpet player, giving a

blast on his instrument that made Jana's ears ring and sent monkeys scattering from the nearby roofs into the forest.

"I'll go inside," she told the musicians, "and see how it sounds in the salon. Start playing, all right?"

Inside, she walked around the tables arranged in the salon and eyed the small area set aside for dancing. The band, meanwhile, was playing "The Twist," which Jana had recently heard wafting from the roller-skating rink. She leaned through the window and said to the musicians on the verandah, "It's still too loud."

After some heated argument, the musicians shifted the drums, made the trumpet player stand farther back, and resumed playing. This time the music was too soft. This is like Goldilocks tasting the porridge at the house of the three bears, Jana thought.

"Perhaps you can stand a wee bit closer," she cried to the trumpeter.

"Madam has very precise requirements," the man said grumpily, but he edged in.

A few more adjustments, and Jana decided the sound was fine, whereupon some of the musicians unrolled bedrolls and settled down for a nap and others disappeared into the bazaar in search of food. Jana wondered whether any of them, on return, would remember where he was supposed to position himself.

She glanced at her watch, did a double take, and headed upstairs at a sharp clip. In the bathroom, she started running the bathwater, then dashed back into the bedroom to lay out her clothes on the bed and the new costume jewelry on the dresser.

Returning to the bathroom, she stepped into the tub and gave a squeal. Freezing! Everyone else in the household had already used up the hot water, it seemed. No time to do anything about it now, she decided, and quickly scrubbed in icy water, emerging bright red, tingling all over, and giddily euphoric.

◄ᢒ Bring the Family

It was now after dark. Lights blazed in the Central Bazaar, and strings of tiny Christmas-like bulbs lit up the gate to the Jolly Grant House. The guests were arriving—singly, in pairs, in families, in brigades, in swarms. Jana could greet a lot of people by name, recognized others by sight, and was completely ignorant of the identities of many more. A band of Tibetan men marched in, festively dressed in sun-yellow tunics and black pantaloons, followed by a cluster of Tibetan ladies dazzling the eye with a rainbow of striped aprons over their long dresses. Mary nudged Jana and tipped her chin in the direction of a particularly stunning young woman with thick braids to her waist. "Look, Jana mem—that's the scarf seller that Lalu likes."

"Hiya, beautiful!" shrieked Mr. Ganguly from Tilku's shoulder, making the young woman throw a startled glance in the bird's direction.

The area under the *shamiana* was getting increasingly crowded, and the rest of the courtyard was packed, too. Undeterred by the crush, people continued to stream through the gate and overflow into the side yard and onto the verandah.

"Mary," said Jana, "how many people have we got?"

"Thousands," said Mary.

"Surely not *thousands*," Jana said. "Hundreds?"

Mary stood her ground. "Jack sahib kept inviting. And Katarina mem, too, was always telling people, Come, come, bring your family."

It was the "bring your family" part that did it, Jana thought. Take, for example, the Ramachandrans. When Jana had made the initial guest list, she'd figured that the Ramachandran family would number nine, counting the seven children. But how on earth could she have forgotten Aunt Putli? Let alone Ramachandran's nephew Teddy and Teddy's wife, Twinkle, and *their* two offspring? The fact that a couple of ayahs had come along, too, shouldn't have been a surprise, and pretty young Meenakshi, after all, was a friend of Mary's. Also, she noted, Ramachandran's son Vikram had brought several of his chums. Never mind, she thought, they're so handsome in their St. Bart's school uniforms that no one will complain. Nineteen, twenty, twenty-one, and more people arrived as part of the Ramachandran clan. Mr. Ganguly said, "Namasté" to each one of them, nodding his head each time.

"Padma-ji," said Jana, giving Mrs. Ramachandran a hug, "don't you look lovely!"

Padma, in a mauve-and-honey-colored shot-silk sari, did in fact look lovely—and also cautiously relieved. Her pundit-ji had earlier pronounced blessings on the house, Aunt Sylvia was still alive, and bad luck seemed to have been kept at bay.

"Mrs. Laird, congratulations," boomed Ramachandran, and then he turned to wave in the four minions who worked at the Treasure Emporium. They marched through the gate, bearing a five-foot-high, irregularly shaped bundle sewn up in burlap.

"Just a little memento!" said Ramachandran, who had cheerfully ignored the plea put out by Jack and Katarina for no gifts.

Patting the rough cloth, Jana detected the contours of the statue of the rani of Jhansi and her horse that had recently graced the entrance to the emporium. "You're so kind," she said weakly. "I know they'll love it." Just be thankful, she told herself, that Joan of Arc wasn't also included in the gift.

Families continued to press in from the street. Jack, Jana remembered, had told Rambir and Ritu to bring along Rambir's elderly parents, but somehow no one had mentioned to Jana that Ritu's sisters were coming, too, along with a batch of nieces and nephews.

Then in came Mr. Dass and his sweet, quiet wife with their two well-behaved daughters and one exemplary son, all dressed to the nines.

"Will we have enough food?" Jana said under her breath to Mary.

"God will have to give us loaves and fishes," Mary replied.

"Salaam, salaam," shrieked Mr. Ganguly, who had recognized Feroze Ali Khan and his wife, Zohra, each leading one of their twin toddlers.

"Salaam aleikum," said Jana, and then she said it again—and again—and again, as all Feroze's cousin-employees filed in, with *their* wives and children. "Salaam, salaam, salaam," echoed Mr. Ganguly.

Beaming all over, next Mr. Abinath marched in, and Mr. Muktinanda, and Dr. Chawla, and all of their assorted households. Jana's head began to swim. Where had she seen that dignified-looking man in the three-piece suit? Oh, yes, he was the president of the Rotary club. And could those four young men in red uniforms be the ushers from the Bharat Mata? Maybe Mary had told them to come; she'd been going to the cinema a lot lately.

Before she could figure out who the four fellows were, she had to greet the next comers. "Oh, good evening, Mr. Shah! And Mrs. Shah, how perfectly . . . perfectly . . . perfectly splendid." Perfectly dripping in jewels, Jana had wished to say, taking in the woman's coils of gold and clusters of rubies. Following the Shahs as if on an invisible tether was a formally dressed Deepak, his dark hair carefully slicked back but his bow tie askew.

As the parade of people—barely known, almost known, and totally unknown—continued to file in, Jana was relieved when the familiar figures of Kenneth and Sandra Stuart-Smith appeared. Kenneth was at his diplomat's best in an evening suit and pleated shirt, and Sandra glamorous beyond her years in a strapless red evening gown with rhinestones in her blond hair.

"Marry me!" screamed Mr. Ganguly, causing several people to turn around and stare. Among them was Deepak, who did a double take at Sandra's bare shoulders and fearless décolletage.

"How's the groom?" Jana asked Kenneth.

"Perfectly cool and collected," said Kenneth. "When I saw him at four o'clock, he was reading a book. We had a brief

consultation about the choreography of this event. I'm going to
escort him to the altar."

"Don't lose your way," said Jana. "Who are those people, by
the way?"

She gestured to a group of tall sunburned Scandinavian-
looking couples.

"I saw them in the dining room at the hotel," said Kenneth.
"I heard them asking at the desk if there was any son et lumière
spectacle in town."

"My nightmare come true," said Jana.

Strains of the snake dance from the movie *Nagin* were
already sounding from somewhere around the clock tower
when a rickshaw rolled up very close to the gate. On seeing Niel
Powell jump to the ground, Jana and Kenneth quickly stepped
forward.

Jana held her breath as Kenneth and Niel helped a tiny figure in a pink beaded flapper dress and matching cloche hat
descend. Mr. Ganguly cried, "Hiya, beautiful!," which brought
a smile from the flapper. Clutching Niel's arm, Aunt Sylvia
announced cheerfully to Jana, "Here I am, my dear. Still on *terra
cotta*." Then Kenneth and Niel made a chair by locking arms and
Aunt Sylvia allowed herself to be scooped up and carried to a seat
near the altar.

The snake dance was now a head-filling wail amplified by
drums, trumpets, and tambourines. Jana, familiar with Lal
Bahadur Pun's repertoire, predicted that "Haste to the Wedding" would be next, and she was correct. The fifth repetition
of *that* tune finished just as a throng of singing and dancing
men came up the street to the gate of the Jolly Grant House.
Hoofs clip-clopped on the pavement, snorting and whinnying
sounded in the air, and the salty smell of horse wafted to Jana's
nose. The groom had arrived.

The traditional white mare now at the Jolly Grant House
gate wore a royal red velvet headpiece, matching neck cloth

and saddle blanket, red ankle bracelets with bells, and a crown with a red plume. Marching alongside it was the police force of Hamara Nagar, some officers carrying flaming torches and one holding a red-and-gold umbrella over the rider's head.

A curtain of multicolored beads and flowers hanging from the groom's forehead completely concealed his face. Jana found herself thinking, Wouldn't it be funny if that rider in a gold brocade jacket and black silk trousers wasn't Jack? She wondered if a groom ever got mixed up and went to the wrong wedding.

Kenneth, however, seemed to have no doubt that the man now dismounting and handing the reins to one of the policemen was the groom they were expecting.

"Let's get you ladies seated!" Kenneth said, and quickly marched Jana and Mary to chairs close to where Pastor Mitra was stationed in front of the improvised altar of a table with a huge bouquet of flowers. In his ankle-length white cassock, he looked for all the world like a chubby, cheerful dove.

Then Kenneth went back and led Jack up to his position at the altar. The roar of conversation fell to a rustling, the door to the house opened, and Asha and Bimla and Sandra emerged. Lal Bahadur Pun broke into the march he had been practicing for weeks. Jana figured the entire neighborhood must know it by heart, but suddenly it sounded brand-new, whimsical and triumphant. A lump formed in Jana's throat. She glanced at Mary, who, in spite of her well-known aversion to bagpipes, also had a look of wonder on her face.

Katarina was now on her way across the courtyard, practically floating, her honey-gold wedding outfit shimmering in the soft light of the lanterns. Her dress rippled out over gathered silk leggings, her long scarf fluttered with the slightest breeze, and at her throat and ears, sparkling against her lightly suntanned skin, were Jana's emeralds. Reaching the altar, she smiled up at Jack, who by now had removed the curtain of beads and flowers from his face and stood there serious and composed.

"Dearly beloved," said chubby Pastor Mitra, in a tone so tender that Jana found the tears pouring down her face. Since she had forgotten her handkerchief, she had to wipe her eyes on her sleeve. Mary was letting her own tears flow.

A Housewarming

Out of habit, Mary hovered in the dining room, but since the food was all laid out on buffet tables, she didn't have to serve or replenish the dishes. The bearers hired for the occasion were moving about with trays of champagne. Why, thought Mary, there's nothing to do! Nothing, that is, except to observe, and there was plenty for that. With a canny eye, Mary watched the way people helped themselves. Some loaded up their plates in a giant pyramid of food; others took an experimental amount, ate it, deliberated, and returned for another small helping.

During the planning, Jana mem had said that meat eaters would be likely to drink alcohol and vegetarians to take *nimbu pani,* but this hadn't turned out to be 100 percent true. Mary saw Commissioner Sharma visiting and revisiting the vegetarian buffet but also allowing his champagne glass to be topped off at frequent intervals. Ritu, on the other hand, washed down her chicken curry and lamb kebabs with *nimbu pani.*

Tilku, in his school uniform, circulated with Mr. Ganguly on his shoulder. Taking advantage of good food before going back to boarding school, he helped himself amply to everything in sight.

"You are looking distinguished, Mrs. Thomas," said a voice at Mary's elbow.

Startled, she turned to see Jacob John in his spotless white pressed uniform and new white turban. He'd been to the barber in the bazaar, and his smooth, unlined face looked years younger than on that day when he'd fallen asleep in church. She could practically see her own face in his highly polished shoes.

"I am no more distinguished than you, Jacob-*anna*," she said.

"Is that a new sari?" Jacob John asked.

"Yes, it is. Three days ago, only, I bought it," she said.

"It's pretty enough to be a bridal sari," Jacob John said. "Be careful not to outshine the bride!"

Mary started giggling at that, recalling that the salesman at All-India Saree Jubilee had said the same thing.

"Did you like the ceremony, Jacob-*anna*?" she said.

"Of course I did," he said.

"I did, too," allowed Mary, "although I would have liked a normal European wedding with a white dress. In the church."

"Yes, that ritual was all mixed up, wasn't it," said Jacob John. "Not quite Christian and not quite Hindu. Have you ever seen someone make up their own marriage?"

Mary had not.

Jacob John went on: "Nonetheless, Pastor Mitra pronounced Jack and Katarina sahibs man and wife quite decidedly, didn't he?"

"He did," said Mary. "Beyond a shadow of a doubt, he did, thanks be to God."

"Thanks be to God also that Commissioner Sharma's white mare hardly pooped at all," Jacob John said.

This reference to horse excrement constituted such a departure from her friend's usual propriety that Mary let out a squeal of laughter. She tried for a moment to look disapproving and failed utterly.

"Listen now to Jana memsahib playing the violin," she said, in an effort to regain her composure.

"Do you like that type of music?" Jacob John asked, as Jana finished to applause and started an encore.

"I'm used to it," Mary said. "I've been hearing Jana mem's music for so long that now it sounds normal to me. Not like that tooting and thumping going on out there on the verandah."

This was a reference to the band from the Victory Hotel, which was just beginning the dance music. As Jack led Katarina to the small area in the salon that had been designated the dance floor, Mary strained her eyes to see if Katarina's waistline looked thick in the wedding outfit, deciding in the end that one could not really tell unless one already knew. Nonetheless, Mary thanked her lucky stars that the pair were now properly joined together. Just try to get them asunder now, Pastor Mitra had said.

The opening dance concluded, the band broke into a livelier number.

"Do you wish to dance?" Jacob John said to Mary. "And drink champagne?"

"NO!" Mary dissolved into another fit of giggling. "But I wish to watch *other* people dancing and drinking champagne. They look so funny, is it not?" She gestured toward Sandra Stuart-Smith, who was trying to teach Ramachandran's son Vikram a dance. "Just look at them hop!" Mary said. "Like people with red ants down their backs."

Jacob John laughed and glanced in the direction of Asha and Bimla. "Look, there. Those missahibs are dancing together. Looking just like twins."

"They *are* twins," Mary said. "I saw them drink twin glasses of champagne."

She giggled yet again, as if she'd had twin glasses of champagne herself, getting silly on something fizzy in the air.

"Mary Thomas," said Jacob John, "have I told you that you are the best woman in the world? The smartest and the most hardworking—and the most beautiful. The queen of my dreams."

"Don't talk rubbish, Jacob John," said Mary. "You've been inhaling champagne fumes."

"I'm not talking rubbish!" Jacob John said.

"Well, then," said Mary. "I'll tell you an idea I've been having."

Taking a deep breath and feeling like a soldier about to do a parachute jump, she asked, "What would you think if you and I joined forces in life?"

"In life?" repeated Jacob John. "In the future, you mean. When Sylvia memsahib . . ." His question hung unfinished on the air.

"No!" said Mary. "Not living like ghouls waiting for other people to die." She gestured to Aunt Sylvia, who was eating a chicken kebab, Mr. Ganguly sitting on the arm of her chair and observing her every bite. "The old lady has some life in her yet. Let her enjoy that life! And let us enjoy our own."

✑ At Every Moment

This, Jana decided, is a jolly good housewarming, if I do say so myself! She looked happily at the crowd of people so obviously enjoying themselves and imagined Grandfather Jolly gazing down from on high—or perhaps peering up from somewhere else. Either way, he was surely approving the scene.

In the salon, Kenneth Stuart-Smith was working the room. What a pro, Jana thought, seeing him stop to chat with Police Commissioner Sharma. She observed with astonishment that Bandhu was *laughing*. Laughing not in his usual menacing way but as if he really was amused.

"Have some champagne, sir," Kenneth was saying.

"Don't mind if I do, my dear Ken," Bandhu answered.

Between the earlier efforts made by Jack and now Kenneth's, Jana realized that her former enemy was being buttered up in grand fashion. No more phony fees for me, she thought with glee.

Close by, Ramachandran and Rambir had settled at a table and were talking politics as if they were at their usual spots in the Why Not?, the only difference being that they were having multiple glasses of whisky instead of multiple glasses of tea. Drifting by their table, Jana heard Rambir say, "But the Americans just don't *understand* about nonalignment."

Jana smiled and paused briefly at the next table, where Mr. and Mrs. Dass and their polite son and two demure daughters were tucking into samosas and crispy onion shreds.

"Mr. Dass," Jana said, "you must congratulate your cooks. The food from the hotel is delicious. Have you had some? I had several kebabs."

Mr. Dass gave her a sly smile. "I don't often eat the hotel food," he said. "I took Mr. Joshi's specialties instead." Glancing at his loaded plate, he tee-heed in a collusive manner.

Meanwhile, the band had broken into "Rock Around the Clock." Jana noticed Asha and Bimla heading for the dance floor with two of Vikram's handsome friends, while Padma's vigilant eye took in every move.

"Are you going to dance?" Jana asked Mr. and Mrs. Dass.

"Oh no, we don't dance," said Mrs. Dass. "But the children will. Go children, go to dance."

Timidly, the three Dass children got out of their chairs and went and stood next to Bandhu Sharma's three boys, whose mother had apparently given them the same order.

Leaving the Dass and Sharma children to size one another up, Jana went back into the hall, skirting Lal Bahadur Pun, who was telling the pretty young scarf seller from the Upper Bazaar that her ankles were as luscious as ripe cucumbers. She continued on to the dining room, made sure that empty platters were being replenished with full ones, accepted a flute of champagne from a passing bearer, and returned to the salon.

Now the party was truly in full swing. The Dass and Sharma children were holding hands and jigging in a circle. The Scandinavian couples had moved into the center of the action, their blond heads sticking up above the crowd. Beyond them, Sandra Stuart-Smith was heading straight for Mr. Shah's son, Deepak, who looked as if he might faint.

"But I don't know how to dance," Jana heard Deepak say, grinning in terror and blushing to the tips of his ears.

"I can teach you in two minutes!" Sandra promised. "It's very easy. I'll show you the box step."

Deepak allowed himself to be guided onto the dance floor, where he clutched a handful of satin from the back of Sandra's gown, trod on her toes, stepped awkwardly back and forth, and never managed to find the beat. Sandra, however, was unperturbed and kept up a running stream of conversation.

"You mean you've never *been* to Kuala Lumpur?" she purred. "But you've *got* to go. And the job sounds great. You'll earn pots of money!"

Jana was chuckling at Deepak's proud but bashful look when a touch on the shoulder made her jump. She turned to find Niel Powell, who had just delivered a tot of whisky to Aunt Sylvia.

"Oh, Niel, there you are!" she said. "Did you have something to eat?"

"I did," he said. "It's a fine spread, by the way."

"I adore our flapper," said Jana. "Last week we were worried that she was about to make her final exit, and here she is."

Niel gave a wry smile. "She *willed* herself back to good health for this wedding. Said she hadn't been to a party since Queen Elizabeth's coronation."

They watched as Kenneth Stuart-Smith crossed the room and sat down next to Aunt Sylvia. Whatever he was saying was making her laugh, and then, unexpectedly, Kenneth was on his feet and helping Aunt Sylvia get to hers.

"Oh no, now what's Stu doing?" Jana asked. "He's not making her dance, is he?"

"No one makes Sylvia do anything," Niel said. "She probably asked *him* to."

Sylvia's dancing, however, was a matter of standing and swaying to the music for half a minute; after which she nodded brightly at Kenneth and, with his help, took the few steps back to her chair.

The band had switched from rock 'n' roll to big band tunes from the war, easing into "A String of Pearls." Often in Bombay, Jana had danced to that tune—or played it—and it had always spelled ease and comfort to her.

"Shall we dance?" Niel asked.

"With pleasure," she said, as they searched for a bit of room among the crush of people. Once on the floor, she was surprised to find how expertly he led her through one turn after another.

"Where did you learn to dance?" she asked.

"Calcutta." He cocked a rueful eyebrow. "My former wife insisted."

"Well, she did you one good deed, at least," Jana said.

"That she did," said Niel. "By the way, your son and his bride are a handsome pair."

"*I* think so," said Jana. "Totally objectively, of course."

"Of course."

As "A String of Pearls" slid into "Heart and Soul," Jana, peeking over Niel's shoulder, noticed that Sandra Stuart-Smith's manicured hand had crept up to the back of Deepak Shah's neck, and Deepak's hand had relaxed its panicky grip on the red satin and was placed firmly on Sandra's back, his fingers in a confident spread. It seemed to Jana that Deepak was now keeping much more to the rhythm of the music, too. "If you come to Washington, D.C.," Sandra was telling him, "I'll show you all the sights. There's more nightlife than here. You'll love it. I guarantee."

"What are you laughing about?" Niel asked.

"At the little dramas going on," Jana said.

"They always are, aren't they?" said Niel. "All around us, at all moments, often without our realizing it."

All around us, Jana thought, and also in our own hearts.

Good-byes and Hellos

⚭ *Packing*

Jack and Katarina's honeymoon consisted of the night (what was left of it) at the Victory Hotel, after which they took a rickshaw back to the Jolly Grant House and started packing to return to Scotland. Jana sat on Katarina's bed and watched for a while, seeing Aunt Sylvia's spoons and forks go into one suitcase pocket, Mary's yellow baby sweater into another, and the red, white, and blue scarves Mary had also knitted into a third.

There were also lots of small mementos people had brought to the wedding: local specialties such as carved walking sticks, Kashmiri lacquerware, copper bowls. Some of the guests had looked for a place to put single rupee notes—or gifts of larger denominations stuck into an envelope, plus a one-rupee note for good luck. Tilku had brought a basket from the salon and watched over it as people threw the money in, then guarded the stash overnight and handed it to Jack in the morning.

"Katya, what do you think? Shall we divide these rupees among Lal Bahadur Pun, Mary, Munar, and Harmendra?" asked Jack. "I'd like to give them more than the average tip."

"Definitely!" said Katarina. "They've given us more than the average visit."

Jack divided the money into four piles and went off to distribute it. Jana, unable to stand any more evidence of their imminent departure, retreated to her own room and lay down on the bed. She was staring disconsolately at the ceiling when there came a tap on the door.

"Yes?" she called.

The door opened a crack and Katarina peeked in. "It's me. Oh! I don't want to interrupt your nap."

"You're not interrupting anything," Jana said, sitting up.

"Returning a loan," Katarina said, coming into the room with a familiar long rectangular box. "And thank you! No one ever borrowed a more elegant item to wear at their wedding."

Jana took the box, smiling at the thought of Katarina stepping out the front door of the house last night on her way to the altar. She opened the lid and looked at the emeralds. They're lovely in spite of their cracks and bubbles, she thought, flawed and beautiful as life itself.

How many owners had these gems passed through? How many Mughal queens, jewel thieves, peddlers, junk merchants, fortune-tellers? The stones twinkled enigmatically. Nothing is in our grasp for very long, Jana thought, emeralds included. Best to pass sparkling things on to others, whether they be necklaces or violin tunes or pickle forks. Besides, she reminded herself, these emeralds aren't mine at all—they're Jack's. He's the one who bought them back.

She snapped the box shut and handed it to Katarina.

"They're yours, Katya darling."

"Oh no," Katarina said. "I couldn't."

"Of course you could," said Jana. "And please do! Wear them in good health and give them to someone else when you're through with them."

"Thank you. I'll wear them on special occasions and think of you every time," Katarina said.

✑ A Departure or Two

It rained in the night, Katarina and Jack's last one in the Jolly
Grant House, and the next morning the paving stones of the
courtyard glistened gray under a tinplate sky. Even the sun has
decided to leave, Jana thought gloomily as she watched eight
porters loading one another up with Jack and Katarina's luggage.

Requiring four men to carry her, there was the rani of
Jhansi, still wrapped in burlap.

"The perfect gift for air travelers," Jack groaned. "Can't we
leave her behind?"

Katarina said, "We can check her straight through at the
Delhi airport. Just think how wonderful she's going to look in
the entry at home! She'll be an instant conversation piece for
anyone coming through the door."

Jack rolled his eyes but gave in. "Okay, rani girl, you're
coming with us," he said, patting the horse's flank through the
wrapping.

Good-byes, how Jana hated them. "Come back soon, safe
journey, thank you so much for a lovely visit . . ." All the oft-
repeated phrases—the rituals of separation—reeked with over-
tones of possible danger, uncertainty over when they would see
each other again, reminders that a string of golden days had
come to an end.

The entire household insisted on accompanying the travelers to the taxi stand, so the rickshaw that had been hired took
off packed with nothing but luggage, and everyone else walked.
They were a tired group of people—as Mary said, pulled down.
In contrast to the day when Jack and Katarina had arrived, they
were all in their workaday clothes. Except for Tilku—he was
dressed to go back to school in his once again immaculate blazer,
creased trousers, and spit-shined shoes.

When they reached the barricade at the edge of town, the

sky had lowered, and Jana felt a few drops of rain. As they waited for Mr. Kilometres, making desultory conversation, the regional bus lumbered in and shuddered to a halt. Several passengers stumbled gratefully off, colliding with those who were trying to get on, and getting in the way of helpers who were tossing suitcases up onto the roof.

Mary said, "Tilku, climb on quickly or you won't get a seat!"

Tilku hung behind for a moment, looking as if he might turn around and bolt for the Central Bazaar, but then he squared his shoulders and said good-bye to the family, one by one.

Katarina said, "Captain Tilku, I have confidence that you'll be fierce in school." Tilku nodded and tried to look fierce.

Lal Bahadur Pun said, "Don't worry about those other boys!" and Tilku shook his head and tried to look blasé.

Mary said, "Going to school is lucky, you'll see"; and Munar and Harmendra said, together, "See you later, small brother."

Jana stepped forward and gave him a hug. "It *will* be better this time," she said. "And if it's not, we'll get you into a better school."

Then Jack and Tilku shook hands. "Remember everything I told you," Jack said. "You'll manage."

"I will manage, Jack sahib," Tilku said. "What's that expression? *Illetigibus non carmidumdum?*"

"Something like that," said Jack, and Tilku climbed the steps into the bus.

When the bus had rumbled off, leaving a cloud of diesel smoke that temporarily made everyone hide their noses in their scarves or sleeves, a rickshaw arrived and disgorged Mr. Shah of Priceless Gems. With him, dressed in a suit and tie and carrying a small brown suitcase, was Deepak.

"Mrs. Laird," Mr. Shah announced, "your children are leaving now, no? I know what you are going through! My wife and I are crying to see our son go out the door. Just after the wedding at your house, he told us that he had been offered a very prestigious job with the Standard Oil Company. You know Esso?"

"I do," said Jana. "Congratulations, Mr. Shah. You must be very proud of him."

"Oh, I am," said Mr. Shah. "I've always said to him, 'You go and conquer the world, my son!' *Finally*, finally, he listens to me. I told him, don't pay the slightest attention to your weeping mother or your heartbroken father in the store. Just *go!*"

"One problem," broke in Deepak. "I can't just *go* if my taxi doesn't show up. I'll miss the train in Dehra Dun."

"We're waiting for our cab, too," said Jack, just as Mr. Kilometres barreled into view.

"Hello, Mr. and Mrs. Laird! We must pack quickly!" Mr. Kilometres cried, jumping from the car just as a streak of lightning split the sky and a deafening clap of thunder made them all jump. At the sight of their piles of luggage, he opened the boot and seized a long rope. In seconds, he was expertly lashing the rani of Jhansi to the roof. As he added the largest suitcases, the rain came crashing down in sheets. Jack and Katarina gave split-second hugs all around, hastily gasped their good-byes, and jumped into the back of the cab.

"Is there another taxi on the way?" Mr. Shah cried to Mr. Kilometres.

"No, sahib, I didn't see one," Mr. Kilometres cried.

Out the window, Jack yelled, "Deepak, you better come with us." Deepak, not needing a second invitation, leaned forward to touch his father's feet in a photo-finish speed farewell.

"Bye!" he cried, and leapt into the front passenger seat, where he sat hugging his suitcase.

Mr. Kilometres gave the luggage a final whack, tied one more knot in the rope, and slammed the boot shut.

"Safe journey," Jana yelled.

"Not to worry, Mrs. Laird! Until next time!"

His windshield wipers better work, Jana thought, as the taxi disappeared from sight. Mr. Shah, weeping and wiping his face with a large white handkerchief, got back into his rickshaw.

"Home!" shouted Mary. "Let's go home."

"Home!" shrieked Mr. Ganguly.

Only partly protected by their umbrellas, Jana and Mary and Lal Bahadur Pun and Munar and Harmendra ran through the rain back in the direction of the Central Bazaar. With tears streaming down her cheeks, Jana felt as if she too needed windshield wipers, the street scene was such a blur.

~⚬⨍ Hamara Nagar 24

By the next week, the town was in the full grip of the annual monsoon rains. "No excitement these days," Ramachandran and Rambir observed during lunch at the Why Not? No excitement? Jana wasn't so sure: Mary was going about with a cryptic smile on her face (Lal Bahadur Pun said she was in love with Jacob John), and Lal Bahadur Pun was composing new songs at the rate of one a day (Mary said they were in honor of the scarf seller in the bazaar).

As for Jana, there was indeed some excitement. She was about to move into the modern world, and today was the day.

In midafternoon, during a break in the rain and drizzle, three telephone-installation wallahs arrived at the gate. With one eye on the sky, Jana stationed herself in the courtyard and watched as they uncoiled wire from a huge spool and prepared to run it from the street to the house. It's an umbilical cord, she thought. Only you connect it instead of cutting it.

Now one of the men was standing on the verandah outside Jana's bedroom, noisily drilling a hole in the wall and making a mess of the exterior paint. An hour later, the wire was attached to the pole in the street. It sagged to the paving stones and swooped up over the verandah railing.

"Pull it up!" yelled the men on the ground level.

"Pull it up!" Mr. Ganguly repeated. *"Buddhu!"*

"Hush," said Jana to the bird. She heard a rumble of thunder and tried to suppress the image of someone being electrocuted by brushing up against a dripping electric line. The men, however, were unconcerned. They shouted in triumph as finally the wire was taut and secure.

"Finished outside, madam!" the men cried. "Now we are putting the phone jack inside, okay?"

"Where do you want the telephone?" the leader of the crew asked.

"On the bedside table," Jana said. Months from now, if news of Katarina and Jack's baby came when she was asleep, Jana wanted to be able to reach over, pick up the receiver, and know about it immediately.

Taking Mr. Ganguly inside and upstairs to the bedroom, she watched as the final connection was made and the big black instrument with its round grinning dial was put in place. When the phone wallah lifted the receiver, a loud buzz sounded in the room.

"Hoorah!" Jana said.

"We'll just now do a test," the man said. He dialed the operator, said a few codes, and hung up. A couple of seconds later, an earsplitting ring filled the room, to the delight of Mr. Ganguly, who shrieked and whistled, too.

"Pick up, madam," the phone man said.

On the other end, a male operator's voice resounded as if it were coming from the bottom of a canyon. "Placing a test to Hamara Nagar 24. Was your ring audible, madam?"

"It was very audible," said Jana.

"You are connected, madam!" the operator said triumphantly. "You may call Hamara Nagar. Or Dehra Dun. Or London. You may call wherever you want."

"That's too wonderful for words," Jana said. "If I want to call Glasgow, Scotland, what do I do?"

"You ring me!" the operator said. "And then stand by. Or sit by. Or even lie by! For just a few moments. Posthaste, I will patch you through."

"Much better than going to the PTT," Jana said. "I'm going to try it in just a few minutes."

Meanwhile, the phone wallah was gesturing for her attention. "We are going, madam. Kindly put your signature on this paper."

Glancing at her watch, Jana calculated that since it was five in the evening in Hamara Nagar, it was roughly lunchtime in Glasgow. Perhaps it was a bit rude to interrupt their lunch, she thought, but at least it was likely that Jack and Katarina would be home. She went down to the kitchen and found Mary, who in turn sent Harmendra to fetch Munar and Lal Bahadur Pun. Ten minutes later, all of them were standing in the bedroom as Jana placed the call.

"The lines are very busy today," said the same operator, suddenly not as cheerful as he'd been earlier. "I will call you back in three-four hours."

By ten o'clock, however, there had been no return call, and Jana fell asleep on the bed with her clothes on. When a piercing shrill brought her bolt upright, she was surprised to see daylight through the window. These days, with the skies gray from morning until night, it was hard to tell what time it was, but her watch said eight o'clock.

Footsteps sounded on the staircase, and the next moment, Mary, Lal Bahadur Pun, Harmendra, and Munar were standing at her bedroom door.

"Pick up, Jana mem! Pick up!" Lal Bahadur Pun cried. The phone rang again, and she dived for the handpiece.

"Your call to Glasgow has gone through," the operator announced.

Jana glanced up at the others and nodded vigorously, gesturing at them to come closer. They rushed to the bedside and pressed in, trying to hear.

"Hello?" came the voice of a very sleepy Katarina.

"Katarina darling! It's you!" cried Jana. "We've got phone service!"

"I see," said Katarina groggily. "I'm so glad."

"Are you two all right?" said Jana.

"We are fine," said Katarina.

"Is Jack there?" Jana strained her ears as in the background a second sleepy voice grunted and mumbled something.

Then came "Hello, Mum" from Jack. "Is something wrong?"

"I'm calling you as promised, the minute I could!" Jana yelled. "Only it took a while to go through. Can you hear me?"

"This connection's quite good, actually," Jack said. "There's really no need to shout."

"What time is it there?" Jana said.

"Er . . ." Jack paused. "It's two-thirty in the morning."

"Oh. Well, I am *so* sorry to wake you up. Honestly, I didn't mean to."

"No trouble," said Jack.

"The others want to say hello, too," Jana said, and passed the phone to Mary.

"Hello, Jack sahib!" said Mary. "How are you?"

When everyone had said, "Hello, how are you," and all had learned that everyone else was fine, Jana took back the phone.

"Jack, are you still there?" she asked.

"I am," he said. Katarina was distracting him with some news, which he now reported. "Katya says she can feel the baby moving."

"Oh, my!" Jana said, recalling the magic of such a moment. "You kicked a lot, as I remember. We thought you were going to be a football player."

"Perhaps we've got a ballet dancer here," Jack said. "Well, Mum, this is costing you a lot of money."

"Bother the money," said Jana.

Jack chuckled, but said gently, "We should get some sleep now. We've both got a full day ahead."

Jana sighed. "I suppose you have. Well, I'll hang up, then. Write soon."

"We will," said Jack.

Jana added in a tone of greatest urgency, "Call us the *minute* that baby is born. Don't send a telegram. *Call!*"

"Of course we'll call," Jack said.

The phone conversation was drawing to a close, like a curtain coming down on a play. Jana said reluctantly, "Well. I'll let you sleep. Take proper care of yourself. And Katarina."

And then she hung up, the click of the receiver in its cradle giving her a sense of loss. A letter could be reread; a phone call, only imperfectly remembered. When it was over, it was over.

"How much did that call cost?" Mary asked, her mind running in more practical channels.

"A lot," said Jana.

The phone rang again, loud and shrill, and Jana lunged for the receiver, this time getting only a dial tone.

"What?" she said, and the ringing noise sounded again. She put the handset down, and there was a third ring, which finally made everyone realize that it was coming from the salon.

"Mr. Ganguly is calling us," Mary said.

Chortling loudly, Lal Bahadur Pun clapped his hands. Munar responded with an unexpectedly feminine-sounding giggle, which was so comical that Mary started laughing at *him*. Harmendra, losing his scared and dim-witted expression for the first time since he'd arrived, also chuckled, his eyes lighting up with glee. Jana looked at all four of them laughing and felt swept along by their mirth. She started to laugh, but then she felt the tears streaming down her cheeks, too.

"What's wrong, Jana mem?" Mary cried.

Jana shook her head. "Nothing." Nothing that being in two places at once wouldn't cure, she added to herself.

• • •

When the others had left the room, she washed up, got dressed, and braided her hair. She stared at the phone for a good long moment. Why, she could dial Niel! Should she? Why not—he'd even *urged* her to and told her his number. "Call me when your phone is installed," he'd said. "Hamara Nagar 10."

Feeling a surge of modernity and power, she dialed the number. Instantly, though, she realized she'd made a mistake of one digit and had reached Hamara Nagar 19.

"Hello," said a male voice. "Aaj Kal Printing Press, this is Rambir speaking."

Oh well, she thought, why not talk to Rambir?

"Are you at work *already*?" she asked.

"Why, yes," Rambir said. "Is anything wrong? Are you at the PTT?"

"No," said Jana. "I'm at home! Hamara Nagar 24."

"Congratulations," Rambir said.

"Thank you," said Jana. "Don't forget we have lunch with Ramachandran next Tuesday at the Why Not?"

"I won't forget," Rambir assured her.

They hung up, and Jana lifted the receiver again, this time dialing more carefully.

Niel answered on the fifth ring.

"Did I wake you up?" she asked.

"Good heavens, no," said Niel. "I was just going out the door when I heard the ring. Where are you calling from?"

"Home!" she said. "The phone has arrived!"

"Congratulations," he said. "Tell me the number."

She said, "Hamara Nagar 24."

"I think I can remember that," he said. "Shall I come by after my last patient?" He paused, apparently checking his book. "I should be all done here by four o'clock."

"Yes," she said. "Come then!"

She hung up and looked at her watch again. Seven and a

half hours until four o'clock—and then another half hour for Niel to walk from his office. She went down to the dining room, where Mary had set a single place for breakfast.

She ate her poached egg and toast and looked at her watch again. It was pouring rain, and the day promised to be very slow indeed. She went into the salon and sat at the table, fiddling with the fortune-telling cards in front of her. Time dragged by, and no customers came in. She wasn't surprised; that was what happened when the monsoon rains came. The tourists and summer people went back to their homes on the plains below, and business dropped way off.

"Jack?" Mr. Ganguly asked. "Katarina? Tilku?"

"They've all gone," said Jana.

"Sad bird," Mr. Ganguly said mournfully. Then he gave an alarmed squawk, and Jana looked up to see Lal Bahadur Pun in the hall, his bagpipes in hand.

"What is it, Lalu?" Jana said.

"One idea, Jana mem," he said. "I thought of it when you sent your tunes to see if someone would publish them. Could you write down the marches I composed? I too would like to offer my work for publication."

The thought of working on bagpipe music in the confines of the salon gave Jana pause, not to mention the unsettling effect it would surely have on Mr. Ganguly. Also, she suspected that pipe tunes, with all those long skinny grace notes, would be hard to transcribe. Nonetheless, she agreed perfectly with Lal Bahadur Pun. His music was original and should be recorded for posterity. In fact, his compositions could make up *The Jolly Grant House Collection: Volume II.* Not that she could be sure that Volume I would see the light of day (it was still sitting on some music publisher's desk), but still.

"Lalu," she said, "rather than playing indoors, what if you *sing* the tunes to me, phrase by phrase, and I write them down?"

"I can do that, Jana mem," he said. "Don't mind my voice, though."

She went to the sideboard and got out staff paper, quill pens, and ink.

"Okay," she said. "Let's begin."

GLOSSARY OF TERMS

Many of these words have alternate spellings.

aaj kal   nowadays; here, used as the name of a fictional printing press

akka   affectionately respectful Tamil term meaning "elder sister"

almirah   a freestanding closet or wardrobe

aloo paratha   flatbread stuffed with potato

anna   a coin worth one-sixteenth of a rupee

anna   affectionately respectful Tamil term meaning "elder brother"

aré   an expression of surprise, dismay, or alarm

ayah   a nursemaid or lady's maid

badmash   a villain, scoundrel

bahut   very much, a lot

bapré bap   an expression of surprise, dismay, or alarm

barfi   a sweet, solid confection made of condensed milk and sugar

bearer   a waiter

Bharat Mata   the personification of Mother India; used as the name of a popular film; here, the name of a fictional movie theater

biri   a small cigarette consisting of a twist of tobacco in a tobacco leaf

brinjal   eggplant, aubergine

buddhu   a stupid fellow

chal   let's go (from the verb *chalna,* to move)

chaprassi   an office messenger, functionary, servant, porter

charpoy   a wooden-framed bed or stringed cot

chokidar   a watchman

dhansak   a savory stew containing lentils, vegetables, and meat; popular with the Parsi community

dhobi   a laundryman

dosa   a type of South Indian crepe

ekdum   right now, immediately, completely

gulab jamun   soft, spongy, ball-shaped sweets made of milk solids, flour, sugar, and other ingredients, deep-fat fried and soaked in syrup

Gurkha   a soldier of Nepalese origin in the British or Indian armies

hajji   a person who has made the pilgrimage to Mecca

halwa   a sweet, dense confection made from seeds, nuts, vegetables, flour, etc.

hill station   a resort established in the mountains, at first for colonial rulers; later used for general tourism

Hindi-Chini bhai-bhai   Indians and Chinese are brothers; a slogan from the 1950s

idli   a small cake or dumpling, usually eaten for breakfast or as a snack

ji   a suffix indicating respect; also, an expression of assent or inquiry

jungli   rough, rustic, wild, ill-mannered

kabariwalla   junk dealer

kameez   a tunic, shirt, or dresslike garment

khatm hogya   it's done, finished

khud a precipice, cliff, or mountainside

ki jai victory to, hooray for

laddu a ball-shaped sweet made of various flours and sugar

mehndi skin decoration with henna or other colorings

memsahib ma'am, Mrs.; may be shortened to *mem*, informally

mochi shoemaker

mubarak ho! Congratulations! Blessings! Good wishes!

mundu a long piece of cloth wrapped around the waist

namaskar hello, good day, or good-bye, somewhat more formal and respectful than namasté

namasté hello, good day, or good-bye

Nehru, Jawaharlal the first prime minister of India

nimbu pani lemonade

ophrysia the Himalayan quail, thought to be extinct; here used as the brand of a fictional beer

pinky water familiar term for a solution of potassium permanganate, used to disinfect foods

pukka good, genuine, solid, completed (literally, "cooked")

Radio Ceylon a popular radio station established in 1923; now the Sri Lanka Broadcasting Corporation

sahib sir, mister, man of importance

salaam aleikum an Urdu greeting; hello or good-bye (literally, "peace be with you")

salwar loose trousers, usually tapered and fitted at the ankle

samjhé? Do you understand?

samosa a small triangular-shaped pastry with a savory filling, usually fried

shamiana ceremonial tent

shanti peace

shrimati   polite form of address meaning Mrs.

subedar-major   a senior rank for a viceroy's commissioned officer in the Indian Army during British rule (similar to a noncommissioned officer elsewhere)

tabla   a small Indian hand drum, played in pairs

tamasha   a big commotion or to-do

tonga   a horse-drawn cart

tota   a parrot

vanakkam   a respectful Tamil greeting; hello, welcome

wallah   a person associated with a particular trade, place, activity, or situation

zindabad   long live

ACKNOWLEDGMENTS

Heartfelt thanks to:

my agent, Suzanne Gluck, who launched me on the Jana Bibi adventure,

my editor, Marjorie Braman, who has guided me through all its phases,

my first reader, Lee Woodman, whose loyalty never flags,

editor Joanna Levine and publicist Leslie Brandon, who make the process fun,

and

copy editor Bonnie Thompson, who improved each manuscript immeasurably.

Woodstock School friends Suzanne Turner Hanifl, Hank Lacy, Bill Tammeus, and David Wagner sustained me with their encouragement and support. Charlene Chitambar Connell and Steve Fiol answered odd queries with good humor.

Veterinarian Cinthia Fulton graciously shared her knowledge of parrots.

Treasured friends George E. Miller and Jeannie Miller inspired me with their lore and their enthusiasm.

Evelyn Roberts boosted my local outreach efforts.

Information about emeralds came largely from Fred Ward, *Emeralds* (Gem Book Publishers, 2010).

ABOUT THE AUTHOR

BETSY WOODMAN is the author of *Jana Bibi's Excellent Fortunes* and *Love Potion Number 10*. She spent ten childhood years in India, studied in France, Zambia, and the United States, and now lives in her native New Hampshire. She was a writer and editor for the award-winning documentary series *Experiencing War,* produced for the Library of Congress and aired on Public Radio International.

Please visit www.betsywoodman.com.